THE MYSTERY OF
THE CAPE COD
TAVERN

ALSO BY PHOEBE ATWOOD TAYLOR
available from Foul Play Press

THE CAPE COD MYSTERY
OCTAGON HOUSE

Phoebe Atwood Taylor

THE MYSTERY OF
THE CAPE COD
TAVERN

AN ASEY MAYO MYSTERY

A Foul Play Press Book

The Countryman Press
Woodstock, Vermont

Copyright © 1934, 1961 by Phoebe Atwood Taylor

ISBN 0-88150-047-X

This edition is published in 1985 by Foul Play Press Books, a division of The Countryman Press, Woodstock, Vermont 05091.

Printed in the United States of America

FOR
WILLIAM · T · BREWSTER

NOTE

All of the characters in this book are entirely imaginary; so is the town of Weesit, even though it bears the name of an existing neck of land on Cape Cod.

THE MYSTERY OF
THE CAPE COD
TAVERN

I STARTED for Capri and I landed in Weesit.

At two o'clock I set out for Commonwealth Pier; at four I was comfortably settled in my favorite cabin on board the "Merantic," looking forward to a pleasant winter in Capri; at five o'clock I was the sole occupant of a red plush day coach, being slowly rattled toward Cape Cod, Weesit, and Prence's Tavern.

Like most drastic shifts of plans, mine was due to a telegram—a brief, unadorned little message from my nephew Mark, which will take its place as far as I am concerned with "You may fire when ready, Gridley," and "England expects every man to do his duty."

It said: "Need you immediately Prence's Tavern Weesit. Train leaves South Station 4:30."

On the face of it, there was nothing particularly remarkable about the message. But Mark had supposedly sailed for Brazil on September nineteenth, exactly a week before. I'd even sent ten new detective stories and five pounds of raspberry creams to his boat.

What on earth was the boy doing in Weesit, and why should he demand his aged aunt?

There seemed only one sensible way for the aged aunt to find out, so I took it. In fourteen minutes I collected my trunks and cases, and postponed my sailing for a week; in fourteen minutes more I was on the Cape train, rumbling out of the South Station. I am exceedingly fond of Mark Adams III, even if he does sound like a speed boat.

Without sacrificing truth to a feeble pun, Weesit meant little to me. I've covered considerable territory in my fifty years, but I'd missed Cape Cod, probably because it's so near Boston. Of course I'd heard of Prence's Tavern, though it was by no means as well known Wednesday afternoon as it became Thursday.

Two hundred years ago the Prence family had made the place famous as an Inn; four years ago Eve Prence, its present owner, had come home from Paris and turned it into a tavern again, although this time it became more of an informal rendezvous for writers than an actual hotel. Eve Prence was a well-known writer herself, but legend was fast forcing her into a class with Rosa Lewis and Mr. Fothergill.—I say "legend," because there seemed to be no end to the remarkable publicity stories which Eve Prence launched every few weeks, with clock-like regularity, about the tavern, her famous· guests—and herself.

Offhand I remembered tales of false fires, fake hold-ups, hidden jewels, and the yarns of transatlantic flyers who'd stopped off en route to Le Bourget for cups of Eve's renowned coffee. There were still other stories which Mark described as "Pure Boccaccio, out of Arabian Nights by Gesta Romanorum."

I knew Mark knew Eve Prence, but I'd no idea he

had ever stayed—or had any intention of staying—at her tavern. It occurred to me that Mark might have become involved with Eve in some compromising situation, but I promptly dismissed the notion. A pre-Harlow blonde had taught Mark both discretion and the price of being a rich man's son during his first year at Cambridge. I had personally, with my own two hands, throttled that frame-up before it reached the ears of Marcus Adams II.—In our family we omit "Junior" and "Senior" and simply number the living Marcuses.—Anyway, Marcus II has a genuine Bostonian antipathy toward headlines.

In the lonely if stuffy splendor of the red plush day coach, I brooded about Mark's S.O.S. until somewhere below Brockton, when a chubby conductor ambled into the car and demanded my ticket.

"I left too hurriedly to buy one," I told him, "so I'll have to pay you. Weesit."

"Weesit?" His pink face grew pinker and he eyed me and my seven leather cases. "Say, I bet you're another writer goin' to the Tavern."

Somehow that assumption annoyed me. "Do I," I demanded, "*look* like a writer? Most people tell me I look like their aunt in Newton Center."

"But you got a typewriter!" He seemed to feel that clinched the matter.

"Only," I said tartly, "because I'm the only person in this world who can read my own handwriting. I'm going to Prence's Tavern, but I'm no writer."

"I see." He sounded disappointed. "Well, the Tavern's

a great place. I lived in Weesit all my life, and I must say it's been fun havin' those writers around. Most of 'em's funnier than the artists down in Provincetown. All the time huntin' what they call local color. They got a pretty famous crowd there now, though there ain't anywhere near as many as there was a few weeks ago. Most of 'em's real nice, except for that kid of Lila Talcott's, the woman that writes children's poetry. Like I told my wife, his mother might be able to amuse other people's kids, but she couldn't do much with hers. Acted like he'd been brought up in a reform school. Anthony Dean's there, too."

"Tony Dean, the playwright?"

"Yup. Red-headed an' a regular giant, he is. Got *his* son with him, too, only his is grown up. Blind. Writes poetry. I forget his name."

"Norris, I think. I've read some of the poems."

"I tried some, too," the conductor confessed, "but I couldn't make anythin' out of 'em. Pretty punk, I thought. No rhyme. Then," he seated himself on the arm of the opposite seat, "then there's that Alex Stout, the feller that's always gettin' banned in Boston. And Mark Adams, he's just come back again—"

"Mark—back again?"

"Yup." The conductor didn't seem to notice my intense surprise. "He's one of them coffee Adamses of Boston. He's been down off and on since last winter. You heard of his aunt Elspeth Adams, haven't you? She used to be a lady golf champ, and now she rolls around the world gettin' mixed up with riots in India and Hitlerites in Germany. She's a great woman!"

"I'm glad," I told him a little self-consciously, "that you think so. But—what about this Adams boy? Does he—er—write?"

"He *says* so." The conductor winked elaborately. "But I think he's fallen for Eve's sister, Anne Bradford. She—"

"Fallen for—how old is she?" I demanded. "Eve's forty-three if she's a day, and Mark's only twenty-five!"

"She's only a step-sister," he assured me. "About twenty-three. Nice girl. We like her in town. Always smooths things over when Eve gets rambunctious and riles folks. Asey Mayo, he's been workin' at the tavern, and Asey Mayo said—"

"Who's Asey Mayo?" I interrupted. "The name's familiar."

"Familiar?" The conductor looked at me with obvious disgust. "I should think it would be! Say, if you don't know who he is, you don't deserve to! Recognize writers an' Adamses right off the bat, but you don't remember who Asey Mayo is! Huh! Say, any one meetin' you at Yarmouth, or you goin' to take the bus?"

"Bus? Doesn't this venerable train go all the way to Weesit?"

"Mornin' train does, but we don't."

"Well," I said philosophically, "if I'm not met, I suppose I shall bus. How do you get home?"

"I don't, to-night," he said, killing all my hopes of

begging for a lift. "Or to-morrow either. Got some vice-president or something comin' to-morrow, and we got to take him on a special to Provincetown and back. Go through Weesit around twelve and three. You'll hear us."

"Hear you?"

"Sure. My wife's an invalid. Got hurt in an auto accident four years ago, and she gets worried about me. So Pete or the other boys just toot special when they go through town so's she'll know I'm all right. This your first trip to the Cape? Too bad. You'd ought to of seen the Cape in the old days."

From then on I listened in a charmed silence to a monologue on Cape Cod in the old days, punctuated only by occasional interludes during which the conductor had to wave lanterns outside. Even if I'd wanted to stem the flow of anecdote with questions about Mark and his Anne Bradford, I doubt if I should have had the chance. By the time we groaned into the Yarmouth station, I felt as though I'd spent practically my entire life in the town of Weesit.

"My name," the conductor said as he deposited me and my luggage on the platform, "is Bill Harding, and I'd be glad to do anything I could for you in Weesit, Miss—Mrs.—Miss Um. The bus don't seem to be here, but it'll come. We go on to Hyannis."

He stepped deftly onto the bottom step of the day coach as the train rumbled away into the darkness.

I shivered as the damp east wind bit through my coat, and gazed gloomily around the dimly lighted station. There was no sign of the bus and no one seemed at all interested in its arrival except me. There was no sign of Mark, who, I thought, might at least have had the common decency to come and meet his elderly relative after his peremptory summons, whether he was in love or not.

Several people strolled up, peered curiously at me, then climbed into cars and withdrew hastily, as though the sight had been more than they could bear. At the other end of the platform two men were piling mail bags into a small sedan. I decided to stroll up and ask about the bus, but before I could reach them, they hopped into their respective cars and drove away. I began to understand how lepers feel.

The station agent, whistling a mournful minor ditty, climbed into his truck.

"Bus'll turn up sometime, lady," he said in a sad, tired voice. "Most always does. Probably got a flat."

It was nice of him, but it didn't encourage me much. I sat down on my largest case, and pulled my fur collar up about my ears. Softly, but with a certain amount of thoroughness, I cursed the bleak platform, the shrill wind, the gull that shrieked somewhere above me, Cape Cod and Cape Codders, and even Mark, for starting me on this probably senseless expedition. I'd been all prepared to step off the train and be a general Aunt Fix-it. The lack of any reception whatsoever came as a distinct blow. There is, after all, no more let-down feeling than being left at a station. And it seemed to me that Mark might have warned me to bring along a chicken sandwich.

"Even," I muttered hungrily to myself after twenty congealing minutes, "even a station ham. In fact, I shouldn't scorn an unbuttered cracker—"

Two headlights appeared as sudden beacons of hope, and I jumped to my feet. But half a look told me that the machine was not the long awaited bus. It was a long shining roadster, the twin sister of the one Marcus II had forbidden my buying in August. He said the car was rank extravagance and thoroughly unsuitable for me anyway; but it seemed to harmonize with its present driver, a tall rakish man in corduroys and a hunting jacket, who strolled up to me, swinging his broad-brimmed hat in one hand.

"Miss Adams?" he asked pleasantly. "If it is, I'm sorry I'm late. If it ain't, I'm just sorry."

I had a fleeting impression of twinkling eyes and a long narrow face.

"I'm Miss Adams, but—"

"Good. If all these bags is yours, I'll put 'em in the rumble."

"They're mine," I began, a little disconcerted by his matter-of-factness, "but I'm afraid there's been some mistake. I—"

"Didn't Mark—"

"Oh, did Mark send you? Where is he? Why didn't he meet me himself? What's wrong?"

"All that," he grinned, "is a long story. S'pose you wait till we get goin'. I bet you're prob'ly in a hurry to get some fodder after bein' jounced from Boston in ole eight-forty. How'd you like ole eight-forty, by the way?"

"If you mean the train, it was a novel experience," I told him, "including the conductor."

He chuckled. "Bill Hardin', huh? Well, you'll never know more about Weesit than you do now. Yessir, ole eight-forty's sort of like Plymouth Rock, just about as d'pendable, an' moves about the same speed. Oh—I plumb forgot. My name's Mayo, Miss Adams. Asey Mayo."

"You're very good to come after me, Mr. Mayo," I said.

The man's drawly dialect charmed me completely. Whatever and whoever Asey Mayo was that I couldn't remember, clearly he was a true Cape Codder—and a competent one. He was packing away my cases with that benign lack of haste which usually indicates complete competence. And he sounded exactly the way I'd always expected a Cape Codder to sound—no final g's to his words, exceedingly flat a's, and no r's at all. He slurred his vowels and ran his words together in a way that out-New-Englanded New England. "Eight-forty" became "atefotty."

"Very good of you," I repeated. "And why isn't Mark on his way to Rio? What's he doing in Weesit?"

He smiled as he fitted the last case into the rumble seat. "Changed his mind, Miss Adams. Men do, sometimes, same as ladies. There—mind the top down?"

"Love it." I stepped into the roadster, and sank back

against the squashy cushions. "What a superb car! Is it yours, Mr. Mayo?"

"Uh-huh," he said casually, as though it were usual for all Cape Codders to drive sixteen-cylindered custom-built monsters. "I like big cars. Bill Porter sent me this from his fac'try last month. I used to work for the Porters. Now—"

"Porters!" I said excitedly. "That does it! *Now* I remember who you are! My memory's slow to start, but once it begins to function—wait, now. I've got the headlines. 'Asey Mayo, Porter Hired Man, Solves Sanborn Murder.' 'Asey Mayo of Wellfleet, Former Seafaring Man, Solves Gilpin Killing.' And there were others, too. Lord, no wonder that conductor blushed to think I didn't remember who the famous Asey Mayo was! I'm chagrined—"

"Uh-huh." His voice held an amused note. "I'm sort of glad you are. Y'see, *I* couldn't r'member who the famous Elspeth Adams was till I pumped Anne Bradford. N'en *I* did a little headline delvin'. 'Elspeth (Kay) Adams Wins Golf Match with Prince of Wales; Putter Did It, Says Prince.' 'Elspeth (Kay) Adams Lost in Sahara.' 'Elspeth (Kay) Adams Swims Hellespont'— say, did you really?"

"It was twenty-five years ago," I said apologetically, "but nothing ever came of it. Mr. Mayo, we're quits. You forget my headlines and I'll forget yours. Now, about Mark. Tell me everything, Mr. Mayo."

"Between headliners," he said, "it's Asey. I hate

handles. Well, point is, Mark didn't want to go to Rio much without seein' Anne. So he did."

"Sounds romantic now," I commented, "but wait till brother Marcus hears his son is courting in Weesit instead of embarking on his life career of coffee in Brazil! Mark is going to become involved with what an astrologer would call malefic aspects."

"He would, only he figgered his cruise boat'd take six weeks, while a plane'd do it in a week. Thus presentin' him with five weeks to gambol in. He can get there the same day his boat's s'posed to land."

"Good. That clears up why he's in Weesit, and how he's going to get out of it without meeting fate in the form of his father. Now, what's wrong, why does he need me, why has he sent you—and what's this girl like?"

"I got sent to pave the way. He thought you might be peeved at havin' to change plans over him. It's— well, it's a queer sort of business. But b'fore I go into it, I'll tell you about Anne, just so's to r'lieve your mind. She's as good as they come, Miss Adams. Good fam'ly, good lookin', good sense of humor—but no money." He looked at me from under his bushy eyebrows.

"You can't make me erupt over that," I said, "though brother Marcus will froth and bubble. I don't even need to ask if he knows about her. He couldn't, for the tumult and the shouting would have reached me."

Asey nodded. "He don't. Mark was scared his father wouldn't let him come down if he asked, so he didn't ask. I sort of gather that his father is boss of all he s'veys."

"He is. I often wonder how Mark turned out so well, considering the constant supervision. I grasp it now, Asey. Mark wants me to see the girl and prepare his father. Is that it?"

"Well," we passed two trucks as though they were a single stationary dump-cart, "yes'n no. Fact is, there's c'nsiderable op'sition now from Eve Prence."

"From Eve Prence?" Amazingly enough, it had never occurred to me that any one could ever find any possible reasons against marrying into the coffee Adamses. The contrary has usually been the case.

"Just so. Eve seemed to approve, first off, n'en she changed her mind."

"But what can she have against Mark?"

"She ain't got nothin' against Mark."

"See here," I said, "if she's nothing against him, she must have something against her step-sister, and that's absurd! What *is* wrong?"

"It's goin' to be hard to explain. But somehow, Eve seems to have somethin' against Anne. It's stranger'n all get-out. Seems's if, on Sunday, Eve took Mark aside and told him some one was tryin' to kill her—"

"What!"

"Yup. Somebody'd shot at her, she said, Saturday. Mark didn't take her serious, thinkin' it was the beginnin' of another Tavern pub'licity story, an' Eve got so mad she upped an' hints it was Anne that was behind it."

"I never heard of anything so ridic—what did Mark do?"

"Blew up like a Roman candle. N'en Eve took him out to the woods an' showed him the bullet hole, in a tree. Right in the middle of a grove she's like to sit in a lot. Said some one's shot an' missed, an' hinted some more that it was Anne. Mark still didn't b'lieve it, but he come to me an' told me. Eve was so def'nite that he thought we ought to do somethin'. I found out from Eve when it happened an' then hinted back to her that fifteen people was willin' to swear Anne was in the post office at the time, but it didn't do no good."

"But what motive—why was—Asey, I can't understand it!"

"Neither can I nor any one else. Eve said to me that Anne knows she'll get the Prence money when she dies, an' she seemed to think Anne wanted it to marry Mark. That's her story, an' she's stickin' to it, God an' snappin' turtles notwithstandin'. This mornin' Mark an' Eve had another set-to, an' Mark was all for leavin'. But he didn't want to leave Anne. She's broke an' hasn't any place to go even if Mark had the money to get her there, an' I gather his father didn't provide for anything like that, anyways. Anne'd have to stay at the Tavern 'less she went with Mark. Mark bein' incog., that's dif'cult. Wants to marry her, but he's fearin' the wrath of Boss Adams. An' so forth an' so on. This aft'noon, Mark yelped an' said he was goin' to wire you to the boat, you bein' the only person he knew that could be r'lied upon to settle anything. N'en he got cold feet you might be mad at changin' your plans, an' findin' him here, an' b'cause of Anne, an' not tellin' you about her—an' so forth an' so forth. So," he chuckled, "he bulldozed me into comin' up after you an' settin' everythin' straight."

"I see," I said. "It's a large order, if you ask me. Just because I rescue him from a chorus girl is no reason to think I'm a Habakkuk. I'm far from being *capable de tout*. Why didn't Mark come along?"

"Well," Asey said slowly, "it's just humanly pos'ble, you know, that some one *might* be tryin' to kill Eve. Y'see, after Mark told me about the bullet, I went to the grove to dig it out; thought I might find out somethin' from it. Bullet was gone. Some one'd been there b'fore me, an' dug it out. *Was* one, too. Mark'd seen it."

"What! Who did it?"

Asey shrugged. "Heaven knows. Anyway, seemed sort of wise to keep an eye on Eve, just in case whoever dug that bullet out was in earnest. So Mark's lookin' after her. We both been. Y'see, I was refinishin' some old furniture for her this summer, so I'm just takin' my time about finishin' refinishin'. Like I told her to-day, seem's if I'd never finish. I told her I liked to work at night, so I've been stayin' there last few days. That's the story."

"What d'you think I can do?" I demanded.

"Well, you could take Anne away, but that wouldn't solve no problems about Eve an' this bullet business, providin'—"

"Providing that the bullet business is authentic and

not another Prence publicity yarn. After all, Asey, she's made up such fabulous yarns that an attempted-murder story wouldn't seem too—well, too bizarre."

Asey agreed. "But just the same, we can't be sure. I'd hoped you might stay here a while an' do a little canny questionin'. Put the screws on Eve an' drag out what's behind this an' if it's a fake or not, an' what's makin' her so s'picious of Anne, an' if she really is, or is just bein' p'verse. Both of them kids is all worked up into a lather over it, an' I'm kind of worried my-self."

We turned off the main road to a narrow tarred lane that wound like a snake through thick woods of scrub pine. Then we turned again onto an oystershell drive-way that scrunched under the tires. Suddenly an im-mense Colonial house, lighted from top to bottom, loomed before us.

"'Less you're in the writin' business," Asey said, "it takes a headliner to get into this place. I guess your headlines roused 'em to action—just look how lit up they are for you!"

He stopped the car before the arched front door and helped me out. I tried to lift the heavy iron knocker, but it refused to be lifted.

Asey examined it and laughed.

"That," he said, "will be little Eric Talcott an' the liquid c'ment. Did Bill Hardin' mention that hellion?"

He pushed the door open and we stepped into a large wainscoted hall. For a second we surveyed the scene before us and then I gasped.

Grouped around the foot of the steep stairs were half a dozen people. But they weren't looking at us. They hadn't even noticed our entrance.

Their eyes were riveted on a limp figure in jersey slacks and an orange jumper. A woman—I'd seen too many publicity pictures of her not to recognize Eve Prence, sprawled there in a heap at the foot of the great staircase.

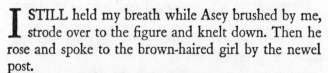

2

I STILL held my breath while Asey brushed by me, strode over to the figure and knelt down. Then he rose and spoke to the brown-haired girl by the newel post.

"Whisky an' spirits of 'monia, Anne, an' call Doc Cummings. An' hustle. She's just knocked out."

The universal sigh of relief sounded like a factory whistle.

"What happened, Mr. Dean?" Asey asked.

"I—we—none of us know, really." For all his six-foot bulk, Tony Dean looked as frightened as a baby. "It just happened. Just now. She must have tripped down the stairs. We were in the blue room," he jerked his head toward the sitting room on the right. "We—we heard a sort of bump and a crash just after we heard your car on the shells. Is she—really all right?"

"May have smashed somethin'," Asey knelt down again as Anne Bradford returned, "but she's alive."

I glanced at the long steep staircase and shivered. Years ago in London I'd seen Billy Kent-Brown fall to his death on a similar flight. It seemed incredible to me that Eve Prence actually could have tumbled down the entire length or even a part of it, without killing herself. I wondered if she hadn't fainted at the foot instead of falling.

It was more than five minutes before Eve Prence opened her eyes, and by the time Asey and Tony Dean had carried her into the blue room, the doctor had arrived.

I knew there was nothing I could do—I've always hated people who diddle about helpfully in emergencies —so I went over to a window seat by the front door and sat down by myself.

Anne and Asey were in with the doctor. I'd liked Anne enormously in the few minutes I'd seen her; she seemed sensible and clear-headed, more than I'd ever been able to say of any of Mark's previous girls. The quick comprehensive glance she'd shot at me was no mere look of casual recognition; I felt I'd been sized up as a prospective relative, and I liked to think I'd passed the test.

The rest of the people wandered around nervously, upstairs and down. They paid no attention to me at all—I don't think they even saw me. I recognized Alex Stout, who was even thinner than the book review sketches pictured him. I'd often heard of human toothpicks, but aside from a Hindu fakir in Peshawur, Alex Stout was the first I'd ever seen. He hovered solicitously about a small blonde girl,—Lila Talcott, I decided,— who seemed to enjoy his hovering. Both of them were not quite as calm as two Mexican jumping beans. Tony Dean dashed hither and yon with cloths and towels and basins of hot water, which he slopped freely over

the floor, and the youngster Eric followed him like a
buzzing mosquito. There was no sign of Mark at all,
which both bothered and puzzled me.

The doctor's diagnosis, when he finally emerged with
Anne and Asey, was cheerfully brief.

"She's sprained her left thumb," he said, "and that's
absolutely all. How she escaped crushing every bone in
her body is something I can't understand. She says she
fell the entire length. It's sheer Prence luck. Keep her
quiet for a day or so—she's naturally a bit jittery. Asey,
you and I and Mr. Dean had better get her upstairs."

During the general hubbub of reaction, Eric suddenly
discovered me. It was gratifying at that point to be
noticed even by a ten-year-old.

"I'd forgot you," he said, "and I bet you're starved.
Anne had everything ready for you in the kitchen.
Come along and I'll show you."

I followed him through a green living room on the
left of the hall into an enormous dining room. Beyond
that was an equally enormous old-fashioned kitchen.
I'd forgotten, what with Asey's news and Eve's fall,
that I'd been hungry, but the clean spicy food odor of
that kitchen turned me into a ravenous pig.

"There's your tray on the table," Eric said. "Everything's on it but biscuits Anne was keeping hot in the
oven. She was going to make an omelet. Will you? Or
shall I boil the eggs for you? I boil eggs," he added
proudly, "very well indeed."

"You may boil them." I felt, as I attacked the fruit

cup, that I could have downed them raw. "How d'you happen to know about everything?"

"I've sampled," he said airily. "I wanted the cherry in the fruit cup, but I didn't take it. Soft or hard?" He picked up an immense hour glass.

"Medium, and you may have the cherry—"

"Don't you *like* cherries?" he asked with the usual childish suspicion of one who offers delicacies.

"Yes," I said, "but clearly you like 'em more."

"Thanks. The intelligentsia," he made a sweeping gesture which seemed to include all the Tavern guests, "are pretty stingy with cherries."

I smiled. That comment made me feel I understood Eric. He was just another prodigy who'd been allowed to express himself too much and been spanked too little.

"D'you know where Mark Adams is?" I asked.

Before he could answer, Anne burst into the kitchen, followed by Asey and Mark himself, who hugged me, fruit cup and all, till I was weak.

"Oh, Miss Adams," Anne said, "we'd lost you—and what an awful welcome—and I *do* hope Eric—"

"He's been most kind," I said. "Mark, desist! Your aged aunt's no dancing bear and she's utterly exhausted! Eric's been very helpful indeed. And how is Miss Prence?"

"Anne," Eric said, "if you're going to tell me to go, you'd better not! Miss Adams is very amiable and kind, and—"

"Upsey-daisy, Rollo." Asey casually picked him up by

the collar of his shirt and the seat of his minute shorts. "Where'll I dump him, Anne?"

"Just thrust him in the blue room and tell Tony to keep an eye on him."

Asey departed with his squirming burden and Anne busied herself with making coffee.

"In spite of his crazy upbringing," she said, "Eric's really all right. Has Asey told you?"

"Yes," Mark said, seating himself on the board over the soap-stone washtubs, "has he told you? And, Kay, you were a swell to come! A perfect swell!"

"You know perfectly well," I informed him with what I hoped was the proper lack of emotion, "that if you yelled for help eighty leagues under the sea, I'd put on a diver's suit and sally forth. Asey's told me, Mark, but it's hard to understand, except that what nice things he said about Anne are undoubtedly true."

"Kay, you lamb you!"

The two of them hugged me till I shouted for mercy.

"But," Mark went on, "we don't get the idea either, Kay. It just seems to be that Eve's got this—this mad notion that some one's trying to kill her. And she's insinuating that it's Anne—"

He broke off as Asey returned. "I've sent Eric's mother up to stay with Eve," he announced, "an' Eve wants to see Miss Adams soon's she's fed. Mark, where was you durin' all this?"

"In with Norris Dean, listening to his radio. You see," Mark explained for my benefit, "Eve had so many writers who yowled about noise that she sound-proofed the second floor. It's uncanny. Norr had the radio going full tilt, and probably you never heard it. Asey, I'd really been keeping an eye on her. She said she was going to work in her room till Kay and you came."

"Okay. Betsey gone to the movies?"

"Second show," Mark said. "Kay, you'll dote on Betsey. She's the real cook of this establishment. And, Kay, we're depending on you to iron this foul business out. You and Asey. Look, you agree with everything Eve says, and get into her confidence, and see if this is a fake or not. Find out what's up."

"Consistent agreement," I said, setting down my empty coffee cup, "is rarely the way to any woman's heart, but I'll see what I can do. And I'll do all I can."

I followed Asey to the front of the house, up the steep staircase to a corridor on the left. Asey knocked at a door, and Lila Talcott let us in.

"Thanks, Lila." Eve Prence's voice was fully as beautiful and cello-like as legend said. "You needn't bother to stay. Miss Adams, for many reasons I'm delighted you decided to come down. People say this place is a madhouse, though, and I'm afraid you've just had sufficient proof to agree with them."

"I don't think that. I think you're remarkably lucky."

As I shook her hand, I noticed the intense pallor under her olive skin. Mark's description of her, long ago, as "spectacular looking," was a distinct understatement. She was seven years younger than I, but she made me feel like a tottering hag. In her brilliant mandarin pajamas with embroidered dragons leaping about, she resembled nothing so much as one of those willowy women out of a fashion magazine. I am of the build which kind people refer to as "stocky."

"Very lucky," I repeated. "When I came in the hall with Asey, I thought you were dead."

She laughed shortly. "I said madhouse," she stubbed a cigarette out in an ash tray beside her, "and I—I meant madhouse. Now, Asey—now do you—believe me?"

"B'lieve you? What d'you mean, Eve?"

"I mean," she said slowly, "that it's just my luck—and some one else's misfortune—that I'm—not dead. Oh, don't stare at me! Don't stare at me as though I were a jibbering idiot! Asey Mayo, you saw that string that tripped me! You know you did!"

"String?" I could feel myself blink. "You can't mean that some one—"

"I mean that I tripped, but it was—no accident." She had, I thought, an actress's flair for spacing her words. "There was a string—tied across the head of the stairs—six inches from the floor! I saw it. I tried to stop myself. But I was going too fast. I'd heard the car—my window was open. I wanted to be at the front door to greet you." She paused. "Well, I was."

"Eve," Asey said, "whyn't you tell us this the second you come to?"

She looked at him scornfully. "And have you laugh at me and say I was crazy—delirious! If I hadn't skiied enough to know how to break a fall! If I hadn't sense enough to relax when I found I couldn't stop! Asey, you saw that string! You know you did!"

"But I didn't, Eve," Asey said gently. "I didn't."

"I'm afraid!" There was so much terror in her voice that I jumped. "I'm beside myself, Asey! All these people are my friends—Anne—what shall I do?"

"You're sure there was a string?" Asey asked.

Eve didn't deign to reply.

"Okay," Asey said. "My first guess is Eric. I'll go—"

"It isn't Eric!" Eve said angrily. "He plays practical jokes because he knows Lila won't say anything, and people will think her a fool. But he couldn't think of any such diabolical thing as this. Don't you realize—if the string's gone—if I'd killed myself—don't you realize —no one would ever know!"

I found myself gripping the arm of my chair as though it were trying to get away from me. I'm usually sensitive to voices, but none I'd ever heard on the stage or off ever moved me as much as Eve Prence's. Low, vibrant—you had to hear it to understand its full power.

But Asey, just the same, left to get Eric; the youngster promptly seated himself on the bed when they returned.

"Awf'ly sorry, Eve," he said earnestly. "Does your thumb hurt much? I sprained my ankle once last year in Palma and I bawled like hell. I was running after a street car to mail a letter."

I smiled as I remembered the mail boxes on Mallorcan trams.

"Listen, Penrod," Asey said, "d'you tell the truth?"

Eric considered. "Always," he confessed a little sadly, "except to Lila. She likes to think I've got a—a heaven-born imagination."

"Did you tie a string 'cross the top of the front hall stairs to-night so's Eve would trip?" Asey's voice was stern.

"No," Eric answered promptly. "This is the first time I've been upstairs since noon. I washed for dinner out in the kitchen. That is, Betsey washed me. Say, I never thought of that string idea—there's a little flight in Lila's duplex in New York—" His eyes shone.

"Got any string at all?"

"Only on my fish pole out in the barn."

A general turnout of his bulging pockets produced no damning evidence; indeed from the heterogeneous collection which included two semiconscious earthworms, peanut brittle and several small crabs, I decided that Eric was a normal youngster in spite of his vocabulary.

"How long since you used your .22?" Asey asked.

"They took it away from me a week ago. Just because of an old hen. She'd have died pretty soon, anyway. I think," Eric gave proof of his heaven-born imagination, "it was epilepsy. She was very droopy."

"Okay." Asey grinned. "I guess you ain't quite so ruthless as I thought. Will you be good enough, Tom Brown, not to speak of this string business to any one?"

"Why?"

"As," Asey said solemnly, though his eyes twinkled, "as a favor. Pers'nal favor."

"Very well," Eric slid off the bed. "I won't. I'd like to, but I won't. I'm going in and listen to Norr's radio."

"Don't bother Norr about my fall, will you?" Eve asked anxiously. "Don't even speak of it!"

Eric shook his head and departed.

"Norr," Eve explained, "is Norris Dean, Tony's son. Blind, you know. He—broke his ankle two weeks ago. Has a cast on it. The poor boy would have had an awfully dull time without his radio, one of those elaborate affairs that brings in European stations so easily. Well, Asey, what's to be done—something must be done!"

"I was wrong about Rollo," he admitted. "Guess I just seen him at the wrong time. Huh. I wish you'd spoken up about this string right off. We could of sort of taken it in our stride. Now—well, best thing I can think of is to round everybody up, find out where they went after dinner, track 'em down one by one, till they heard our car, or your fall. Then we could 'lim'nate. I—"

"You mean," Eve sounded incredulous, "to—to subject my guests to the—the indignity of cross-examination? It's unthinkable!"

I bit my lip. Considering the indignities she'd heaped on some of her past guests in the way of newspaper stories, it seemed to me she was displaying undue consideration. I thought Asey's suggestion sane and logical.

"Well," Asey looked thoughtfully at Eve, "s'pose you come right out in the open, Eve, an' tell me who you s'spect. I'll see he—or she—leaves town inside an hour."

"All these people," Eve said with dignity, "are—are my friends. I've known them for years. And Anne—she —I couldn't accuse any one, Asey. I couldn't."

"Eve, you been hintin' you thought Anne was tryin' to kill you. D'you think she tied this string you think you seen?"

"I did see it."

"All right. You seen it. But let's sift this out. D'you s'spect Anne?"

"You can hardly expect me to—to accuse Anne," Eve retorted. "Not here, and not now! Not with Miss Adams present! After all, I've no—no right to prejudice her. That's final!"

"Very well," Asey said. "You're boss here. But if you won't accuse any one, an' you won't let me try to find out where people was, exactly, from dinner time till you fell, so's I might find out who slipped up an' tied the string, I'm sure I don't see no way out. I think you're makin' a wrong move."

"But if—if I should do either—think—Asey, think of the publicity!"

That word "publicity" struck a false note. Up till now, Eve had made herself the object of all my pity. But now the sympathy aroused in me by her recital and by her beautiful voice, suddenly dissolved. I began to think things over quickly.

No new Prence story had appeared in the papers for several weeks. One was due.

It was the beginning of the winter season. If stories of attempts to kill Eve Prence reached the papers, they'd be pure headline material. It seemed clear to me that she expected either Asey or me to argue with her that publicity didn't matter if her life were involved, that questioning people or accusing some one was the only way out.

Thus the story would get about, become headlines, and Prence's Tavern would do a rushing business in the dull season.

Then there were two other sides.

If I weren't already for Anne, I could see where Eve's reticence in naming her might have prejudiced me far more than any out-and-out accusation. If you suggest that some one is guilty of a certain thing, people are far more likely to believe you than if you tell them so definitely.

And indisputably, the fact that Mark and I were at the Tavern would add great spice to any newspaper story. In spite of brother Marcus's hatred of the press, the coffee Adamses are well known to the public.

I was sure of one thing. That fall was a fake. I'd thought when I first looked at the stairs that she couldn't have tumbled down them and lived to tell the tale. Now all her melodramatic reluctance to take the obvious courses emphasized my belief.

"Well," Asey said, "I s'pose I can stick around an' keep an eye peeled, but—"

"Oh, Asey! Please do. Please! I'm so—so frightened! It would make me feel—safe!"

She was overplaying her part badly. But I was no longer being taken in, and I didn't think Asey was.

"Now," she went on, "you must be exhausted, Miss Adams. I'll ring for Anne and have her show you your room—I've moved every one down on this floor. Asey, you're elected to play chess with the patient until the doctor's little white powders take effect."

An hour later, with most of eight-forty's penetrating cinders scrubbed off me, I sat up in my maple spool bed and tried to read a book of Eve's I'd found in my room. But my thoughts went wandering to Eve's tumble, and Mark and Anne and all the rest of the complicated business.

It occurred to me that I might possibly have misjudged Eve cruelly. Perhaps she *was* telling the truth, though I couldn't believe that her suspicions regarding Anne were true. I'd let myself be swayed by preconceived notions of Eve, and a lot of snap judgments and rationalization. No one but Eve had seen the string, but it came to me suddenly that if there had been one, it had to be fastened to something—tacks or pushpins. I decided to investigate.

Slipping on a dressing gown, I went out into the hall to find Asey kneeling by the head of the staircase. He looked up at me and grinned.

"No holes," he said. "Couldn't of been Eric's c'ment 'cause the paint's okay. If there was a string, t'was tied on."

"Asey," I said, "what d'you make of this?"

"Don't get it, Miss Adams. It's like Step'n-Go-Fetch-It Carver said last week about the gold standard. You can rum'nate a lot an' get jawed at a lot about it, but nothin' jells. Bullet might of been an acc'dent, an' this might of been 'magination, but I don't feel sure. She couldn't of laid it on so thick if there wasn't somethin' b'hind it."

"If I were in her place," I said positively, "I'd have cross-examined and accused and seen to it the person I suspected were on his way. If you ask me, this is a publicity stunt. She wants us to raise the hullabaloo and make it seem sincere. I'm going to bed."

Asey smiled. "Wa-el," he said, drawling a little, "I wish I was. But I'm goin' to set out here an' kind of ponder. 'Member the boy that cried 'Wolf,' Miss Adams? We'd be pretty sorry if this *was* a wolf."

I pooh-poohed the idea. "Wolf, nothing. She wants us to turn a mosquito into a leopard. But the spots don't fool me. You take my advice and go to bed."

I slept late Thursday morning; the previous day had been more wearing than I'd thought. After an early luncheon, Asey asked Mark to drive to his house in Wellfleet for him.

"I need some clothes," he explained, "an' I don't like to leave."

"Fiddlesticks," I said. "You two go, and I'll hold the fort. It's all nonsense, this business. You've been up all night, Asey—go along with Mark. If you won't sleep, at least get a little fresh air!"

Mark agreed with me, but Asey shook his head.

"S'all right, but s'pose—"

"No supposing about it," I interrupted. "Your being here, after all, wouldn't really stop any one from killing

Eve if his mind is made up. And personally, I don't in the least think such is the case. But I'll stand guard."

Asey hesitated. "Well," he said, "I ought to see my cousin Syl Mayo, an' I ought to go to the bank. I—well, I'll go, but I don't feel quite right about it. Eve's asleep up in her room now, but keep an eye on her from a distance, Miss Adams. I d'pend on you."

I went into the green room and picked out one of those best-selling novels you're always promising yourself to read when you get time. But around half past two I'd stood all the stream of consciousness I could. I crossed the hall to the blue room, intending to write a letter. But Tony Dean was at the desk, his glasses perched high on his forehead like a pair of aviator's goggles.

"Come in," he said. "I'm not working. Tried to, but I went for a walk instead. Just got back. Norris has been asking all day if you won't come in and see him. Will you?"

"Certainly," I said. "I've read his poems."

"Good. I'll run up and see if he's company-minded at the moment. Got to change my shoes, too. I soaked them at the back shore."

He shook his head when he returned. "Norr's asleep," he said, "and I didn't wake him. Poor boy, it seems he always has more than his share of troubles. His mother died when he was born, you know, and he lost his sight ten years ago, when he was fourteen. Week before last he stumbled into the open cellar bulkhead and broke his ankle. His favorite German program's on at three," he glanced at the clock, "in ten minutes. Perhaps he'll wake when the clock strikes. I hated to disturb him."

"I can see him later," I said. "What's all this script scattered about? Another play?"

He nodded. "It's awful," he said. "Look—you wouldn't care to listen to it, would you? I've tried it on the crowd here till they scream at the sight of it. The second act's got me licked."

I sat down in the biggest chintz-covered armchair. Practically no famous playwright had ever entered my life before, and absolutely none had ever suggested that I lend my ears to their efforts.

"Begin," I said. "I'm honored."

"You'll probably be bored to death. I'll begin with the first act. It's bleary in spots."

He read—very well, I thought, for over half an hour. But he apologized when he finished.

"Norr reads much better than I," he said, getting up and opening the door. "He's got a Braille copy—uses a Braille typewriter. Let's see if he's awake. I'd like him to do that foul second act—"

He broke off as a dull clanging sounded.

"What's that weird noise?" I asked.

"It's Norr's cow bell. Sounds queer because his door's closed. You're hearing it from the windows. He wants me. Won't you follow?"

Picking up his script, he raced out of the room and went up those heart-breaking stairs two at a time. I followed more leisurely to the front left chamber.

Tony Dean stood in the center of the room; it

seemed to me that he was white under his tan. I could feel myself grow white as I looked about.

Norris Dean sat in an easy chair beside a radio, perhaps ten feet away to the left. There was a violin in his lap, and his injured foot, grotesque in its cast, was resting on a stool.

On the right of the fireplace sat Eve Prence, her head and shoulders bent over a low cobbler's bench. The rest of her body, doubled under her, was still on her chair.

On her left shoulder was a wide splotch of red.

This time I knew there could be no doubt about it.

Eve Prence was dead. She had been stabbed. Asey was right and I had been wrong. Eve's cry of "Wolf" was genuine. And because I hadn't believed it, it was all my fault.

3

~~~~~~

"**D**AD!" Norris's voice was taut and nervous. "Dad, is that you? Something's wrong—where's Eve? She came in here to listen—is that you, dad? Where's Eve gone?"

Tony Dean's agonized eyes met mine.

"It's me, son. Wait—wait a moment."

"Get Asey," I said, astounded that I could speak so calmly. "Telephone—do something!"

"But—" Tony pointed to Norris, "I can't leave him here alone—or you, either—"

I remembered the boy's bell. "Ring that," I told him. "Yes—ring! I think I hear a car coming up the driveway. Maybe it's Asey and Mark."

Picking up the bell from the table by Norris's chair, Tony swung it furiously.

I don't suppose I shall ever forget the scene before me during that awful clanging minute. On one side of the fireplace the blind boy sat helplessly, a strained confused look on his face; on the other side was Eve Prence, hunched over the cobbler's bench. Before the open window stood Tony Dean, the muscles on his arm showing under the rolled-up sleeves of his blue shirt as he rang the bell back and forth.

Almost automatically I found myself noting discon-
nected details about the room; the old-fashioned pic-
torial paper which showed two gentlemen in knee
breeches and plumed hats making their way to a castle
beside a waterfall; a Chinese chippendale table; an old
clock on the mantel above the high fireplace, whose
clipper-ship pendulum bobbed unceasingly over painted
waves; a pair of antique pistols on the chimney panel;
a shaft of sunlight which pierced the rose damask
curtains and made a pool of light on Eve Prence's short
black hair.

Then Mark rushed into the room and stopped short,
aghast at the scene.

Then Asey appeared. His keen blue eyes hardened
as he took in the scene, and he bit his underlip until it
showed white. I turned away. There had been no reproach for me on his lips, but I knew as surely as
though he had uttered the words that he was blaming
himself for what had happened—and me. After all,
I'd persuaded him to leave when he hadn't wanted
to—and I'd said that I would look after Eve!

Asey crossed the room, leaned over the still figure
for a second, then rose and shook his head.

"Dad!" Norris said. "Dad! What is it? What's the
matter? Who's here? Eve—where's Eve?"

Tony Dean looked at me appealingly, but I couldn't
force myself to tell the boy, either. Asey drew a deep
breath and took command of the situation.

"Norris," he said, "we're goin' to take you into your
dad's room—"

"Asey, is that you? What's the matter? Why do I have to be moved? Oh, I *know* there's something wrong! I've felt it for minutes—Asey, tell me!"

"I'll lift him," Tony said quietly. "I always do it— Mark, you help. Asey, if you'll steady his cast. Son, we're going to take you into my room. I want you to—to go, and I want you, just for a few minutes, not to ask any questions. Miss Adams, will you open the connecting door and take the cover off the bed?"

Mechanically, like something that had been wound up like a spring, I turned right and walked across the room. But before my outstretched hand could touch the knob, the door was opened from the other side.

Anne Bradford stood there. Her face was perfectly white save for a bright spot of color on either cheek.

But it wasn't her color or her breathlessness that made me start. In her left hand was an old double-edged carving knife. Its bright blade was spotlessly clean—but there were drops of water on it.

I looked blankly at her and at it. Then I suddenly realized that a tap was running in the bathroom beyond.

"Anne!" I was so shocked that I couldn't do anything but repeat her name dazedly. "Anne! Anne!"

Asey's eyes opened wide and Tony's jaw dropped. Mark gasped. Obviously they had made the same inference I had—that Anne had just washed the blade of the knife.

"If both of you," Asey said, " 'll just step aside—there. Easy—"

They passed by me and laid Norris on the bed. Anne peered into the other room, and then looked at me with her eyes full of terror.

"Eve," she said haltingly. "Eve—?"

"Dad," Norris's voice was hysterical. "I can't stand this any longer! You've got to tell me what the matter is. Is anything wrong with Eve? Is she hurt? She was all right at three o'clock, when the music began. Is she—is she dead?"

No one said anything.

"Oh, she is, she is! Anne—you're here! You, oh, you did it after all! Eve came in late last night and told me how you'd tried to kill her—with that string. And before—with a gun! And now—now you have! She said she expected to be shot or stabbed—that must have been it—stabbed! Stabbed before me—before my eyes!" He laughed wildly. "My eyes—that can't see—stabbed—"

"Norris, stop!" Tony's voice was like steel. "Stop! There's no excuse for hysteria even from you!"

The boy covered his face with his hands and sobbed bitterly; if he had said another word I think Mark would have beaten him.

Tony turned to Asey. "Shall I call Doctor Cummings —or who—or what?"

"Yup. He's actin' as med'cal examiner this month while Hurlburt's sick. Tell him to phone the county people to come right off. Now," he faced Anne, still standing there grasping that ugly knife, "now—"

"Asey, she wasn't really stabbed?"

He nodded.

"Oh!" She gave a little cry and the knife clattered to the floor. Asey promptly picked it up and laid it on top of a chest of drawers.

"Anne, you just washed that off there in the bathroom, didn't you?"

The tap was still running and gurgling.

"Yes. Yes, I did."

Mark started to speak, but Asey motioned for him to be still.

"S'pose you tell us why. An' where you come from. An' what you're doin' here."

"Eve told me Norr wanted a chicken for dinner tomorrow," Anne said in a small voice. "And Lem Dyer killed one, and I was cleaning it, out beyond the chicken yard. Lem didn't have time. He had to go clamming and the tide was coming in. I thought I heard Norr's bell while I was out there. I knew Eve was asleep, and I thought Tony was out, so I started up to see what Norr wanted. The cats were around, and I had to find a safe place to put the chicken—Snooks and her kittens are terrible thieves. Then I heard the bell again. I—well, I put the chicken in a pail and covered it, and started in. I—I brought the knife along with me. It was bloody, so—I came up the back stairs by the balcony,— and I stopped in there and washed it off. The," she wet her lips, "the bell was so loud then. It frightened me. I—I don't know why I stopped to wash that blade. But I did. Is Eve really—was it—"

"Yup. Anne, is that the truth?"

"Word of honor, Asey!"

"Honor nothing!" Norris burst out. "You're lying! You came in here and stabbed Eve with your knife. Then you went in to wash it off. Yes, I know you killed her! She said you wanted the money. She said you knew this place and the Prence money would be yours when she was dead! You—"

Mark was almost on him before Asey grabbed him.

"Stay put, Mark, an' keep quiet. Stay out of this! An' that's enough from you, Norris!" Asey's voice was pure quarter-deck. "Did you get the doc, Tony?"

"He was just going on a call, but his wife ran after him. He'll be right over, and he'll call the police. Asey, do we have to—can't you attend to everything? Aren't you a constable or something?"

"I'm nothin' at all any more. This," he shook his head as he sat down on a sea-chest at the foot of the bed, "this isn't goin' to be—Anne, when did Lem Dyer kill that consarned hen?"

"I don't know, exactly. Around half past two or quarter to three, I guess. He called in the kitchen door and told me, and then he went off clamming."

"Where's Betsey?"

"She's been away since half past one. I think she's down in the back garden, weeding, and getting to-matoes for pickle."

"Oh, Lord. Miss Adams, where was you an' Tony?"

'Together in the blue room. We were there from ten minutes of three till we came up here."

"Anne," Asey said, "isn't there some one that was

around near you from the time Lem left till you come upstairs?"

She shook her head. "Not a soul I know of. Eric hasn't been around since lunch. Lila and Alex have gone off somewhere, to the ponds, I think. But why does it matter so?"

"It matters," Asey said, "b'cause there ain't no knife in that room that I can see—"

"Oh! Oh, then you think—of course you must! You think I stabbed Eve and then came in here and washed —oh, it's too terrible! I didn't, Asey! I swear I didn't!"

There was no reason for me to believe her, but I did. Sometimes you simply know when a person is speaking the truth.

Asey picked up the knife and went into the front room.

"I think I b'lieve you," he said when he came back. "But Anne, this ain't goin' to be easy. I don't know how the county fellers is goin' to feel."

"You mean—that awful Quigley man?"

"I do. New deal," Asey spoke to me, "wasn't so hot down here. District attorney an' the sheriff an' their bunch are mostly a gang of ex-bootleggers, an' some of 'em ain't so ex. Been musclin' in on pol'tics till they got a strangle hold. If only Parker was here—but he's out of office an' gone to the west coast. They're tryin' to get this bunch out, but they ain't been able to do it yet. Anne, this knife's awful like the one that was used!"

"But Norris was in there," Anne said. "He can prove—"

Asey raised his eyebrows. "Yes. Yup. Uh-huh. He was. Norris, will you tell us now just what happened?"

"Anne," Norris said angrily, "Anne killed her! She—"

"What you s— what you heard, son," Asey interrupted. "What happened. Not what you think. Shut up, Mark!"

"This morning," Norris said sullenly, "dad carried me out on the back balcony and I stayed there till after lunch. The sun was awfully hot, and it made me sleepy. I went to sleep. I woke when the clock struck three and snapped on the radio. It was on the table by my elbow. Dad had set it before he went out for a German musical program I like. Fifteen minutes of Anton Braun—but that wouldn't mean anything to you! Anyway, Eve usually listens to it, too, if she's around. She heard when I turned it on and came in during the announcement."

"Where was she?"

"In her room." Norris jerked his head toward the next room. "Doors were all open between her room and this and mine. She came in and said she was going to listen and wasn't it hot, and her thumb ached. Then the music began. After it was through, I snapped the radio off and played back one of the movements on my violin. I play by ear."

"How long did you play?"

"How long? How can I tell? Then—"

"Wait. Did you an' Tony hear the music?" Asey asked me.

"I didn't," I said. "I was too busy listening to Tony read his play, down in the blue room."

"I'm afraid I'd shut the door," Tony said rather sheepishly. "People have heard that play so many times that I was ashamed to have any one find me reading it again to Miss Adams. I opened it just a second before Norr's bell rang."

"I wonder was the hall door closed up here?"

"Yes," Tony said. "I'd come up around half past two and I closed it then, myself. All the corridor doors were closed."

"Huh. Then I guess no one'd of heard the music anyway," Asey said.

"Then how was it they heard the cowbell," Norris demanded, "and not the music?"

"B'cause the blue room's on the other side of the house, an' the door wasn't opened till just b'fore you rung. But your window's open in front an' so was the front door. The chicken yard's on this side, but I'd say a cowbell'd be more aud'ble out there than your violin or any radio program. Now, you played your violin, Norris, an' n'en what?"

"I stopped and asked Eve a question. I'd forgotten a couple of bars, and she has a terribly keen musical memory. She didn't answer. Sometimes she's broody, so I waited. I didn't think anything about it. Then I began to feel queer. The silence was so dead—and so—flat. It grew. I got worried and rang the bell. I've used it since I couldn't move to get to the regular push button."

"Notice the time when you come up?" Asey asked Tony.

"Around three-twenty-five, I think. I'd read my first act to Miss Adams, and it takes half an hour, more or less, to read. We began to read at ten of three."

"I think that's right," I said. "I looked at the clock when I came in, but I didn't actually note the time."

A horn sounded outdoors and Tony went down and brought up the doctor. Asey touched me on the arm.

"You'n Tony'n Mark'n Anne run along downstairs," he said. "I'll be with you later. The doc'll stay here."

"But Norris," Tony began.

"Doc'll look after him."

Down in the blue room Tony flung himself on a couch and rubbed the back of his head till his red hair stood up on end.

"I thought," he said dully, "I'd felt everything. I thought if I'd missed a few emotions, I'd given 'em to characters. But this—my God! Eve murdered! Norris —accusing Anne! Everything happening in front of that boy, who couldn't hear because of the music and who couldn't see anyway. Anne, oh, Anne, I believe you! But why did you have to bring that damn knife upstairs?"

I agreed with him entirely.

"But it won't matter," Mark said complacently. "People will know she had nothing to do with it. It—"

"It will matter," Anne said quietly.

"It will not! I—"

"Don't, please," I said wearily. "All I can think of is that the whole thing happened because I didn't do my watching job as Asey expected me to! It's all due to my negligence, the whole wretched business!"

"It is not," Mark said stoutly. "It probably would have happened no matter what you'd done."

"Perhaps. But there was no reason—"

"Miss Adams," Anne said, "it's not your fault. Nor Asey's. Neither of you should reproach yourselves— I mean, rather, what we've got to do now is to find out who did it."

With perfectly steady fingers, she lighted a cigarette. She seemed to have regained her composure more quickly than any of us. I knew she felt no less deeply than the rest of us, but she had correctly diagnosed the situation. The future was more important than the past.

"I'd say," Tony spoke up, "that we'd better look after you! You know, Mark, I'm afraid they *will* leap on Anne. Asey thought so, too."

"It's pretty bad." Anne blew out a long cloud of smoke. "If you'd set out, Tony, to write a chain of circumstantial evidence about some one, you couldn't have done any better. Eve's money comes to me— there's a motive. I'm on the scene after she's been stabbed, with a knife I've just washed off. And Eve told Norr I'd tried to kill her. She said more or less the same thing to Mark and Asey and Miss Adams. But she would have impressed it on Norr, who believes it. And when he believes anything—"

"He believes it," Tony interrupted grimly, "to the complete exclusion of everything else. He's such a—a fire-eater! He doesn't just believe in things passively. It wouldn't do the slightest bit of good to ask him to keep quiet about what Eve told him. He'd just say it all the more. And he was fond—tremendously fond—of Eve. Maybe he'll calm down when the police come, though."

But all of us knew he wouldn't.

"I can't see," I said, "why he didn't hear, even with the radio going, or his violin. I always thought a blind person had a very keen sense of hearing."

"Norr has," Tony said, "pretty much. But when he listens to music, he listens all over. Same way when he plays. Intensity is his—well, Asey?"

"Doc says she was killed instantly." Asey sat down and pulled out a vile-looking corncob pipe. "Stabbed b'tween the fifth an' sixth ribs. Double-edged blade. Prob'ly seven-eighths of an inch wide."

"Asey," Anne said, "that knife of mine was—"

"Yup. Double-edged an' seven-eighths of an inch. Only—the doc thinks yours is too thick. He can tell more later. An' Norris's already told the doc all about what Eve said. Boy's fit to be tied. The doc's given him somethin' to quiet him, Tony."

"Asey," I said despairingly, "what's to be done about this—and Anne? You've been decent not to blame me, but now I—"

"Miss Adams, we ain't goin' to talk about that. Prob'ly there'd always of been some split second some one'd been nappin', when the feller that done this would of hopped in. From the looks of it, I'd say I'd prob'ly been less help than you. But—we ain't got the

time for that. We got to find out who done this. An'
there's one more thing I can tell you. I know—"

"You know those police will take Anne," Mark interrupted bitterly. "Well, I won't stand for it! We'll
get a lawyer and we'll—"

"Wait up, Mark. These fellers have been roasted to a
crisp in the papers lately about a lot of things. Road
houses, gamblin' joints, kidnapin',—a lot of things
they ain't bothered with much 'cause they was mixed
up in 'em themselves, most folks think. Now, they're
goin' to jump into this business an' pick some one
quick. They got to. N'en they'll get praised for 'ficiency
an' carryin' out the duty of the Com'nwealth of Mas'-
chusetts, an' the honor of the nation, an' with all that
praise, the taxpayers'll forget all they been beefin'
about. An' there ain't no doubt, with that knife, but
what they'll pick on you, Anne."

"Look here," Tony said, "why do we have to tell
'em the truth? I can give you parts—and Miss Adams
and I can alibi Anne—"

"I thought of parts, too. But can you get an am'chure
cast of five, includin' Norris, letter perfect in the next
ten minutes? 'Nough so to stand cross-examinin'?"

"You're right," Tony said. "They'd get us all."

"I don't see why," Mark protested. "If this crowd is
as big a bunch of crooks as you think, I don't see why
we have to tell the truth."

"Yup. But there's Norris. No silencin' him. An' one
lie'd lead to 'nother, an' it'd get awful' involved-like.
Lies do. Make matters worse all 'round."

"I won't let Anne bear the brunt of this," Mark stormed. "If they take her—if we let them take her, she'll be branded a murderess for the rest of her life! I won't—"

Anne went over and sat on the arm of his chair.

"Listen, Mark. There's absolutely nothing to be done. If I'd taken any other knife, it might have been all right. But I know more about these men than you do. Asey's right. It's not going to be fun, but once they've taken me, Asey and Kay and you will be free to get me off. And I know you will. Don't worry about headlines,—the rest of you will probably figure lots more than I shall. You're all glamorous copy, and I'm nothing at all. And—"

"But they can't get you off without trials and proof and—Anne, you can't! And father,—oh, Lord, when father—"

Anne rested her cheek against his for a second.

"I know. But—it's the way things are. And Asey'll fix everything. You can't kick against the pricks, Mark, but Asey and Kay and you can remove the prickles—"

A blowing of sirens announced the arrival of the gentlemen from the county.

"Okay," Asey said. "Mark, keep your temper. Anne, my hat's off to you. I'll get you out of this if it's the last thing I ever do."

The law entered. As Tony whispered contemptuously, you could cast two gangster movies from the crowd of them without visible effort. In fact, as far as I was concerned, there was a certain aura of old silent picture days about the whole performance. It wasn't real.

Looking over the bull necks, red faces and prognathous jaws, I understood better what Asey had been driving at.

The most unpleasant-looking one of all, his derby still on his bullet head, demanded the doctor and the corpse in one breath.

"Yes, Mr. Quigley," Asey said politely. "This way."

"Mayo, huh? The ol' sleut'. Well, brother, we won't need you. Parker might, but we won't."

His bass laugh rumbled as the crowd trooped upstairs.

In half an hour, they all clumped down, beaming complacently from ear to ear. Quigley stepped forward.

"Which one's Anne Bradford?"

Anne crushed out a cigarette and faced him.

"You the one, sister? Give you five minutes to get your things together for a little trip to jail."

4

I THINK it was the cocksure briefness of his command which made me completely realize for the first time the enormity of what had happened and the ominousness of what was to come. Quigley's reaction was exactly what we had expected, but none of us, not even Asey, had expected him to react quite so abruptly.

"Ain't you," Asey's voice had a purring note, "ain't you even goin' t' ask a few questions, Mr. Quigley?"

Quigley guffawed. "Questions? You may have needed 'em, Sherlock, but I don't."

"Just the samey," Asey persisted, "ain't it pos'ble you might be takin' a leetle mite too much for granted, mebbe?"

He spoke with a far broader Cape Cod accent than I had heard him use before. Quigley noticed it and shook with laughter.

"Mebbe," he said, mimicking Asey's tones, "mebbe 'tis. Mebbe 'tain't. I'll ax a couple, Sherlock, effen it'll help you any."

Asey's eyes gleamed. "So do," he said, seating himself. "So do."

I wondered what his purpose was in egging Quigley on, but when he looked at me, casually, and then glanced at the clock, I knew. He was playing for time. Why, I didn't know.

"Okay. Miss Bradford, you're broke, and you was to come into the Prence money when your sister died, wasn't you?"

"Yes, Mr. Quigley."

"Lost your job last winter and had to come and live on your step-sister, didn't you? And you're planning on marrying a rich man, too."

"Yes, Mr. Quigley."

"You was upstairs with a knife when the body was found, wasn't you?"

"Yes, Mr. Quigley."

"A knife with a two-edged blade. And you'd just washed blood off that knife, hadn't you?"

"Yes, Mr. Quigley."

"The blind kid upstairs says Eve Prence told him last night she knew you was out to kill her, for the money."

The veins on Mark's forehead stood out. He never, I thought irrelevantly, looked more like the Sargent portrait of his grandfather than he did at that moment, with his light hair tousled, his gray eyes flaming, and the classic Adams jaw jutting out as far as it could jut.

"Well," Quigley barked, "what about it?"

"If Norris told you that, I suppose he spoke the truth, Mr. Quigley. It is possible that Eve may have said that to him. I don't know."

"But you can't prove it was a lie, can you?"

"I cannot prove, Mr. Quigley, that she did not say that."

He beamed. "There—no. Thar. Thar you be, Sherlock. Suspicion, threat, motive, weapon, on the scene. Nobody else there except the blind kid with the busted ankle, and he don't count. She admits everything."

"But," Asey said quietly, "she hasn't admitted that she killed Eve."

"She don't need to. No other knife around. I got enough."

"Did the doc say it was the knife that done it?"

"He said he wasn't sure, but there ain't no doubt."

"There was other folks here," Asey began, but Quigley interrupted.

"Yeah, but they wasn't around, was they? The boy upstairs said his father and a woman were down here together and every one else was out. If they was out, they ain't got nothing to do with it. Five minutes, sister, to pack your duds. No funny business, either. Run up with her, Mike, an' watch her. Say, you," as I stepped forward, "who said you could go?"

"I am Miss Elspeth Adams of Boston," I said in my best Bostonian voice, "and I am going to accompany Miss Bradford upstairs."

"I didn't give you no permission—"

"Your permission, my good man," I said coldly, "will not be neces'ry in the least."

I am proud to be able to state that he even gave me room to pass.

Within the appointed five minutes, we were back

downstairs. Anne was pale, but I marveled at her composure. I've often flattered myself that I possess a certain amount of poise, but mentally, I gave the girl a medal. She might have been setting out for an afternoon tea party.

As we reached the bottom of the stairs, a small man with a walrus mustache appeared and took Anne's bag. He was neatly dressed in a blue serge suit and he seemed considerably out of breath.

"Syl Mayo," Mark whispered in my ear. "Asey's cousin."

"Well," the little man said blandly, "we're all set, Anne."

"Say," Quigley demanded, "what do you think you're doing and where do you think you're going?"

"I'm goin' with Anne. Pro-tem counsel."

"Say, you—"

"Mr. Mayo's my counsel." Anne never batted an eye. "Isn't it all right, Mr. Quigley? I'm allowed one, aren't I?"

Quigley swallowed hard, but Syl escorted Anne out to one of the police cars and got in beside her. I knew now why Asey had stalled for time, and I thoroughly approved of his plan. In Syl Mayo, Anne would have some protection from Quigley and his bull-necked friends, and Asey would be able to keep himself informed of whatever went on.

"Mayo touch, huh?" Quigley looked contemptuously at Asey.

"S'all proper," Asey assured him politely. "Syl's never

practiced much lawr, but he got admitted to the bar in 1899, when he was young an' han'some. Helped him a lot in the real estate business."

"Smart, huh? Yeah," Quigley taunted, "but just the same, the great Asey Mayo wasn't smart enough to keep Eve Prence from gettin' killed, was he? You stick to digging clams, brother. Clams instead of clews and you catch lobsters instead of murderers. Lobsters and clams are just about your speed."

He got into his car. "I left two men upstairs with the doc, and one's going to stay here and keep an eye on you. None of you leaves this town, nobody that's here at the Tavern, till I say so. That goes for you, too, Sherlock."

The three cars roared off.

Asey's lips were still smiling politely, but his eyes were chunks of frozen flame.

"One lobster," he murmured, "I'd take a lot of pleasure catchin'. Huh. We'll get goin' now."

"We better had!" Mark finally exploded. "We were crazy to let them take her! I should have said I did it—"

"At which they'd simply have taken you along too," I told him. "I know how you feel, Mark, but no gallant gesture of yours or any one else's would have made the slightest bit of difference to that crowd of jowled hogs. Quigley decided on Anne, and he took her."

"But she—she was so meek!" Mark gulped.

"An' just you think," Asey suggested grimly, "what'd happened if she hadn't 'Yes-Mr.-Quigley'd' all over the place. Stop'n think. If she'd got Quigley peeved at her, it wouldn't of been much fun after she got away from here. That bunch didn't stop at nothin' when they racketed around, an' they ain't stoppin' any less because they happen to be at the top of the heap. Quigley's thoughts on this matter was all done an' browned an' frosted with choc'late squiggles. He was goin' to pinch Anne, an' it's a dum sight better she went easy than otherwise."

"If they lay hands on that girl or third degree—"

"They can't, now. B'sides, thank God, all that county bunch ain't crooks. They's a good lot of honest underlings up there that knows me an' Syl. Quigley ain't pop'lar with 'em. He knows it, but he can't fire 'em. Once Anne's there, she's all right. An' Syl'll see to it she'll get there all right. He's got his orders. I phoned him after the doc come. There's a lot of St. B'nard in Syl for all you could pour him into a pint bottle."

"But Asey," Mark said, "this is such a ghastly business! We can't get Anne out of this rotten mess without trials and things, if they indict her. Not unless we might find out who killed Eve, and the chances are we may never—"

"Chances may be so, but we got to," Asey interrupted. "We just plain, plum, outright, up an' down *got* to. But b'fore we go into a huddle, we'll just mosey into the settin' room an' close the door. Quigley's fellers might be the long-eared kind."

We followed him into the blue room.

"I'm all balled up," Mark said. "Where *was* every one when this happened? In fact, where the hell *is* every one right now? Lila and Alex and Betsey and Eric—where are they?"

"Gone," Asey said, waving his hand casually. "Vamoosed like peas in a shell game. Anne said Lila an' Alex'd gone for a walk. Marathon, 'parently. Betsey was diggin' up a garden. Lord above, I sh'd think she'd of had time to plant a century plant an' reap it! As for Eric, well, Frank Nelson is just two other places altogether. P'raps he's gone hitch-hikin' again."

"What I want to know," I said, "is,—who *did* try to kill Eve last night? Who put the string across the stairs? And how? And who took it away? And when?"

"Think of something easier than that, Kay," Tony Dean said, getting up and stalking around the room. "By the way, I can't 'Miss' you any more. You don't 'Miss' people who've been through things like this with you. Anyway, you might have found out about that string business last night, but to-day—after this—never! Everybody was milling about, anyway. And to be entirely frank, even if I'd gone upstairs myself after dinner, I'd never admit it in a thousand years."

"Well," I said, "what about the bullet, then?"

Asey shrugged. "Bullet's gone, an' so's the string. F'r all we know, neither of 'em might of been true, even in the face of all this. An' if they was so, they might not all of been done by the same feller, you know."

"Not the same person? Why not?"

"Wa-el, if I set out to shoot any one, I'd shoot. I wouldn't use trippin' strings an' daggers. I'd kind of stick to one method. An' it might be some one was cashin' in on the first two—"

The door burst open and one of the most ample women I'd ever seen in my life cannoned—literally cannoned—into the room. I knew it was Betsey Dyer, the cook, even though I'd not happened to have seen her before.

"Asey Mayo," she commanded, "you start right in, right in at the beginnin', an' tell me every single thing. What's been goin' on here? Is Eve really dead? I dreamed of white hosses an' caskets Saturday night, an' I told her it was a sure sign of death, but she wouldn't —what's been goin' on?"

"You just give me a chance," Asey said, "an' I'll tell you." Briefly, he told her the story. "Now," he concluded, "where was you all this time?"

"Where was I? D'you mean to say them—them bootleggers has gone an' taken Anne—"

"Uh-huh. Don't bristle, Betsey. We know how you feel an' we feel the same way, but right now we got to find things out."

"Feel? I feel about Eve, but I ain't feelin' so much about her as Anne," Betsey announced with stark honesty. "I worked for Eve off'n on for twenty years, an' for her fam'ly too. I liked Eve all right. She had her good points same as any one else, an' it's a pity, if she had to die some time, she couldn't of died—well, proper. But Anne—my Anne!" she sighed. "Where was I? I was down in the back garden. Went down about half past one. No one ever thinks of that garden 'less

it's me, for all it's Lem's business. I needed some tomatoes to try out a new pickle recipe I cut out of the
Globe. 'Twas from the same woman that sent in that
beach plum jelly that was so good an'—well, after I
picked the tomatoes, I says to myself, Betsey, I says,
you can't use all them tomatoes in a hundred years. So
I took a basket an' marched off to Sadie Hardin'—poor
sick woman all alone, with her husband traipsin' off
on ole eight-forty all the time. N'en I stopped in at
Elmer Snow's an' he give me some crabapples, an'
then I went to," she reeled off a string of names, "an'
then I come home."

"How'd you—"

"I went upstairs to see when Eve wanted dinner—
everythin' was all ready before I left, an—if the doctor
hadn't stopped me, I don't know as I wouldn't of hit
those men! I never seen such nasty rude things in all
my born days!"

She didn't seem in the least out of breath, though as
far as I could see, she hadn't paused during her recital.
I learned later that that was only a sample of how
Betsey could, and did, hold forth.

"Did you see Eric, or Alex Stout, or Mrs. Talcott?"
Asey asked.

"Eric, he popped up an' helped me pick tomatoes for
a while, an' then he wandered off. Cut his hand, he had,
an' it was bound up. He ate three raw onions before
I—"

"Hand cut?" Tony whistled. "Did he say how it
happened?"

"Why, I never!" Betsey sat bolt upright. "Why, Mr. Dean! Eve was stabbed—hm. He said he'd been cuttin' a fish pole an' his knife slipped. Oh, but I don't think— no. Eric told me the truth. He always tells the truth to every one 'cept his mother. It's her own fault he don't to her. I've told her any number of times you got to dis'pline children, an' she don't even try. Alex an' Lila," Betsey's sniff disposed of that couple, "they *said* they was goin' to walk up to the ponds. You can't tell, of course. They really might of. Asey, I've just thought of him."

"Who?" Asey didn't seem at all confused by Betsey's sudden transitions.

"Why, that man I met. Just after I took the path from the back garden. It struck half past two by the Con- gr'gational church clock not five minutes later. This man jumped out of the old path like a rabbit. Knew he wasn't even a summer person, b'cause his pants was pressed an' he had on a felt hat. Not a cap or a yachtin' cap. Said he was takin' a short cut, an' I told him he was takin' a short cut on private prop'ty into a swamp, but I showed him the way to town. Said he'd run out of gas."

"We'll check up on him," Asey said. "Know him again?"

"I certainly would. He had beady little pig eyes an' a mole on his neck, just like Georgie L.'s youngest, and he had a scar on his cheek."

I didn't like the sound of that. There is always something slightly sinister about a scar. It suggested stabbings, moreover.

"Huh. Well,—oh."

A car drew up before the door, and Asey rose.

"Ambulance," he said briefly, and left. He appeared a few minutes later with the doctor, whose face was a deep rich crimson.

"Those," he said with effort, "those creatures! Those so-and-so utterly asterisked be-such-and-suched and so-forth-and-so-oned things! I can't talk. I can't utter a word. I'm unable to express myself. Norris is all right, Dean," he answered Tony's inquiry. "I gave him a sedative, much against his will. But, oh, those men!"

"We know," Asey said sympathetically.

"One of 'em, ironically named Just, is going to stay. Just is the lesser of the two evils, but if you ask me, what this country needs is a good black plague to purge us of all similar evils!"

We laughed—we couldn't help ourselves—for the first time in what seemed years.

"I mean it," the doctor went on. "I'm deadly serious. I've heard of, lectured on, examined and even treated low-grade morons. It comes as a complete shock to find that my knowledge of such specimens is entirely elementary. There, I feel a little better. And I'm almost convinced you guessed right, Asey. Anne couldn't have used that old carving knife to stab Eve."

"Why not?" the question burst from all of us.

"Well, the blade used to kill Eve was seven-eighths of

an inch wide, and so was the blade, unfortunately, on Anne's knife. But hers is far too thick."

"Why didn't you tell Quigley?" I demanded. "That would have got Anne off, wouldn't it?"

"I told Quigley. I said that the wound had been made by a knife resembling Anne's, but that I was nowhere near convinced that hers did it."

"Why didn't—what did he say?"

He said it was a minor matter, or words to that effect. Said it *had* to be the right knife. If, at that point, Anne's knife had been a meat chopper or an early Germanic battle ax, it would have made no difference to Quigley. You see, Norris had already told his story. I told Quigley that I'd given Eve sleeping powders, that she was under the influence of a drug, and that anything she said to Norris last night could hardly be considered evidence. He assured me that when any one accused some one of trying to kill them, they meant it. Those are his very words. I asked him if it were a personal observation, but he didn't answer."

"I don't understand," Mark said, "why, if Quigley was told that knife was not the one—"

"Mark," Asey said patiently, "I been tryin' to screw it into your head for hours that this wasn't goin' to move accordin' to Hoyle an' the book of et'quette. When Quigley gets the doc's r'port, he'll just see to it a knife is found that meets spec'f'cations, an' call her knife a plant. Oh, yes, Anne can deny it—but he'll say —*wouldn't* she?"

"Asey," Mark said, "you're letting yourself be carried away by your own imagination. No—"

"I ain't, but I wish I was. Two months ago there was a rob'ry in a Wellfleet store. People got mad 'cause nothin' was done. N'en a feller in Truro was 'rested. They'd found a tin can with some of the cash in it buried outside his barn, they said. Feller said he didn't know anythin' about it, but he couldn't prove he was just sittin' around doin' nothin'. I know the feller, an' I b'lieve him, but he's doin' time. Y'see, they really had dug up that can, but they'd stuck it, first off, in there so's they could! An' I can tell you a couple more such-like stories. Did they take the knife, doc?"

"No. I decided it was the better part of valor for me to keep it. I had the same notion, that they might doctor it. They took pictures of it—they took pictures of everything, as far as that goes, and they said if I had to examine it, I probably had to."

Asey nodded. "One thing, they'll either have to doctor that, or plant another in the house here. We'll keep the knife long's we can, an' see to it they don't do no interior dec'ratin' here. You better give it to John Eldredge, the bank pres'dent, doc. He'll see it's tucked away careful for you. He ain't forgot how his bank was robbed."

"Right." The doctor picked up his bag and rose. "I'll do that. We've got precious little, Asey, but we can make a fight—"

He stopped short as Eric bounded into the room and crashed squarely into him.

"Didn't see you sorry hi every one I'm starved," Eric said in a lump as he got to his feet.

"How," Asey demanded without any preamble, "did you cut your hand?"

"Knife slipped while I was paring down a branch. Dinner ready?"

"Where've you been all afternoon?"

"Yoicking around. Up town, in the barn, in the garden. Where's Anne?"

"Cut your hand?" The doctor finished picking up the odds and ends which had spilled out of his bag. "Let's see it."

"Don't bother," Eric surveyed the gory rag. "It just bled a lot because it was the same place I'd cut last year in Palma. I was hacking off a slice of turron. You know," as the doctor raised his eyebrows, "that pasty candy stuff with the almonds and fruit in it. Looks like a long bar of Castile soap. Anyway, I tied it up with my handkerchief, and it stopped bleeding after a while."

But the doctor took his hand and removed the rag.

"Wah, what a mess! Come out, young man, and let me fix that up. What did you do, jam the whole blade in?"

"Most. Say, you all look—"

"Wait," Tony said, "I'll get a basin of water and bring it in. Then Asey can—"

"What's wrong?" Eric asked. "Where's Eve?"

"Look, Eric," Asey said, "this is important. I want to know just where you been since two o'clock."

"Two? I guess I was back from town then. Then I went out in the woods and cut a branch and my hand, and then I picked tomatoes with Betsey and ate some onions. Then I didn't feel very well so I went up in the barn loft. I looked down through a crack into the old grain room and saw where Tony'd hidden his fishing rod. And," he sighed, "I took it, and I'm not supposed to, and on the way to the pond—"

"Which pond?"

"I was going to Horse Leach. Anyway, I heard some one and thought it was Tony, so I ducked. It wasn't Tony, though, and when I got out of the bushes I'd smashed a joint of the rod. But I went up to the pond and got a turtle. See," he produced it, "isn't it a nice little one? I walked it home most of the way and that's why I'm so late," he concluded.

It was the most naïve explanation of lateness I'd ever listened to in all my life.

"Walkin' a turtle," Asey said. "Hm. What'd the man look like?"

Eric described Betsey's stranger, even to the mole and the scar.

"Okay." Asey nodded. "What about the cut, doc?"

"Too jagged and all the wrong size, if that's what you mean. Let's see your knife, son."

Eric produced one of those amazing knives with at least a dozen cork screws and reamers and screwdrivers attached—but the short, chewed-out blade testified to his truthfulness and his innocence.

The doctor bandaged his hand and Eric surveyed it proudly.

"Where's Eve?" he asked. "I want to show it to her. It's a bigger bandage than her sprain."

We all looked at each other. It was not going to be easy to explain to Eric. But Tony did, as gently and as kindly as any one could have.

Eric's eyes widened and his lips quivered.

"Eve—oh, Eve! She—she was—too! Oh, no! Eve!"

With a cry he rushed from the room and we heard him pounding up the stairs. Then there was an almighty crash.

With one accord we all dashed after him.

He was up in the front left chamber, Norris's room. The crash had come, apparently, when he knocked over the radio, now on its side on the floor.

Eric stood on a chair in front of the fireplace, wrenching from the panel above the mantel one of the old pair of flintlock pistols I'd noticed earlier in the day. He tugged it free, jumped down, and started to run from the room. Asey caught hold of him just as he crossed the threshold.

"Eric, what in time is—"

"Let me go, Asey. Let me go!"

"But what are you goin' to—"

"I'm going to shoot— I'm going to shoot who did it! I'm going to find out and—"

Asey gripped the double barrels, but Eric held firmly onto the handle.

In his frenzy the child seemed to have the strength of a man.

Then Asey stumbled backwards. The barrels and the gun were in his hand—but Eric still held part of the handle.

And attached to it was a dagger.

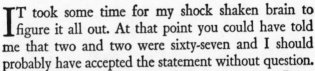

5

IT took some time for my shock shaken brain to figure it all out. At that point you could have told me that two and two were sixty-seven and I should probably have accepted the statement without question.

Mark said he had heard of such a weapon. Long afterwards he sent me a picture of a pair at the Metropolitan Museum, with a description which is far more clear and accurate than anything I could ever manage. The pistols at the Tavern were exactly the same.

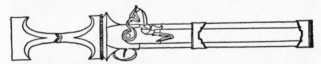

"A double barrelled flintlock pistol, length 19″, barrel length, 10½″, has a dagger lying between the barrels. Over and under barrels are fired by one lock on the right side working with an automatic double pan, —the top half slides back automatically for the second shot. The barrels are inlaid with gold and mounted in silver with a T-shaped butt that pulls apart to reveal a dagger with an 11″ blade that lies between the barrels. The band of engraving in the middle of the grip hides the joint where it comes apart to form the dagger handle.

Pistols supposedly of Balkan origin, circa 1800 A.D."

That was the description Mark sent me, which I digested and finally understood much later. At the time I could only say that the pistol somehow had a dagger hidden inside it,—somewhere.

And even now I do not care to remember how that blade looked.

Asey took it from Eric just a split second before the youngster dropped it. Striding over to the desk, he spread a clean piece of paper over the blotter, laid the dagger on it and pulled a ruler from a pigeon hole.

"Seven-eighths of an inch wide," he said as he replaced the ruler.

"That's the weapon that was used," the doctor said, "without any shadow of a doubt. My Lord above, what luck to find it! Those guns could have sat on the wall forever, and only collected dust—we'd never have known, probably, if the boy—"

"Now," Tony interrupted, "now all you've got to do is to get fingerprints, and you're all set! Asey, this is—"

"Nunno." Asey shook his head. "If there was any fingerprints at all, Eric's smeared 'em up. An' if you ask me, whoever was brainy enough to think of this thing was likewise canny enough to make sure there wasn't no prints. I'll give him that much credit right here an' now. Daggers in a gun! Betsey,"—she had clambered upstairs in our wake, "I never knew about this business, did you?"

"My good heavens on earth, no! If I had, I'd of told

you. Why, Asey Mayo, I've waved dusters around them things ever since I been here. Great-great-grandfather Edmund Prence—"

"The Captain?" Tony asked.

"One of 'em. There was a dozen Edmund Prences that was captains. Well, he brought 'em home from Europe or China or India or some place like that, years an' years ago. A hundred years, I guess likely. Them guns always been here that I can remember. But I never knew there was any daggers inside 'em. An' I'm pretty sure Eve or Anne never did."

"I've looked at 'em for three months," Tony added, "but I never knew, either. Why, it's clear enough now that that band of engraving might be where the handle would come apart to form a dagger handle, but I never thought of it before."

"C'lumbus," Asey murmured, "an' the egg."

"And Norr's played with them and felt of them, and so has Eric," Tony added.

"Yes, but I didn't know there was any dagger," Eric said in a small voice. "I—oh, I wish Anne was here. I'm going to—to blub."

Betsey gathered him up against her capacious bosom.

"Come along with Betsey, lamb. This ain't any place for you, with your sick hand an' all. An' I got a lovely duck for your supper—"

"Don't want any old duck," Eric sobbed.

"And," Betsey whispered in his ear, "and—"

He was brightening a little as she carried him out.

"Well," Mark said, "this clears Anne completely, doesn't it?"

Asey looked at him cryptically. "Think so? Think again."

"Why, doesn't it?"

"Nun-no."

"And why not?"

"Of course, Mark," I said, "of course, it doesn't. Why, it only makes matters worse! Much, much worse, doesn't it, Asey? The knife Anne had wasn't the knife that killed Eve. But here's the knife that did, right here in the room. And Anne was up here. And until we can prove that she wasn't up here from three till we found her,—well, they'll assume she did it and say that the knife the doctor's got is only a blind. Or a fake. Asey, what'll we do?"

But he was already doing it. The dagger was back in the gun, and in another minute, the gun was back in its old position over the fireplace.

"No one," he said, "need ever know about that till we're ready they should. Just— Golly, I forgot that feller Just. He'd ought to come ramblin' around to find out what all that noise was. Mark, you run downstairs an' tell Betsey an' Rollo not to let a peep out of 'em about this gun an' dagger business. Tell 'em to say it was a rat we come upstairs chasin'. An' remember that, the rest of you."

"What about Norris?" I asked.

"Door into his room's shut. Don't think he'd of heard."

"Besides," the doctor added, "he's undeniably asleep by now."

Mark had returned from the kitchen before a drowsy looking man strolled into the room. Mr. Just was the least alert looking officer of the law I ever recalled having seen.

"Anything wrong? Thought I heard something." He yawned extensively. "I was taking a snooze on a couch in that green room. Nice couch."

"Glad you liked it," Asey said heartily. "It's yours for the d'ration of your stay here."

"What was that noise?"

"Only a rat."

"Rat?"

"Rat," Asey repeated patiently. "Rat. You know. Eats cheese. Came out of the settin' room, went up the stairs an' run in here. We tried to catch it. That's how the radio got upset."

"Get the rat?"

"Nope. Must of gone in where this moldin's loose around the fireplace."

Just went over and examined the molding minutely.

"I guess that's right," he said. "Quig's pretty smart, huh?"

The doctor sighed. "There are undeniably brains extant in our universe at the moment beside which that of Quigley rates with Napoleon."

Just nodded. "Yeah," he said. "Quig's bright. Say, you people ever eat in this place?"

Mark rose to the occasion.

"Meals," he informed Just, "are necessarily secondary considerations right now, but if you'll accompany me down to the kitchen, I'll see what can be done."

"Huh?"

"Follow me." Mark spoke very distinctly. "Follow me for food."

"An'," Asey added, "you give Mr. Just the best this house has to offer. Extend, as you might say, our hospital'ty. Extend it a lot."

Mark accepted without enthusiasm his order to keep Just out of the way indefinitely.

"I'll do my best, Asey. I—I suppose we could always play ping-pong in the cellar."

"I like a good fast game of ping-pong," Just said delightedly. "That's white of you guys!"

Asey shook his head after they left. "He's bluffin', ain't he, doc? God A'mighty, he must be!"

"He's not. I thought at first, too, that no human being could be as stupid as he seemed, but I was wrong. After he eats, we will. I don't feel that I could face the Just table manners at this point, neither can I leave this situation now. It's far too tense. I only hope Mrs. Cooper's baby doesn't decide to come, but I bet it will. They've always been an inconsiderate family. What now, Asey?"

"Tony, you take my car—nope. Guess you better take a 'lectric torch an' go on shank's mares, an' find that errin' couple, Lila an' Alex. They've erred long 'nough. I want 'em. Don't tell 'em what happened. I'll do that after I found out what I want to know from 'em."

"Can I have a sandwich first?"

"Yup, but eat it on your way."

Asey's ultimatum made me think of Henry Ford's when, years ago, people wanted colored Ford cars: They can have any color they want so long as it is black.

"All right," Tony said resignedly. "But will some one look after Norr?"

"Yup. I'll call Syl's wife Jennie. She can come over an' help Betsey. Betsey's pretty capable, but she ain't superhuman enough to look after Eric, an' Norris, an' the Tavern an' us."

"Marvelous man," the doctor said appreciatively, as Asey left with Tony. "Brain like Euclid, imagination like Scheherazade, shrewd as any Yankee tin peddler, and a sense of humor,—well, words fail me. I always wanted to see him in action."

"Tell me something," I said curiously. "How old is Asey? I simply haven't been able to make up my mind. There are lines in his face, but he doesn't move or walk like an old man."

"Actually, Miss Adams, I couldn't tell you. He had a cold once eighteen years ago, when I first came to Weesit. I examined him then, and I remember asking him his age. He told me to guess, and I've been guessing ever since. Some day I'm going to look in the Wellfleet town records and make sure."

"Does he have any regular business?"

The doctor laughed. "He's been a sailor, he's an expert mechanic, he's a splendid cook and a fine carpenter. He worked for old Captain Porter for years, and Syl Mayo says Porter left him very well off. Syl thinks it's awful that Asey continues to work around, cutting grass and painting and chopping wood. 'Jack of all trades,' Syl says, 'master of 'em all, an' he don't need to lift a finger! An' you ought to see him in his city clothes, with that slick car Bill Porter give him!' It simply burns Syl up."

Asey came back, grinning. "Jennie's on her way," he announced, "an' the op'rator says she was just goin' to call you, doc. Mrs. Cooper wants you to hustle fast an' quick. Take my car, if you want."

"Take on sixteen cylinders after four,—no, three,—to-day? Don't be silly. I'd die of fright. Asey, I'll drop in when I can, and I'll cherish the knife. Anything I can do, let me know."

With a wave of his hand, he departed.

"Nice feller," Asey said. "He's only subbin' for Hurlburt, but I must say he's doin' his part. Huh. Don't know's this's just the room I'd choose to chat in, but I want to set an' brood. I want to get things straight. Eve Prence come in here a little after three. Say 3:01. She was alive an' well an' spoke to Norris. They listen to the radio till 3:14½, or thereabouts, if you like split seconds, an' it was a fifteen minute program. Then Norris snaps off the radio, picks up his fiddle, an' plays. Don't know how long, but it's prob'ly six minutes or so. Then he stops. Feels somethin' wrong. Rings his bell. You an' Tony come up from the blue room, an' Eve's dead. You right b'hind Tony?"

"If you're thinking that Tony might have stabbed Eve before I got here, it's impossible," I told him. "In the first place, I wasn't thirty seconds behind him, and he couldn't have taken that gun off the wall in that time, let alone stabbed Eve and put the dagger back. Besides, Norris would have heard,—the music was over."

"Yup. But if you'd been very far b'hind him, I'd do a lot of heavy cross-questionin', just the samey. Somehow it's hard to keep in mind there was a witness here that wasn't a witness really. Well, you an' Tony was in the blue room from ten of three till three-twenty-five. You two is out. I've been wonderin' about how helpless Norris was. If, on a pinch, he couldn't of got up an' got that dagger down. But he couldn't of, not in a hundred years. B'sides," Asey added with a smile, "his bandage is all spandy clean. So he's out. An' I b'lieve Anne's story."

"So do I."

"An' I b'lieve Betsey Dyer. Be easy enough to check up on her, anyways. She never spent ten minutes of her life without talkin' to a dozen people. An' I think Eric's out. Murder's kind of too adult even for him."

"That leaves only Lila and Alex Stout."

"Yup, an' the stranger with the mole an' scar. Strangers are kind of scarce this time of year. Usually they ain't more'n half a dozen strangers in town from Labor Day till M'morial Day, 'cept for corset salesmen an' such. An' Lem Dyer was around, too. We'll have to look into him. Huh, there's little enough to start with,

Miss Adams, with six folks 'liminated right square at the start."

"Didn't you find anything in the room that might be a clew?"

"The doc an' I combed it pretty thorough, but there wasn't anythin' we could find. It's all a lot of hooey a person can't go into a room an' stay there any length of time without leavin' some track'n trace b'hind. They can. An' I know if I was to murder any one, I wouldn't leave no clews 'less they was false ones. Well, we got four people to look into, an' I'm bettin' Lem Dyer's out at the start."

"Why d'you think Eve was killed?" I asked. "Wouldn't it help if you could think of the motive?"

"I been thinkin'. There's two gen'ral motives. Money, an' r'venge. Money's out of this business, as Anne gets everythin' Eve had, an' Eve was too clever to have any one owe her money. It's a snap no one killed her b'cause they owed her an' couldn't pony up. That leaves r'venge."

"Revenge? Why should any one want to revenge themselves on Eve?"

Asey smiled. "Well," he said, "there's lots of reasons, Miss Adams. The—"

"Between headliners," I said firmly, "it's Kay."

"Miss Kay, you tell me your impression of Eve Prence."

I thought a moment. "Stunning looking," I said at last, "clever, intelligent, shrewd. Um—"

"Yup, she was all of that. But before anythin' else,

she was as spectac'lar as Fourth of July fireworks before the Fourth got to be sane. She play-acted herself into any scene she happened to land. Now, you seen her doin' the gracious hostess that'd been done wrong to, didn't you?"

"Yes, but—"

"But she overacted. I seen you feel it when she hinted too little about Anne, an' groaned about public'ty. If she hadn't been actin' so hard, I'd of paid a lot more 'tention to that string affair. Same way, if she hadn't acted so about the bullet, I'd have taken that more serious. Now,—at four o'clock yest'day I seen Eve throw a bunch of carrots at Anne, an' toss a punkin at Betsey. She was bein' the temp'ramental chef, see? That is," he grinned, "it'd of been temper in others, but in her it was temp'rament. Just the samey, she took Anne in when she was busted, an' paid all Betsey's hosp'tal bills when she was sick last year. I seen her be a lady of the manor at town doin's, fairs an' town meetin's, till you wanted to sock her. But when she heard the Weesit budget'd gone on the rocks, she passed over a bank book an' said 'Fix it up.' I known her to torment Lem Dyer about the garden an' grounds till he cried, an' I seen her give half her wardrobe to a woman in Well-fleet that got invited to New York but hadn't any clothes to wear. You begin to get what I mean?"

"I begin to. She was temperamental, and dramatized herself every minute. Always played a part."

"Just so. You'll realize that more'n more. Every rose was a bokay to her, an' every egg a nog. Everythin' was just a little bigger than it really was, an' you could sort of feel the limelight hit it when she looked at it. She could be Griselda in the mornin' an' Mae West in the evenin' an' almost anythin' from Peter Pan to Queen M'rie durin' the day."

I laughed. "You make her sound like a chameleon."

"She was, sort of. Sometimes you could like her as much as you'd like anybody, an' then the next minute you'd want to stick pins in her. There wasn't one Eve Prence; there was a million. After you got to realize that, you could sort of set back an' enjoy her. That's what I did, all the thirty years I known her. She's been back to town off'n on, you know, though she ain't lived here all the time but the last four years. Anyway, after you got to takin' her the right way, the nasty things she done didn't matter. You knew she'd be the first to help you when you was down'n out. Her lies didn't matter, b'cause to her they wasn't lies at all. She b'lieved all her actin'."

"You might have been able to take her as she was," I said, "but it would take an awfully calm, intelligent person to figure that out."

"Anne did an' Betsey did," Asey said, "but not a lot of others. Yet you couldn't help likin' Eve. Well, anyway, the intell'gent person don't kill, as a rule, 'cept in self-defense. You can raise your eyebrows at that, Miss Kay, but s'pose you tell me just what p'centage of your friends is murd'rers?"

I admitted the justice of his statement.

"Okay. Intell'gent person who's out for r'venge,"

Asey went on, "b'cause he hates some one somethin' awful, he's got two things he can do. He can just beat it an' figger justice is the Lord's, or he can torment the person he hates till that feller wishes he was dead an' buried. There's a million ways to torment a person that'll hurt 'em more'n killin' ever could. Death's over, —like Eve's,—in a second. But you can make a livin' person wish he was dead for years an' years. Tell stories an' lies against him. Turn his friends. Hurt his rel'tives. Boycott his business. There ain't no end to torment. But—"

"But," I interrupted, "the fact remains that intelligent people do commit murder."

"Uh-huh. Bringin' what I was sayin' plumb down to the point, any one of these folks here could have run away if they'd hated Eve, 'cept Anne, an' we'll take it for granted right now her story's true. But they didn't run. See?"

"You'll have to fill in more than that," I said. I have always openly admitted since I was a child in school that I had to have all the steps from A to Z written out in full before I began to understand the theorem.

"All right. Eve hurts some one, an' they d'cide to torment her. Now, Eve bein' what she was,—intell'gent an' shrewd as all the Prences,—she'd of got the idea almost b'fore they started. N'en what'd she do? She'd play the pers'cuted heroine an' torment them back more'n they ever begun to think of doin' to her. Get it now?"

"I think so," I said slowly. "You believe that whoever killed Eve didn't start out with the exact intention of doing so. Probably some one took seriously one of her rôles, or her temperamental outbursts, and decided to torment her for revenge. But she tormented them, and egged them on to a point where reason didn't count. They were just going to kill her,—and did. My grammar is involved, but the thought is crystal clear."

"That's the way I feel," Asey said.

"But couldn't you begin with the string episode or the bullet business?"

"Like Tony Dean said, no one'd tell the truth about the string, now. An' there ain't much to start on with the bullet gone. An' prob'ly it wasn't the same one, an'—"

"Asey, you don't mean that three separate and distinct people were attempting to take Eve's life!"

"Miss Kay, Eve could annoy three people an' set 'em against her, an' then torment 'em back, all at the same time, just as easy as pie. Or a dozen. She's juggled people an' their feelin's all her life. I sh'd think she'd of known you couldn't keep on stickin' pins forever without sittin' on a needle some day yourself."

"It must have been some one in the house," I said, "otherwise how could they have known about the dagger in the gun?"

"The gun's been here a hundred years," Asey said. "An' Prence's used to be the gatherin' place for all the town. Used to come here m'self with m'father when I was young to visit ole Cap'n Matt. This place's been a tavern four years, an' God only knows how many

writers lived in this room. Saturday's bullet might have
come from some person Eve tormented Saturday; last
night's string might of been tied by the person she tormented yest'day; this afternoon's dagger—well, your
guess is as good as mine. Might of been some one here
now, or some one here four years ago, or fourteen. An'
heaven knows writers ain't no easy folks to cope with.
They're such 'daptable critters. They'd agree with the
devil himself to get what they call a new reaction.
Always nosin' out copy, an' next to actors they're the
only folks I know that can lie with a straight face."

I was willing to wager that none of them ever got
any reactions or copy out of Asey unless he intended
them to, and I said as much.

He grinned. "I give 'em a lot of what they like to
call 'local color.' I didn't know just what it was, first
off, but after I got on to it, it seemed to come real
easy to me." He chuckled. "Seem's if local color's just
the p'mento an' parsley an' lemon sauce you stick on a
fried flounder to make it filley of sole. Some of the
local color I let myself get parted from's goin' to make
a lot of good Cape Codders joyful some day. Oh, you
here, Jennie? This is Syl's wife, Miss Adams."

The plump, red-faced Amazon who bustled into the
room was only a degree less ample than Betsey. The
tiny Syl Mayo, I thought, would probably be lost in
half her shadow.

"I'm here," she said. "I been here some time. Don't
this business beat all? Ain't it awful? Betsey's next
door lookin' after the blind boy, an' I got your supper

ready down in the dinin' room, an' I put the little feller to bed. But he says he wants to see you."

"Okay. We'll go in before we eat."

I followed him around to the long hall on the other side of the house. Eric's was the last room down.

As we entered, he tossed the book he'd been reading, —and I noted with pleasure that it was an old copy of Oliver Optic,—down on the floor.

"Say, Asey," he began sheepishly, "I'm awf'ly sorry I kicked up such a row. I—I didn't mean to—to blub— and all. I don't often. But you see," he pulled a blue dotted handkerchief from the pocket of his scarlet pyjamas and blew his nose vigorously, "you see, that's the way—well, daddy was stabbed, too."

6

IF the boy had hurled a stick of dynamite at us, he couldn't more successfully have startled us out of our senses. I'd been startled out of my senses so many times in the past twenty-four hours, though, that I was gradually becoming accustomed to it.

"It was in Madrid, six years ago," Eric went on rapidly. "Lila and daddy always liked Spain, but it gives me a pain in the neck. It used to be fun to watch Alphonse and his family and the guard, but Spain's no good any more. Nothing to do but play soccer on the ramblas or ride bikes in the Retiro. I like New York, myself. Why, there's only three tall buildings in all Madrid!"

"Did they," Asey found his voice, "ever find out who done it, son?"

"You mean—daddy? No. Lila was awf'ly broken up. We went to Palma after that, mostly. Lila never speaks of it. Or—or daddy, either."

"Lila," Asey said, "huh! Don't she ever look after you, son?"

"Not very often," Eric admitted honestly, "but I get along all right. I want to go to military school, but Lila says it'd break my spirit. That's why I'm—uh—a bother sometimes."

"To force her into lettin' you go?" Asey smiled. "I see."

"Yes," Eric said sadly, "but Lila doesn't seem to catch on. Sometimes I don't think she's very intelligent. But," he added quickly, "she's shrewd. The—well, take the way she's going after Alex. That's not very intelligent, but it's shrewd. And pred—pred something."

"Predatory?" I suggested, still slightly dazed.

"That's it. Alex favors military school, though, so I'm for him. Thanks for coming in, Asey. I wanted to tell you—and maybe you could say something about military schools for me. There's one near Boston I'd like a lot, I think. I sent for the catalogue."

"I'll do it," Asey promised. "Anythin' we can do for you b'fore we go?"

"You could open the window. My feet are all warm and I hate to get 'em cold again."

While Asey opened the window, I pulled the covers up around his neck, tucked him in and kissed him.

"'Night," he said sleepily.

Asey shut the door. Neither of us spoke till we got downstairs.

"God A'mighty," Asey said, "like the doc says, words fail me. What a life that kid must of led! Huh. We'll see to it he goes to that school."

"We," I said briefly, "will."

"An' that mother of his! An' his daddy was stabbed,

an' no one knows who did it. We'll look into Lila a little more deep-like."

I agreed. "Asey," I said, "I've been thinking. If Eve was trying to break up any match between Mark and Anne, isn't it possible she might have been trying to break up any possible goings-on of Lila and Stout? Wouldn't that have been, perhaps, a tormenting factor?"

"It ain't quite the same thing," Asey said, "but it sure is a tormentin' factor. I had a couple of leadin' questions to ask brother Stout about somethin' that went on last night, an' this—yup, it's b'ginnin' to perk up a bit, this business."

"What d'you mean that it's not the same thing?"

"Well, I can see where it'd of done Eve good to bust up Mark an' Anne. Anne was a big help here. She worked like a slave. Scrubbed floors, waited on table, subbed for Betsey, washed dishes, an' messy work like pickin' chickens. She earned her keep, an' for all the purse-tossin' Eve did, she was as chary of spendin' pennies as any Cape Codder. But gettin' Lila an' Alex mad'd of lost her three cash customers, includin' Eric. Don't forget, Eve made a good livin' out of this place. You got atmosphere an'," he smiled, "local color, an' genuine antiques full of worm holes r'sultin' from time, not a machine, an' good food, an' plenty of quiet, an' n'en you got a good, first row seat for Eve Prence an' her c'lebrities. An' you paid for it through the nose. I don't think Eve'd of tormented Lila an' Alex enough to get 'em too roused, but we'll go into that later."

We finished our meal hurriedly. It didn't startle me to find that neither of us was particularly hungry.

From the cellar I could hear an occasional yell.

"Mark an' the arm of the lawr," Asey said with a grin. "Ping-pongin' it. Where d'you s'pose that gangster learned ping-pong? Well, let's go up an' give the rooms of this missin' couple a once-over. There's always a low, sneakin' pos'bility they might of run out on us. We'll see if they left their city clothes b'hind."

We stopped outside of the front right chamber—a duplicate, I guessed, of Norris's room on the other side of the house. Asey turned the knob, but the door didn't open.

"Locked," he said. "That's p'culiar. Never knew a door in this place to be locked b'fore."

"Listen!" I took hold of his arm. "There's some one in there!"

Faintly—Eve's sound proofing was remarkably efficient—we heard Stout's roar.

"For God's sakes will one of you bastards let me out of here?"

Asey looked at me and grinned. Then he put his lips to the keyhole.

"Where's the key? Who's got it?"

"How the hell should I know? Ask Eve."

Asey straightened up. "'Ask Eve.' Huh. Maybe Betsey'll know."

But Betsey didn't.

"Good Lord, Asey, I can't even think of a likely place to tell you to hunt in. We didn't use keys more'n once in a dog's age, an' Eve never knew where her key ring was from one year's end to another. Least, she pretended not to. Said she hated keys. Never locked trunks or bags 'cept the express comp'ny made her, n'en I always had to put the keys in a box an' mail 'em on ahead of her, special deliv'ry. She kept the old carriage house locked, but—"

"Uh-huh. Well, I'll holler in to Stout to p'sess his soul with patience, like Job, an' we'll see if we can't rout 'em out. Keys must be here, else Stout couldn't get locked in. Huh. Wonder how long he's been there?"

Betsey pursed her lips. "Mr. Stout's a nice man," she said primly, "an' easy to cook for—no fussin' an' fumin' about mixin' proteins an' starches. But I must say, I can see where his books'd be banned in Boston, sometimes!"

During the next thirty minutes we went through more nooks and crannies of that tavern than I had ever suspected could exist. There was no movable object that we did not move, look into, under or behind. There was nothing stationary that wasn't minutely inspected. At last the key ring turned up—in the small tee pocket of Eve Prence's golf bag, thrust far back into the darkest corner of her closet. By that time I was so exhausted that I felt as though I'd been put through a wringer.

"Where," Asey murmured ironically, "d'you keep your keys? Oh, I keep 'em in my tee pocket. Rimes.

Keys-tees. Nice'n simple, once you get on to it. Wonder if she kept her spare change in the ice box."

"What?"

"Simple," he said. "Gold—cold. That wasn't so good. I'm sorry."

"Did you notice," I said, laughing, "those pictures of Tony and Alex on Eve's dressing table?"

"Yup," he answered as we walked across to Stout's room. "She always has pictures of whatever famous men's stayin' here, on that table. Nice of her, but it must of been a bother, always switchin'. Well, here goes for Mister Stout. Persn'ly I'd like to wait a bit longer an' get him a little madder 'fore I let him out, but I—"

"Why?" I demanded. "Why d'you want to get him madder?"

"B'cause the madder folks is, the more chance you got of wanglin' the truth out of 'em. Calm person can lie like a rug. Mad feller can't. He don't stop to do no thinkin'. I'm sort of int'rested to know how long he's been in there an' who locked him in an' why."

I agreed with him. There was something in the situation which bordered on the fantastic.

After two false starts, Asey found the right key, and swung the door open.

Alex Stout was in a towering rage. I'd always thought it took a fat man to achieve a complete state of apoplectic anger, but Alex was so mad that for once I didn't mentally comment on his thinness.

"Two hours!" He pointed dramatically towards the mantel clock. "Two hours I've called for help and no one in this foul establishment has had the common decency to—"

"How long you been in here?" Asey interrupted interestedly.

"Since two o'clock this afternoon! Eight hours! And I—"

"An' you only called for help the last two? What you do the rest of the time?"

"I took a nap," Stout said with dignity.

Asey and I shook with laughter.

"It's no laughing matter," Stout said angrily. "A man—"

"Who locked you in?"

"Eve. A man has some rights—"

"Yes—yes. But why'd she lock you up?"

"She was annoyed with me. Perfectly silly. A man—"

"Just so. But why was she annoyed?"

"Look here, Asey, it's no business of yours to—"

"Maybe not. But I r'lease you from bondage an' you call me names an' don't even say thanks, an' didn't it 'cur to you no one heard you callin'? No one would, 'less you'd opened your window an' yelled. We all thought you was out walkin' with Mrs. Talcott, anyway. She ain't back, an'—"

"She isn't? The fool," Stout said hotly, "the utter fool! She probably jumped into that mud puddle and got mired. I told her she would."

"What mud puddle?" Asey sat down on the bed and motioned for me to take a chair. "An' when did the mud puddle happen?"

"It was perfectly absurd, the whole business." Stout was cooling off. "We were on our way to the ponds, and we came across this mud puddle. A perfectly enormous one. It seemed that Lila'd just written some foolish child's verse about what fun it was to jump mud puddles, and she insisted that we jump it, because she wanted to see if it *was* fun."

Asey and I broke down. There is probably nothing funnier in the world than the scornful *reductio ad absurdum* with which one writer can demolish another's work.

"I," Stout went on, "refused to do any such senseless thing. We argued about it, and I turned around and came home. Probably she tried to jump the puddle and sank into a miry place and stuck there. Like a quicksand. By the way, Asey, what d'you call a quicksand when it's mud, down here?"

"Quick mud," Asey said promptly. I thought of his remarks concerning local color and inwardly giggled. "This is—what happened then, Mr. Stout?"

"Oh, I came home, and went in to see Eve for a minute. She asked me where I'd been. I'll admit I was still annoyed with Lila, so perhaps I answered her a little brusquely. She got mad, then, and said—oh, well, no need to go into that. She was jealous. I stalked off in here, intending to take a nap. I'd worked last night until two, and again this morning. I was taking my shoes off when I heard the key turn in the lock. It was just two. I've been in here ever since. The next room's empty, but Eve must have locked or hooked the connecting door, because I couldn't budge it. There, that's the story. I'm sorry if I was abrupt with you, but I *was* mad. Where's Eve? I'm going to tell her just how foolish I think she is."

He got up and started out of the room.

"Wait a sec," Asey said. "Set down, Mr. Stout."

Once again the story of Eve, and of the afternoon, was told. It was rapidly being reduced to a ten line formula.

Stout sat down heavily on a chair.

"Good God! And I—slept through that. It's—oh, Eve said last night that Anne was at the bottom of that tripping business and I told her she was crazy. She—she was in here late last night, you see—"

"I know," Asey said casually.

"You know?" Stout glared at him. "What do you mean, you know? Why should you?"

"I told Eve I'd keep an eye on her, an' I did. Pity I wasn't on my job so well to-day. Yes, I seen her come in here after two."

No wonder Asey had told me he had some questions to ask Stout!

"And," Stout said a little belligerently, "you didn't see her leave, and you thought—"

"I didn't see her go," Asey interrupted crisply, "an' I didn't do any thinkin'. It wasn't my job to."

"I'm sorry, Asey. I—I don't know what I'm saying. It's all—well, you see, Eve was my wife."

The renowned Adams aplomb broke into small pieces like a dropped tinsel Christmas-tree ornament.

But Asey didn't appear startled at all. He simply leaned back and crossed his long legs and drew out his pipe.

"S'pose," he suggested, "you just tell us all. It might be simpler."

"Very well. If I'm incoherent—well, you'll see why. I married Eve thirteen years ago in Paris. I was twenty and she was thirty. I left her the week after the wedding."

He smiled wryly and lighted a cigarette. "You want to know why? It's funny now, but it wasn't then. I had a swell book planned. Told her all about it, long before we were married. It was going to be—oh, one of those books that will go down through the centuries. You know. Every writer has at least one of them in the back of his head. Keeps it there on purpose, I think, to console himself for what he actually writes. Well, the week after we were married, Eve's newest book came out. It was mine."

"You mean she'd swiped your story?"

"She'd swiped the plot. I'm glad, now, that she did. It jolted me into writing for a living instead of pretending to be an author with a soul and a message. Somehow I've never thought of any great novels afterward, but I've a curious feeling that literature has greatly benefited thereby." He smiled. "But it hurt like hell then. It took me a long time to realize that she hadn't meant anything by it; she hadn't stolen the plot the way the average writer might have. She just knew she could write the thing better than I, and she could, and she did. It never seemed to occur to her that she'd stolen it. That was what—what hurt so, then. I didn't understand Eve then as I came to later."

"You went back?" I said.

"Oh, yes. I got over it and went back. There was something about Eve that fascinated me. Always had and always would. No matter how she injured you or tormented you, there was always something that drew you back. Perhaps you two aren't the sort who touch 'Fresh Paint' signs. Or play with matches. I still do. I never could see why I went back. I think it was her mind. It was a remarkably stimulating mind."

"Yup," Asey said. "Yup, it was all of that. You ever see minin' engineers blow up a mount'n—little charge of dynamite here, little charge there? Well, her mind was stimulatin', just like that."

Stout laughed. "You're right, Asey. But living with Eve was never an experience you could call dull. Of course, each time I went back, something else happened. Some part she'd be playing at the moment would send me dashing away. I always realized later what an ass I was to take her seriously. I always swore there'd never be another time. But there always was, and I always boiled over. Eve was a marvelous actor. I've often thought she'd have been a great success on the stage, the only drawback being, of course, that she couldn't have played the same part two nights running, or two acts running, for that matter."

Asey nodded thoughtfully. "Real trouble with her was, I s'pose, that she was a real Prence. Prences barged over here with the Pilgrims an' fought Indians an' hewed water an' dug ditches an' gen'rally pr'ceeded to be active. Never was a scrap or a squabble that a Prence wasn't in it, from Concord to San Juan Hill. Eve had all the fam'ly desire for action, but her space was sort of limited."

"You're right," Stout said. "But—what's to be done about Anne? She didn't kill Eve. Couldn't have, not even if her knife was the right one and some one found her taking it from Eve's body."

"I don't know what's to be done," Asey said. "If you was locked in this room, you're the seventh that's out of the line-up. Why did Eve tell that story about Anne to Norris an' you, an' hint it to the rest? Why was she tryin' to get Anne in so wrong?"

"Because of Mark," Stout said promptly.

"What do you mean?" I asked.

"Mark wasn't taken in by Eve the way most men were. He didn't join the adoring circle. I've noticed, during the times he's been here while I have, that while he's made it clear that he thought Eve was a remarkable woman, he left it at that and made a bee line for Anne. Mark didn't ignore her; he was always polite and amiable, but he kept his distance. And Eve pretty much demanded the spotlight. She was jealous of Anne. And Anne was very useful to her. I think that's the only reason."

I was inclined to feel that it was the only explanation we would ever get for Eve's accusation of Anne.

"Do you think," Asey asked, "that she really thought some one was trying to kill her last night?"

Stout hesitated. "I didn't think so then. I thought she saw a chance to be dramatic, and took it. I thought she wanted to prejudice Miss Adams, knowing that if she succeeded, Mark's family would see to it that the affair was quashed. But you can't tell. Maybe she really did suspect Anne. The whole thing's incredible. I can't seem to get it through my head. I always felt that some day, some one would stop excusing Eve and fly at her. I often felt that way myself. Don't know why I didn't, except that I always managed to leave in the nick of time."

Asey's theory about motives and revenge was proving itself.

"Eve tell you about Saturday?" Asey asked.

"Saturday?"

"No matter. You don't think, do you, that your mud puddle might of been a-uh—an ole quick mud, do you, Mr. Stout?"

"No. The only reason I didn't jump it with her," Stout confessed, "was that I had on a new pair of shoes and I hated to get 'em muddy. No, I think Lila's probably pulling the helpless act, though, by George, it *is* late, isn't it?"

"Know anything about Mr. Talcott?"

"Jim Talcott? I met him once in Paris. Very decent sort. He was a foreign correspondent for some New York paper. Died very suddenly in Madrid, about six years ago."

I wondered if he were trying to hide from us the fact that Talcott had been stabbed, or if he honestly didn't know. Something made me suspect that he did.

"Tough for Eric," he continued. "He's a nice youngster. Survived Lila's notions on the upbringing of children about ninety-nine per cent better than any boy I
know could have. Look, don't you think I'd better hop
out after Tony and see if I can't find Lila? Not," he
added hastily, "that I think she's in any trouble, but she
might have hurt herself. Turned an ankle or something.
She's got a weak ankle."

"P'raps," Asey smiled faintly, "it might be a good
idea."

Stout looked at him.

"I—well, it's not just Lila," he said lamely. "I want
to get out, if you know what I mean. Things always
seem complicated when I'm indoors, but once I get out,
they clear up."

"I know," Asey said, as he got up from the bed.
"You sort of realize that the whole dum world's just
two clouds an' a bunch of scrub pines instead of bein'
so bafflin'. Well, I've sent Tony out,—no reason why
you shouldn't take another 'lectric torch an' sally forth
an' see what's happened to Mrs. Talcott. She—what,"
his voice changed suddenly and he pointed to something on top of the wardrobe, "just what, Mr. Stout,
are you doin' with a dupl'cate key to this room?"

7

"THAT key? But—I forgot about that. I—I never used it." Stout moistened his lips nervously. "Eve gave it to me yesterday. You see, Lila'd been making a habit of coming in and interrupting me when I worked during the day. I like Lila, but I wanted to put a stop to it. I worked last night, but I didn't use it, and I forgot about it this morning. The key's been right there where Eve put it when she brought it in."

He sounded as though he were speaking the truth, but undeniably the duplicate key changed everything.

Alex was no longer "out," as Asey said. He was "in." He was definitely as much of a suspect, as far as circumstantial evidence was concerned, as Anne. We couldn't prove she was out by the chicken house from quarter of three till she came upstairs with the knife in her hand. Neither could we prove that Alex had slept peacefully, locked in his room, from two o'clock on.

"That's the truth, Asey. It really is. I didn't stir from this room after Eve locked me in."

"P'raps. But you got to admit—"

"Asey, would I be fool enough to let you even suspect that I had a duplicate key, if I *were* guilty? Of course not. I'd hide the key. Put it somewhere you'd never know about even if you suspected its existence."

"Yup, or you'd be canny 'nough to do just the op'site. I'm sort of familiar with that 'Only a fool'd do it' line. Yup, leavin' the key out in plain sight would be silly, but it's no sillier than your howlin' to be let out, with the windows closed an' the key square at your elbow!"

"Asey, I didn't remember the key! And it never occurred to me to open the window and yell, and I'm pretty sure I shouldn't have if I had. Locked in my room by a woman, and then having to yell for help! No—you've just got to take my word for everything. You've got to!"

"I know," Asey said, "but look at it sort of impartial like, like I got to. You're Eve's husband. You're bein' p'sued by Lila, an' you ain't resisted much. Plum off the bat, you got a motive for gettin' rid of Eve. Did Lila an' the rest know, by the way, that you was married to Eve?"

"Lila didn't, I'm sure. The rest may have, but I doubt it. Since we—we generally lived apart, there didn't seem to be any reason for advertising it. And Eve said it would hamper her—her business, that is."

"Hm. Well, you already admitted they's been times when you was that tormented by Eve that you'd been like to have killed her if you hadn't beaten it. She is killed. Before she's killed, you an' she squabble, an' she locks you up in your room. An' durin' the time she's killed, you're across the hall with a dupl'cate key starin' you in the face! Now, offhand—"

"Offhand," Stout said wearily, "there's as much of a case as the police have against Anne. 'Prominent Scribe Sleeps Through Wife's Murder.' Think of the beautiful headlines. But frankly, Asey, the time when I would have killed Eve was thirteen years ago in Paris. And—I haven't any knife about. And—"

A car horn sounded outside.

"That's the doc's old Klaxon," Asey said, putting the duplicate key carefully in his pocket. "Wonder—"

But before we could get downstairs, the doctor appeared.

"Mrs. Cooper was a false alarm," he said excitedly. "I got two days anyway. Listen, Asey. There's lots to tell you. I found Lila Talcott and Tony Dean, beautifully lost around Jeremy's Hollow. Brought 'em back. Lila Talcott knows about Eve—as things happened, she couldn't help it. Just after I picked 'em up, I met three cars in a row. Some one called out and asked where the tavern was—they were reporters, going to cover the Prence killing. They'd have been here before, but they took the wrong turn."

"Oh, God A'mighty," Asey said. "I forgot about them fellers. Sometimes I wish they'd 'bolish free speech an' news. Thank the Lord, it's too late in the season for the tourist trade. That's a help. Are these fellers here?"

"They are not," the doctor said. "I sent them on down the Hollow road, and if they follow the directions they wrote down, they'll land up somewhere on Great Meadow. And it ought to take 'em a couple of hours to get here, and maybe they'll get stuck. Most people *do* get stuck on Great Meadow. But, Asey, half the town is parked outside the drive. Got the tidings from the radio, I suppose."

Asey sighed. "This is goin' to create what you might call a problem. I forgot I didn't have no one for an outside guard, an' I can't post no 'ficial ones, either. An' b'lieve me, Quigley's goin' to see to it this is smeared all over the papers, an' we ain't goin' to get to —Doc, I got it! Eric!"

"Eric what?"

"What's a good quarantine?"

The doctor slapped his thigh and chortled lustily.

"You've got it! Measles'll do it!"

Alex and I looked blank. "Measles, what?" I asked, "and why?"

"Cinch," Asey said. "Eric's got measles, an' we're quarantined, an'—"

"And it's a particularly malignant case," the doctor went on enthusiastically. "And you've all been exposed, and I think two of you are coming down with it. And you can't leave, and no one is to come in. Strictest orders from me, the chairman of the Weesit Board of Health. Glory be, and I've even got the signs in my bag that I took down this morning from the Rose's place out on the stone-crusher road! All that tribe's just had measles—perfectly logical to assume that Eric wandered over there against orders. Every one knows he wanders against orders anyway. Where's some push-pins? I'll stick a card on the door and one on the gate post and put the gate lights and the front lights on—"

He raced away.

"Asey," I said, "that's a superb way of keeping people from getting in, but don't you realize that you're going to keep yourself from going out? And how will you ever get any proof that Anne—"

"Don't you worry about my gettin' out," Asey said with a chuckle. "I can get out of this place any time of night I want, an' I don't think any one'd know. Daytimes, too, 'less Quigley guards us too careful."

"Invisible cloak?" Stout inquired, "or vanishing cream?"

"Neither. You don't find much talk about smugglin' in Cape hist'ry for the plain an' simple reason that dum few smugglers ever got caught. This place was one of the reasons why."

"Asey, don't tell us there's a passage—"

"There is, an' it still works. When I come here to fix Eve's furniture, I wondered if it did, an' went out to the end, where you come out, but I didn't have the keys to go no further. End door was locked. Like I told you, Miss Kay, I used to play around this place when I was a kid. Y'see, years ago, b'fore the dyke was built, the water used to run in a little river-like, b'hind the tavern where the meadow is now. Ship to dory to passage, see? Made things real easy. That part'll be all right. Make Quigley think he's got us licked, an' that's always nice."

The doctor came back, grinning broadly. "I've put up the placards, and you'd have thought it was the plague from the way the crowd scattered. Oh, and Lem Dyer's here. I told him to take up a stand by the gate and hold people off. He had a shotgun with him, and it's very effective, the whole picture."

"Fine," Asey said. "One thing, doc, Quigley can't get in to do any plantin' of knives. An'—now I got somethin' to tell Lem—"

Lila Talcott came upstairs as Asey bounded out the front door.

"I'm horrified," she said. "Poor Eve—I'm simply broken up! I don't know what to do! Poor Eric, I hope he's—"

"Eric is quite all right," I assured her a little acidly. "Jennie Mayo put him to bed, and Asey and I saw to it that he was all right before he went to sleep."

Somehow it was impossible for me to keep a certain chill out of my voice. I hadn't exchanged a hundred words in conversation with her since I'd come to the tavern, and I held no personal grudge against Lila Talcott at all. But I didn't like her. I didn't like her blonde prettiness or her calculated air of utter helplessness, and most of all I disliked her attitude toward, and her treatment of, Eric.

The boy, however, had been entirely correct about her shrewdness. She sensed my attitude and instantly set about to change it.

"I know, Miss Adams, that you must think I'm a perfectly terrible mother, to leave my boy alone in—at a time like this. But Anne and Betsey have looked after him so competently that I've simply felt he was better off with them. I'm so helpless!"

And she did seem helpless right then. I knew from

what I'd read about her that she was absurdly young to have a ten-year-old son—not more than twenty-six or seven. But as she stood there in her scarlet suède coat, with a pert scarlet feather perched on her beret, she looked about thirteen and a half.

"Don't try to pull the wool over Miss Adams's eyes," Alex Stout said coldly. "She knows perfectly well that you never pay any attention to Eric at all. Where've you been all this time?"

He was trying very hard to pretend that her safe return meant nothing to him, but he wasn't succeeding one bit.

Lila's underlip quivered. "After you—you left me," she said, "I went on to the ponds. And—"

"Did you jump that puddle?"

"Yes, I did, Alex Stout! And it *was* fun. Anyway, I thought I'd like to walk around the big pond, and I did. But I got hopelessly confused when I tried to pick the right path to come home. I found a man who told me, but I missed the turn and blundered about for ages before I came to a road. It was dark, then, and I'm always scared to death. I guess I walked in the wrong direction after I got on the road. Years and years later, after I turned back, I met Tony. I'm so utterly exhausted that I can't think straight. And I still don't really understand what happened to Eve. What was it all?"

Asey, returning, heard her question and sighed.

Once more he told the story, but I noticed that he omitted the incident of Eric and the dagger-gun.

At its conclusion Lila had dropped some of her pose of helpless exhaustion and seemed as genuinely stunned as we all had been, and still were.

"And they took Anne! Oh, that's too horrible! It's all too horrible. You know, it was Eve who introduced me to Jim, my husband. Years and years ago in Paris. I was just seventeen and just out of Miss Grant's—" She bit her lip.

"Your husband," Asey's voice had a purring note, "is dead, Mrs. Talcott?"

She nodded.

"D'you mind if I ask—how it happened?"

"Heart trouble." The answer came readily. "Six years ago in Madrid. Those guns in Norr's room on the wall —was that where the dagger came from?"

Asey swung around to the doctor and Tony. "Did either of you tell her about them guns?"

Neither of them had.

"An' I just said," Asey turned his blue eyes on her, full force, "that Eve was stabbed. I didn't tell you about the guns an' daggers. How'd you know?"

"Why—I just always thought the handles looked like dagger handles! I don't know why I—well, I just assumed that—"

"An'," Asey looked at her, "your husband died of heart trouble, did he? Alex, will you an' Tony go down cellar an' r'lieve Mark? He's been amusin' Just just about as long as any one human critter could stand it. Needn't say anythin' about anythin'."

Tony and Alex obediently left. Asey motioned for

Lila to sit down on the long seat at the head of the stairs.

"Mrs. Talcott, d'you like to lie, or d'you think lies is nicer than the truth? Or d'you want to show us that you got a heav'n-born 'magination, too?"

"What—what do you mean, Asey?"

"I mean you know your husband was stabbed. I know it. An' no one else in this house even s'spected about them guns. An' you know you come back to this house around three o'clock. You was seen."

Asey's bluff would have convinced me, but it didn't touch Lila.

"I did *not* come back to the house, and you can't trap me that way. I'll admit that Jim was stabbed, but," she looked at him, "I didn't want to say so before Alex and Tony. They don't know. I don't know how you could have found out, either, unless you've been forcing things from Eric—"

"Eric told us of his own free will."

"Asey, you can look the matter up. The house was robbed, in Madrid, and several papers of Jim's were taken; he was a newspaper correspondent, you see, and about that time they were having a great to-do over a revolution. I never knew what the papers were, but I always felt Jim'd found out more than was good for him to know. The police said it was just a robbery and that the evidence showed that Jim had tried to interfere, and been killed by the burglars. They were very polite and they bustled around a great deal, but that

was the end of it. They never found who did it. I don't
think they were meant to."

"I see."

"And I'm desperately hungry, Asey. May I go and
get something to eat?"

"Sorry—'course you can. Betsey or Jennie'll look after
you. An' later, will you be good 'nough to tell Eric he's
got the measles?" He explained about the quarantine.

Lila smiled faintly. "He'll love it."

The doctor raised his eyebrows as she went downstairs.

"R'served," Asey said, "for future ref'rence. She's
tired now, but she's got a ten-foot guard around her.
We'll get her some time when she ain't. R'porters'll
prob'ly check her story for me. Now, I got half a dozen
little things to do, an' I want you to phone Quigley, doc,
an' look after the r'porters, an' do a few more things.
An'—where you goin', Miss Kay?"

"I'm going to bed," I informed him. "Let me tell you
that in the course of my life I've meandered into some
remarkably strange situations, but this—this is the most
remarkable! And I'm not as young as I used to be. And
I have a curious feeling that this is only the beginning.
I'm going to take three iron pills and a triple bromide
and sleep while I've a chance."

But once in bed, I found that I couldn't sleep. I wondered about Lila and Alex, and how Anne was getting
on, and where Eve Prence had been taken:—that
thought was not pleasant.

It amazed me to find how calmly, after all, we had

taken the murder, and how inevitably things went on. We had all been shocked. The tragedy of the thing had impressed itself on us, but we still went on. Still moved and talked and got hungry and ate food—and went to bed. We hadn't cried or wailed or gnashed our teeth, or had hysterics. It wasn't that we hadn't wanted to. I know I had, and still did. After all, pounding like a tom-tom in the back of my head was the demanding voice of my conscience: "You didn't watch as you were supposed to, and so Eve Prence was killed!" And I knew it wouldn't stop till Asey had found out who killed her,—and probably not then.

I began to realize the difference between death—natural death—and murder. In the first you felt grief, and sympathy, and a sense of loss, all mingled with the resentful realization that nature was bigger and stronger than you. Here we felt those things; but rushing on top of them like a cloudburst, flattening everything before it, shot the question—Who Did It?

The blinds outside my windows squeaked and rattled, and I could hear a mouse scurrying behind the wainscoting. The old maple bed creaked every time I breathed, and the east wind moaned under the eaves. At two o'clock I snapped on my light, got up and jammed a chair back under my door handle. Then I removed the chair. It would have been all right for the average woman, but Elspeth Adams had a reputation to sustain. Shivering, and wishing devoutly that I'd never been labeled anything but average, I hunted methodically through my luggage till I found the small pearl-handled Deringer pistol which I'd carried around the world with me for years, after a particularly trying experience in Honduras. I'd never needed it after that Honduras episode, of course, but it had always provided a certain aura of security. I tucked it under my pillow and went to sleep.

Eric woke me Friday morning by the simple expedient of rubbing a feather against my nose.

"Hi. I got your breakfast. Look at me!"

He wore a bright blue flannel bathrobe over his crimson pajamas, but his hands, his face, his bare feet— were splattered with neat red dots.

"Eric! You haven't really got the measles?"

He roared delightedly. "Took you in! I thought it would!"

"But what—"

"Mercurochrome. It took Asey an' me about ten minutes. Isn't it swell? I got to wear pajamas and be ready to hop into bed and groan and fool people if they should send another doctor."

"Without doubt you will," I assured him. "If I saw you and didn't know, I'd run a mile. It looks as much like the plague as it looks like measles."

"That's what Asey said. Oh, he says he wants to see you when you're up."

I hurried through my breakfast—Eric snared the cherry on my grapefruit—and got dressed.

Asey was alone in the blue room, before the window. "Mornin'," he said cheerfully. "We got the papers.

Want to see your newest headline? 'Elspeth (Kay) Adams—' "

"I do not," I said firmly, "want to see more. Oh, what brother Marcus will say! Asey, have you heard from Syl and Anne?"

"Yup. Quigley's been so busy gettin' his picture took an' givin' out statements 'bout the speed of the lawr an' the 'ficiency of the new county of'cers, that he didn't bother Anne at all. Say, Syl says the bunch up there— the non-Quigley-ites—was swell. They had to let the r'porters in, but Anne just let 'em take pictures an' said she had nothin' to say. Syl says she's all right, an' every one's lookin' after her."

"Where's every one here?"

"Lila ain't up, Alex an' Tony an' Mark is playin' bridge with Just. He found out Mark once won a tourn'ment with some big-bug, an' I guess that'll keep him out of the way as long as the other fellers can manage to bear up under him. Say, you look 'round Norris's room much yest'day?"

"Well, yes and no." I remembered that awful minute while Tony clanged the cow bell. "I looked around and saw things, but they didn't exactly register themselves on my mind, if you know what I mean. I was too confused to do any more than just look."

"Notice that the door of Tony's room opens into Norr's, so that when it's wide open, some one could have hid b'hind it, an' not been seen by Eve when she come in?"

"Well," I said, "I recall now that the door opens into

the front room, but I hadn't thought out the rest of it. Why?"

"Well, the door opens in an' could hide some one. An' the window's on a line with the door, about three feet b'hind the chair Eve—"

"Asey, d'you think some one came in the window?"

"I wondered, but they couldn't of. Seems's if that window's been stuck since the storm last week. An' there ain't no ladder on the place that's the right size. An' Anne would have seen, from the chicken yard. But—you come up an' let me show you. I can show you better than I can explain."

Upon the white window sill were two small round brownish spots.

"There." Asey displayed them. "What d'you make of 'em?"

"I should say," I retorted, "that the whole house was breaking out in spots! Some one, Asey, undeniably left a couple of cigarettes burning there."

"So I thought. But I kind of 'xperimented. Seems like when you leave a burnin' cig'rette lyin' around casual, you leave the burnin' tip stickin' out. Leastways, I would. An' that'd make the spots be on the edge of the sill, if they come from cig'rettes. But these is square in the middle."

I thought a moment. "That's so. But a couple of cigarettes, left burning on an ash tray, might have burned down and slipped onto the sill and made the spots that way."

"I thought of that, too, an' tried it. It's a smaller mark, altogether. More burned."

"Possibly," I said, "it was a couple of cigars."

"Or two other fellers in St. Looey. But here's the story. When the doc an' I was lookin' 'round here yest'day aft'noon, I seen these spots. Noticed 'em, like you say you noticed things, without havin' 'em perc'late. N'en I got to thinkin', an' asked a few questions. Nasty habit of mine, like Quigley said. Anyways, I found out from Betsey that she cleaned this room yest'day mornin'. An' Lem washed all the paint just b'fore he went out to kill that consarned hen. He swears the paint was all nice 'n white then. No spots here at two. But these was there when we looked, 'round quarter of four. Wasn't put there after three-twenty-five. We know that. An' Norris was alone here till Eve come at three. Reas'n'ble notion would be to say they was put here between three an' three-twenty-five, durin' the time Eve was murdered."

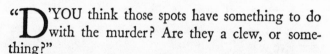

8

"**D**'YOU think those spots have something to do with the murder? Are they a clew, or something?"

"Don't know's I'd go so far as to call 'em a clew, Miss Kay, but on the other hand they're goin' to be fun to think about."

"But see here," I pointed out, "any number of people might have come into the room between two and three o'clock. Norris was here, but you forget that he was asleep. Tony came up around half past two, himself."

"Yup, but he tells me he didn't come into the room. Changed his shoes, looked in at the boy, an' went downstairs again. The shoes," Asey said, "is still wet, if that helps any."

"I wonder, if Eve was in her room, why she didn't speak to Tony? The door from her room to his was open, wasn't it?"

"I asked him about that, too. He thought Eve must have been out of her room, or else she just didn't bother to say anythin'. N'en he looked in at Norris, n'en he come down. But as for any one wanderin' around that room while Norris was in it, I don't think that could 've happened. Plenty times this summer I thought I was walkin' 'bout as heavy as a puff of smoke, but he's heard me. Even Tony, quiet as he walks for a big feller, usually wakes him. Now, them spots didn't just walk onto that sill an' fasten themselves there. Got put there by human hand, an', life bein' what it is, the hand was prob'ly stuck onto a human body. That bein' the case, seem's if Norris'd heard the human body durin' the time from two till three, if it'd been there then."

"Then I suppose those spots were made during the time Eve was killed, but—"

"Seems so. The radio, or Norr's fiddle, one of 'em, drowned out the noise of whoever come in an' killed Eve. You could sort of figger that it hid the spot-makin', too. An' the chances are that the same person done both. 'Course, it's tall figgerin', but seems like tall figgerin' was the only thing we c'd do, here."

"But what are the spots there for?" I asked. "What made them? What good are they? What do they prove?"

"You got me there. I don't know any of the answers; but we got one p'culiar bit to brood about, an' that's a step up. Trouble with this business here is that there ain't nothin' you can put your finger on. Usually when some one plans to kill some one else, they do a lot of plannin'. An' sooner or later, the r'sults of them plans crops up. Or some shreds an' tatters of 'em, at least. When you find a spider's web, you usually can find a spider, dead or alive, somewheres about. But there ain't no trace of plans here. No more'n there was any trace of plans in the bullet an' string businesses. It's hit or miss an' without method, like ole Parson Howes used to say of the New Thoughters."

"You've still got Lila and Alex to account for," I reminded him. "And weren't you going to check up on Betsey's brother?"

"Lem? Lem says he was clammin'. An' if you're clammin'," Asey grinned, "in the town of Weesit at three o'clock, 'bout six hundred an' ninety of the eight hundred an' somethin' inhab'tants knows all about it by three-forty-five. Usually they know how many quohaugs or clams you got, an' how many holes you dug into was only worms. An' they prob'ly can add which toe of which rub'boot had a hole in it."

"I didn't know," I said, "that the Cape was such a curious place."

Asey chuckled. "I'll let you in on some local color, Miss Kay, that's gen'wine a-number-one local color. It's a story my grandfather used to tell an' he said he got it from his pa. Seems's if a stranger come to Weesit an' took a room. Stayed in town a week, an' folks was crazy to find out who he was an' why. He just kind of ignored all the leadin' questions an' kept on stayin'. End of a month, people was in a lather. They got up a del'gation to go to the feller an' ask him, real def'nite an' direct, what he was doin' in Weesit an' what his business was, an' if there was any insan'ty in his fam'ly, which they did. The feller r'ceived 'em real p'lite, an' listened to 'em, an' then he said, 'Gentlemen,' he said, 'I'll c'nfess. I had my choice of bein' hung,'—an' everybody gasps, 'or I could spend six months in Weesit. An', gentlemen,' he says, 'now I wish I'd been hung.'"

Asey laughed. "An' Weesit prides itself on not changin'."

"I don't believe a word of it," I told him, "but I grasp Weesit. What d'you think of Stout's story?"

"It ain't sens'ble, but it's just crazy enough to be true. An' Mrs. Talcott, well, I'm goin' to let her alone an' let her hang herself. She's all set to answer questions, so I'm goin' to wait till she's tired of havin' her answers ready."

As I followed him downstairs, I wondered where and how this man had developed his knowledge of human beings. Had I been in his place, I should have bullied Lila into admitting anything I thought she might be trying to hide. But Asey knew she would be expecting him to do just that, and so he bided his time. I imagined that would annoy Lila. Nothing irritates me more than having to keep quiet over something when I particularly want to be asked about it.

Asey grinned, as though he knew what I was thinking.

"This Talcott woman r'minds me of the wife of a feller named Keatin' I shipped with once out of Sydney. She liked to dress herself up a lot. But Tom, her husband, he'd never say one word about her fancy rigs. Near worried her to death, it did, not to be noticed. One day I says to him, 'Whyn't you speak up when she's put on a new dress, Tom, so's she can tell you all about it?' An' Tom smiles weary an' says, 'Sooner or later, I'll get told, Asey.' Well, it's the same idea."

As we went into the blue room, some one banged at the front door. Asey opened it to a three-inch crack, and took in two notes from some one standing outside on the doorstep.

"Jabe Winter, who's subbin' for Lem at the gate, brought these," he reported. "Says a state cop named Hanson just brought 'em. I know Hanson. He's an ole friend of mine an' one of the straightest guys there is. Guess, just for fun, I'll read my note from Syl b'fore I give Just his from Quigley."

His face clouded as he slowly read through a long message.

"Anything wrong?" I asked.

"Well, it ain't so good. Monday's our deadline. Syl says people been tellin' Quigley they want action, an' he's got obligin' all of a sudden. Got everythin' set for Monday aft'noon. An'—"

"Asey, to-day's Friday! Three days!"

"An' that ain't all. Syl says there's been murmurs about that knife the doc's got. Says he's written a note to the doc to take care. Doc told me this mornin' he was goin' to spend the day pretendin' to shoot things on the marshes, an' it'll take a lot of huntin' to find out just which gunny hole he's in."

"But he can't keep that up indefinitely!"

"Nope, but we can trust the doc. Listen to what Syl says, Miss Kay:

" 'Mahoney told me Quigley's writing Just to stick to you like a leech. He's also posting guards around the tavern to see none of you gets out. I found out from Carter, that man whose sister married Tim Mayo, that Quigley is also going to have the tavern phone tapped. He don't trust you. But I am also giving another note to Hanson to take to Alma Nickerson and Mamie Higgins, the Weesit phone girls. They are both fourth cousins of yours though you probably forgot it.' "

Asey smiled. "Fourth cousins! Syl could r'late me an' him with all Cape Cod if you give him a block of paper an' a couple of pencils with long points. Funny thing about it is, it'd all be true. N'en Syl says:

" 'I told the girls to tell folks they knew that called you to go easy if they had anything important to say, and to ask others who they was, and to be canny about it. You use Lem if you want word sent to me or anywhere, or Hanson. Don't say anything over the phone Quigley could use. The measles are a swell idea as Quigley and his bunch are more scared of getting sick than getting shot at apparently.' "

"Asey," I said, "if he's ordering Just to follow you, what *can* you do?"

"Guess the best thing would be to leave that note to him on the hall table. He can find it by himself, some time. Or it can get infected, an' we'll have to burn it up. Say 'measles' to Just an' he wilts. He told me this mornin' he didn't feel so good, an' he'd never had measles. An' then he give me a blow b'blow description of whoopin' cough. Seems he'd had quite a s'vere case. I told him folks that had whoopin' cough bad always took measles bad. That's why he insisted on playin' bridge down cellar. Farthest place from Eric he could think of."

"But Asey," I said, "what can we do? Anne's taken. We're sure she's innocent, but we can't prove it. Here we are, cooped up, with Quigley's men watching, and we've only got till Monday—"

"An'," he looked at me and smiled, "you don't think I got very far yet."

"I didn't say anything of the sort," I protested. "I simply feel—"

"Don't try to hide things from Swami Asey. Knows all, hears all—cheer up. Go find a nice novel,—they's fifty million of 'em autographed right up to the hilt in the green room, an' set down an' read—"

"Read!" I said disgustedly. "What are you going to do, play marbles?"

"Nope. I'm goin' to r'vise the list of things you'n me is goin' to do t'night after it gets darkish. We can get out then, easy."

"We? You mean, I'm going with you?"

"Sure."

"Why me?"

He grinned. "Might want to play golf or swim a river—"

"Stop it! Why?"

"Well, I want some one with me so's they'll be able

to swear afterwards that the things I find out, if I find anythin', is so. Got every one here all set. Lila Talcott's got to play anxious mother, Betsey'n Jennie've got plenty to do, an' the three men've got to keep Just amused. They all got their jobs, an' yours is witness."

"What are we going to do?"

"Check, first," Asey replied promptly. "Betsey, Lem, Lila, an' Anne if we can. An' the scarfaced feller. Now, I got to check our exit. If I ain't back in an hour," he grinned, "send for a pulmotor an' some pickaxes. But I don't expect no trouble. That—h'lo, son, how's the patient? Say, you keep out of Just's way, if you're goin' to wander 'round. An' stick somethin' on your feet."

"Are you really going out the passage?" Eric asked interestedly, as he seated himself on a hassock.

"Have you—have you been list'nin' outside the door, you—you dastardly villin?"

"Yes," Eric admitted cheerfully. "And the passage is all right. Or it was, a week ago. That was the day I bumped against the panel and it opened, by the stairs. But Eve found the panel swinging open, and followed me and caught me before I got to the end. She spanked me, too."

"Did, did she?"

"She absolutely walloped! Made me promise never to go in it again. She said she was afraid of cave-ins. Say, Asey, where does the passage lead to?"

"Carriage house," Asey said. "Side shed."

Eric whistled. "Gee, that's funny. She told me it went

to the barn! I spent a lot of time trying to find the other end, and no wonder I didn't! Eve was always pretty queer about that carriage house, wasn't she? I mean, the big front door's locked with a padlock, and the windows are boarded up tight, and the shed door's got a lock on it, and so has the side door. I asked her why, once, and if I couldn't go in, and she got awf'ly mad. You ever been in the carriage house, Asey?"

"Long while ago." Asey looked out of the window. "I'd plumb forgotten that shed was locked. I'd wondered 'bout it, too. Know where the key is, Rollo?"

"I hunted," Eric said promptly, "but Eve put her key ring in the strangest places."

"Tell us," Asey said. "Well, Rollo, you f'get about this passage, will you? To every one. 'Lim'nate it from your heaven-born mind. An' now, I feel we could d'spense with your comp'ny. You go be an inv'lid."

"I'd like awf'ly to go with you and see if the passage—"

"No doubt," Asey interrupted, "you would. 'Course, in a mil'tary school, when they say—"

" 'Bye." Eric left.

Asey took Eve's key ring from his pocket. "I'd clean forgot 'bout them locks out on the carriage house an' the shed," he remarked. "An' I r'member thinkin', when I first seen 'em, that they seemed an awful am'chure job. An' when I asked Eve if I couldn't use the shed to work in, she said no, real def'nite. Huh. I'll go try the passage an' see if the keys work."

"May I?"

"May you come? Not this trip. You read a nice book. I'll be all right."

I sat and smoked one cigarette after another, like a portrait of a nervous woman in a tobacco advertisement. Instead of calming me, though, each successive cigarette made me feel a little more jumpy and on edge.

The whole affair of the carriage house was getting Alice-in-Wonderlandish,—just curiouser and curiouser. Why was the carriage-house locked and boarded? And the shed, too? And why had Eve lied to Eric about the passage, and tried to frighten him with tales of cave-ins? I knew perfectly well that Asey had no fear of them, or he would have taken decided precautions before entering.

There seemed only one answer: that Eve didn't want any one wandering about the shed or the carriage house, or the passage, either. Common sense added that there must be some reason why, but I couldn't think of what it could be.

I jumped on Asey when he returned.

"Was it all right? What was there? What did you find out?"

Asey sat down and pulled out his pipe.

"It was all right, an' the only thing I can find out there in the shed is an ole beach wagon. An' a few stray rats. An' I think a skunk's been there recent. I don't understand about that car. Eve's never had one since she's been here. Don't let her guests keep none, either. That's one of the reasons she an' Mark had such a set-to Wednesday mornin'—he said he was goin' to have a car, an' hired an' ole roadster uptown. Well, we'll set out to-night an' see what can be found out."

"But we haven't any car—"

"Yup. We got one. Lem hid mine in the willows b'hind the meadow, last night. We'll use it till we can get somethin' else. It's a sort of not'ceable car. An' we can always hoof it. You'd better put on ole clothes. Don't s'pose you got ridin' things?"

"I have. But what if Quigley calls you up on the phone while you're away?"

"Easy. Lem's goin' to slip in an' be me. He's goin' to say 'Yes-yes' an' 'Nunno,' an' over the phone, one Cape voice sounds pretty much like another. Lila can broad-a for you."

"Wouldn't Betsey know about the shed, Asey, why it was boarded up?"

"I asked her. She said Eve said the town kids was usin' it for neckin' parties, an' she was 'fraid of fire. I—"

The telephone rang. Asey hummed a bar of "Casey Jones" and smiled pleasantly.

"We'll let it ring again," he said, "so as to give brother Quigley ev'ry chance." He went out into the hallway, and removed the receiver. "Yup. Asey Mayo speakin'. Who? Colonel Belcher? How are you, colonel? What? Oh. Why, yes, colonel, I know I said I'd take you out for some cod. Sure. But I couldn't go now. Nunno. We had a murder here," he spoke as casually as though he'd announced he had a cold, "an' we're quarantined for measles."

He held the receiver so that I could hear the violent stream of lurid language which issued from it.

"Yup. Uh-huh. When I get out, I'll be over to see you. When? Fourteen days, I think the doc said. Fourteen days from yest'day at—let me think. Somewheres from six-thirty to 'leven. So many things goin' on, I don't know. Yup. But the cod'll be bitin' just as good then. Sure. Well, don't damn me, colonel. I didn't invent measles. I just got exposed to 'em."

His eyes were bright when he turned around to me.

"That," he said, "was Colonel Belcher. R'tired from the m'rines—"

"I could almost have guessed the marine part," I told him. "Is his name really Belcher?"

"Really is. But you couldn't guess the whole of it, Miss Kay. Y'see, I never said I'd take him out for any cod fishin'. Ain't laid eyes on the man for six weeks."

"Asey, you mean—why, he's probably got something to tell you!"

"Guess so. Wanted to know when the hell I was goin' fishin' with him, an' he wasn't goin' to be here all winter, an' I'd better be over quick."

"And you told him—from six-thirty till—Asey, you're clever."

"But he was a dum sight more realistic. We'll stick him at the head of the list. Now, if the men can pour 'nough of Eve's gen'wine pre-r'peal Cape Cod bootleg gin down Just's throat, just to keep him from gettin' measles, of course, we'll be all set."

Dinner was early that night. Lila, apparently by arrangement, fussed about it. Asey told her tartly that dinner at five-thirty was an old Cape custom, and they called it supper anyway. She continued to find fault with everything Asey said or· did until the end of the meal. Then she took Eric's tray from Betsey and announced coldly that she'd had enough rudeness, and preferred the company of her poor sick son to any healthy Cape Codder living. At that point, Mark kicked my ankle.

"So do I," I said. "I shall not be downstairs again to-night."

Just, whose eyes were more than slightly glazed, decided that he would agree, too.

"Goin' to play bridge," he said with all the finality his slurring tongue would allow. "Come on, boys. Leave the Cape Codder. 'Noyed the ladies, 'noyed Quig, 'noyed everybody. Won't see me neither."

Half an hour later I followed Asey through the panel he coaxed open under the main staircase, and glued my eyes to the small circle of light from his electric torch.

The passage was high enough for me to walk upright with perfect comfort. The air was damp, but fresh. Hitherto my mental picture of an underground passage was a cubistic arrangement of slime, rats, fungous growths and evil odors. I reversed my ideas.

Asey unlocked a trap door and I walked up two steps behind him.

"Carriage house shed," he announced. "Beach

wagon's in the corner. Can't seem to r'member what I ought to about that, though it hits a r'sponsive cord, as the feller said when the el'phant stepped on his corns. I can't c'nect, though."

He unlocked the door, and silently we stepped out into the damp darkness. Gripping the belt of his canvas coat, I padded along behind him through the pine woods and bayberry bushes—and probably, I suspected, poison ivy. We skirted a meadow, jumped a couple of tiny creeks, and then, in a clump of willow trees by a wood lane, we found the car.

"Good for Lem," Asey said. "Right to an inch. Oh, I'm goin' to drive blind, by the way. I'll put on dimmers when I see another car. Don't worry, 'cause there ain't a back road on the Cape I couldn't drive over blindfolded. Bill Porter took me up on that, once, on a crooked strip b'tween Orleans an' Wellfleet, an' he lost fifty dollars."

Ten minutes later we drew up before a long rambling fieldstone house.

Before we could knock, the door was opened.

"Come in, you crazy man, come in! I hope to God the measles are a fake because I've never had the damn things. Why the hell—oh." The colonel, bulky and red-faced, stopped and stared at me. "Elspeth Adams, by the living God! Saw you win your first national title. Prettiest forty foot putt I ever saw. Never could putt, myself. Never got below eighty-five in all my life, as far as that goes. Come in and sit down, Asey, why in hell did you let that blasted gangster take Anne? It's insane."

"Why?" Asey seated himself in a leather arm chair.

"Because from quarter to three till three-twenty-five, I watched her as she sat out behind the chicken house."

9

"TELL us all," Asey said promptly, "an' are you sure of the time?"

"Positive. It's a damn fool habit of mine, noting the exact time things happen. For example, you two came in at 7:53 precisely. I finished playing golf yesterday at 2:06. To-day, at 2:18. The first nine was seven minutes speedier to-day, but I lost four balls coming in. Anyway, I walked home from the club yesterday afternoon. Often do. I had a lot of old balls with me, so when I reached that ridge above the meadow behind the tavern, I pulled out my driver and sliced a couple of dozen into the muck. Then I sat down and smoked a couple of pipes. Beautiful day. I could see Anne sitting out there behind the chicken house the whole time. And as I said, I'm sure of the time."

"How come," Asey asked interestedly, "you didn't call Quigley when you thought of it?"

"Don't be a damned fool, man!" The colonel bit the end off a fat black cigar. "Maybe you've forgotten how one of that man's myrmidons stole my brand new launch last spring, but I haven't! When I read in the papers this morning that Anne supposedly killed Eve during the time I was watching her, I called you. I knew damn well that if you were there, you'd have a finger in the pie, Quigley or not. Won't it help?"

"Help?" I said, as Asey didn't seem to hear. "Of course it'll help! It'll—"

"Look, colonel," Asey interrupted, "you was on that little ridge—it's clear half a mile from the tavern, ain't it?"

"Less than half a mile, I'd say, but not by much."

"Couldn't see Anne's face, could you?"

"No. But I knew it was Anne."

"An' you wear glasses, don't you?"

"Yes. Didn't happen to have 'em on then. I'd taken 'em off when I changed at the club and they were still in a case in my pocket. But I *know* it was Anne. She had on that green sweater suit she wears so much. But it won't make any difference, will it? About the glasses?"

"Last year," Asey said, "Jabe Winter was on main street when the bank was robbed. Standin' by his car, waitin' for Dorcas to come out of the A. & P. Broad daylight. He seen three men come out of the bank. Didn't know, 'course, that anythin'd been goin' on inside. But he noticed the men was strangers. Jabe took a good look at 'em. At their car. At their bags an' briefcases. That was how they caught the fellers, from his story of them an' the car. But Jabe is near-sighted. Didn't have his glasses on. When the expert got through with Jabe an' his eyes, the jury said 'Not Guilty.' Just like Quigley's judge said, it was perfectly clear that Mister Winter, who couldn't d'stinguish two black micr'scopic spots on a piece of purple paper at ten feet, cert'ny was sufferin' from d'lusions when he thought he could recognize three men at seventy-five feet. An' so forth an' so on an' etcetery. See?"

The colonel saw, violently, for several minutes.

"But," he said, "I could always say I had the god-damned glasses on. If they can lie, so can we."

"They won't lie," Asey said. "They'll simply make it silly. Colonel wears glasses. How long since the colonel's eyes was tested. Colonel couldn't see the young lady's face. Colonel was a friend of the young lady's an' wouldn't like to see her c'nvicted, would he? All the colonel seen was a figure in a green dress. Pos'bly Miss Bradford had on a green dress that day, but the colonel can't swear—an' so on an' so forth. It'll all turn out the same way."

"That's absurd, Asey," I said. "The colonel *did* see Anne. He's cleared her completely."

" 'Course he has. I know it an' you know it. But these fellers won't let Anne go on the strength of what the colonel can say. The doc knows an' we know that the knife Anne had wasn't the right knife, but the right one'll compl'cate matters more. If you'd gone over an' talked with Anne an' held her hand, they'd have to let her off. But the way it is, there's a nice big loophole, an' they'll plop right through it. Justice to them guys is the blind lady without the scales. Tell me, how'd you know enough to talk about fishin'?"

"The operator asked who was calling, and I told her I had important information for you. She asked if it was very private, because there was a suspicion of crossed wires. I didn't get her at all, and roared out that I had something to tell you about the murder. She said that was it exactly, and the wires were crossed up the county. Clever girl."

"She's a cousin," Asey said modestly.

"I don't doubt it. Anyway, I finally understood that Quigley was playing games. Asey, what's to be done about this business?"

"First off, I'm goin' to use your phone an' call John Eldredge, the bank pres'dent. He's a notary. Goin' to let you write your story a couple of times an' get it witnessed all legal an' proper."

"Phone's in the hall. It's a pity," the colonel added as Asey left, "that he can't, in addition to finding out who really killed Eve—"

"You think he will?"

The colonel looked at me pityingly. "Of course. But I wish he could put the skids under this rotter Quigley and his crowd.—Get him, Asey?"

"He says he's pract'cally here. I'm goin' to keep one copy, an' let you an' John look after the other. Come in handy if we got to wage any legal battles, an' we may have to, as a last r'sort."

"Anything I can do," the colonel said, "will be done with the greatest of pleasure. Now, Asey, there's one thing more. I mention it only for what it's worth. But d'you know Bill Harding, the conductor with the lame wife?"

"Yup. Sure."

"Well, last Saturday as I was walking home from the club, I saw him flitting around the woods near the tavern. He was acting damn suspicious, and I thought he put a pistol in his pocket when he saw me coming. I couldn't swear it was a gun, but I felt that it was. And I thought, yesterday, that I saw him around again."

Asey's eyes gleamed. "What time was it, Saturday?"

The colonel didn't hesitate. "One-thirty-nine."

"That shot," Asey turned to me, "Eve talked about, that was around ten of two. Huh. I was goin' to see Sadie Hardin' anyway to check on Betsey. Colonel, thank you kindly. That news is help."

"Possibly it is," the colonel replied, "but it's Greek to me."

Asey grinned and enlightened him. Before he finished the story, Mr. Eldredge appeared. The colonel wrote out his story of the previous afternoon, Mr. Eldredge applied his stamp, and Asey and I witnessed the documents.

"Now," Asey said as he tucked his copy into one of the numerous pockets of his canvas coat, "we'll be settin' out. Got a car, colonel, you'd like to donate to the cause? I got a lot of runnin' around to do an' mine's awful easy to spot."

"Three out in the garage," the colonel said casually. "Take what you want. I'd advise the coupé. Leave yours there—Lorne'll look after it—and keep mine as long as you want it. You've my permission to chop it into little pieces if you think it would help to annoy that b—— that Quigley."

We took the coupé and departed.

"I'm disappointed," I said, "that you don't feel the colonel's story will impress anybody. But—what d'you think about Bill Harding's being around?"

"I think it's more'n worth lookin' into. I'm sort of dis'pointed myself, but we're sure now Anne was tellin' the truth, an' that's one thing. You got to realize, Miss Kay, that these fellers is hard to beat. They got Anne. They told the papers so an' bragged about it consid'rable. They ain't goin' to let her go on the say-so of a near-sighted colonel. That bunch's awful eager to see justice done in anythin' that ain't c'nected with their own bunch. Here we be."

He parked the car in a driveway near a small, box-like Cape house.

"Half house," Asey said, beating a tattoo on the back door. "Don't see a lot of 'em now. We'll go right in."

I followed him into a neat little ell kitchen, through a narrow hall into a dining-room. My first impression was of golden oak. I'd forgotten that it took so little golden oak to give such a vast impression of it. Then I looked at the pretty gray-haired woman who sat in a wheel chair by a bridge lamp, and forgot straightway about golden oak, cut glass and Maxfield Parrish prints.

Despite her surroundings, I told myself, this woman was a person.

She looked at me and smiled delightedly.

"Elspeth Adams," she said. "And you wore those riding clothes two weeks ago at the hunt—oh dear me. I shouldn't have said that, should I?"

"Why not?" I smiled back at her. "I did. But how did you know?"

She pointed to a screen beside me. There wasn't an inch of its surface that wasn't pasted over with pictures cut from the papers and the rotogravure sections.

"You're on the top row, left," she said. "Next to that duchess and the nice looking French premier that refuses to pay us money. I hope you're not annoyed?"

"At the premier? I'm honored to be pasted anywhere. Do you—"

"Always paste pictures about? I have since my accident. I pick out the pleasantest looking people from the papers and keep them on the screen for a week or so. Then I change them. It gives me something to do and some one to look at. I don't often get out, you see, and I don't have many people around, though the neighbors are very kind. Oh—I forgot. Do sit down, both of you. And tell me everything, Asey. And what are you doing away from the tavern? Aren't you all quarantined?"

Asey explained about Eric and she laughed. "That's characteristic," she said. "You know, Miss Adams, Asey was one of the first Cape Codders I met when I came to teach school in Wellfleet twenty years ago. He stopped by the schoolhouse at a most propitious moment. I was trying to chastise a boy three times my size. After Asey got through, I never had further trouble in keeping discipline. He completely reversed a most unfavorable first impression of the Cape. I'd been ready to go home at once. What can I do to help you?"

I expected Asey to ask where her husband had been

on Saturday and what he had done the previous afternoon during the time Eve was killed. But he asked instead about Betsey.

"Just wanted to know when Betsey Dyer come here yest'day aft'noon. I'm checkin'."

Mrs. Harding thought a moment. "I put a cake in the oven at two, and when Betsey came, she looked at it for me and said it was done. About quarter to three, I'd say. She stayed and chatted for half an hour or so more, and then she went out and picked some dahlias in the garden for me."

"Good," Asey said heartily. "That settles Betsey. Ain't that a new chair you got, Sadie?"

"Yes. I forgot you hadn't seen it before. You've heard of Bill's uncle, haven't you? The one in Tacoma who discovered us a few years ago, and sends us checks every now and then? His last offering was enormous, and Bill bought this chair for me. It's so much nicer than dragging myself an inch at a time with crutches."

I noticed for the first time that both her legs had heavy, ugly braces on them.

"And," she went on, "that new specialist in Boston thinks that if I do all his old exercises and have the district nurse massage me every day, I may really be able to walk again some time, too. We never could have afforded him without Bill's uncle, either. I've often said to Bill that on the whole, I felt it was a good thing he never found us or thought of us till after my accident. We never really needed his help before."

"When did it happen?" I asked.

"My accident? Oh, four years ago this month. I was walking along the side of the road just below the woods here. Near the fork. It was dark, and it had been raining. I heard a car and stepped to the side of the road—I was two feet off it, easily. Then—the car skidded into a puddle, and the next thing I really remember is a red-headed nurse in the hospital. But I've got along very well. It might have happened that I never came to at all. But even now I shudder a little when I see a beach wagon—"

"Beach wagon!" It burst from Asey and me like a rehearsed chorus.

"Why, yes." She seemed surprised at our explosion. "It was a beach wagon. Whose, we never knew."

"Beach wagon," Asey repeated thoughtfully. "You know, Sadie, I'd almost forgot 'twas a beach wagon. An' they hit an' run, an' you never got a sight of the driver?"

"I never did, but I always had a feeling that it was a woman, though I couldn't tell why. Well, it's all over and done with. Even if we never got insurance money, Uncle Martin—"

"Say," Asey broke in, "I was goin' to ask you. What was that uncle's name? I wondered if it was one of the Hardin's that used to live over near Bound Brook—"

"I don't know about that, but his name is Martin Smith, and he's helped more than any insurance money ever could have. But don't let's talk about my troubles. Tell me about Eve Prence. I shall miss her very much indeed. She dropped in one day shortly after I came back from the hospital, and introduced herself. Ever after, when she was in town, she came every week and she always brought books or magazines or something to amuse me. Sometimes her guests sent her fruit or flowers, and she always shared them with me. I've often said to people whom she'd annoyed that whatever else Eve Prence might be, she was one of the kindest, most considerate people I'd ever met or known. She had no need to bother with a person like me, but she did."

Asey and I looked at each other, and then I began to study the intricate octagonal pattern of the faded Axminster rug. The figures danced an even, measured two-step as I stared at them, trying to figure this out.

Mrs. Harding had been run over four years ago by a beach wagon, driven, she thought, by a woman. Eve Prence had a beach wagon boarded up, locked up, hidden from sight, in her carriage house shed. Eve Prence, moreover, had come home from Paris four years ago. That had been when Mark first began to mention her.

Asey had spoken of it casually, but I recalled suddenly that Mark had told me long ago about Eve's dislike of automobiles, which bordered on a phobia. He'd thought it queer, for she drove a lot in England and on the Continent. But she had never had a car in the states. By her order, no one at the tavern kept a car or brought one there. Lem Dyer had an old truck, but she allowed that because he had to fetch provisions and baggage from the town. Mark had flagrantly disobeyed her command by hiring a roadster, and Asey had said that provoked the flare-up Wednesday morning.

"Yes," Asey said after a pause, "Eve was always kind to any one she thought she could help."

I hardly paid any attention to Mrs. Harding's answer. I was too busy thinking.

After the accident, a mysterious and hitherto unknown uncle had sent checks to the Hardings. Just, as Mrs. Harding said, when they needed help.

Somehow there was only one conclusion left to draw.

Eve Prence herself had been the driver of the beach wagon responsible for Mrs. Harding's accident. Eve Prence herself must have been the mysterious uncle.

No wonder, I thought, that the colonel had seen Bill Harding wandering around the tavern with a pistol!

"Bill," Mrs. Harding was saying, "was awfully upset by the news. He'd expected to be on a special yesterday, but Barney Fisk went instead, and he got a day off."

"Seems to me," Asey said, "he's got a lot of days off lately. Didn't I see him around last Sat'day aft'noon?"

"Yes. Something else was switched then, too. It's so good for him. He can get out of doors in the fresh air, and he loves to walk. Yes, he went to the Masonic Hall to some sort of meeting yesterday, and he was terribly wrought up when he came home."

"How long did that meetin' last?" Asey inquired. "I tore Syl away from it to look after Anne."

"It began around half past two, and Bill didn't get home till after six. I'd heard about Eve over the radio, and I was shocked, myself. But I had to make Bill take two aspirin tablets and he must have had six cups of black coffee at dinner—must you go?"

"'Fraid so, Sadie. We're what you might call A.W.O.L. an'—an' there seems, somehow, to be an awful lot to do. You won't tell a soul we was here, will you? Not even Bill. Where is he to-night, by the way? Ain't this one of his home nights?"

"Yes. He walked over to Nate Hopkins'. Something to do with town meeting, I think. Or taxes. He told me exactly, but I've forgotten. It's been nice seeing you two. Won't you come again, Miss Adams, if you can?"

"If I can get out," I told her, "I certainly shall."

Both Asey and I were silent till we got into the coupé.

"This," Asey said, "is sort of thickenin', ain't it? I ain't a softy, but that woman's pluck ain't somethin' they teach in schools. She come from a rich fam'ly that died an' left her flat busted. Fell in love with Bill when she was teachin'—Bill was better lookin' then'n he is now. She married him. Son died. Bill's fish business went, like all Cape fish businesses gone. N'en he got this job on the railroad. N'en this ac'dent. An' nary a peep out of her. Yessir, that woman's got my vote. She—"

"Asey," I said, "think of her—and Eve coming there —Asey, what d'you think about the beach wagon?"

"Same thing you thought when you sat an' stared at the rug. Eve did it. Prob'ly bought the car in New York'r Boston, an' was drivin' it home. Have to be that, or every one'd known about the car here. Anyways, she went home an' boarded her car up, herself, an' put the locks on the shed, herself. An' then, when it was too late, she begun to think what she'd done. Knew what'd happen to her if she told—then. Not even the Prence name could of saved her. Prence name's saved a lot of Prences in the past, but none of 'em was cowards. Eve thought it over, an' she b'come the uncle in Tacoma. That's a goodish ways off."

"But Mrs. Harding! D'you suppose she knows, or suspects?"

"Nope. She never knew, an' she never must. Huh. It mustn't of been easy for Eve to go there with books an' presents. Only took money to be the uncle in Tacoma, but knowin' Eve an' knowin' Sadie, I can bet that the hardest part Eve ever played was bein' the kind consid'rate neighbor in this p'ticular case."

"It seems incredible," I said. "It would have killed me, had I been Eve, to sit—and listen to that woman's thanks, and see the spunky fight she was making for health—and for—everything. Yes, I think it was probably driven home to Eve that she was a first class skunk."

"But she took it," Asey answered. "That's somethin'. May of been a coward about admittin' the ac'dent, but the way she took to get out of it wasn't so simple, either."

"What about Bill Harding? D'you suppose he knew?"

"Sort of would seem that he didn't, an' yet it'd seem

he did. I don't know. But we're on our way to find out about Bill. Nate Hopkins," he added, "is another cousin of mine."

"Are you related to every one on Cape Cod," I wanted to know, "or is cousin a courtesy title in these parts? It seems to me I've never known as many relatives as you seem to possess."

"Wa-el," Asey drawled, "Mayo fam'ly's been settin' here on this spit of land since 1620. You can c'lect a lot of rel'tives in three hundred odd years—"

"Asey," I interrupted, "I shall personally see to it that some future headline of yours makes mention of the 'Mayflower'—"

"But," he broke in regretfully, as he swung the car into another driveway, "but I never swum no Hel'-spont." He put a finger on the horn and kept it there. "Once I swum Gull Pond, but—"

"Let it," I said hastily, "pass."

He chuckled.

A tall lean man ambled out of the back door of the house on our right.

"No need wakin' the dead," he protested matter of factly, though Asey's finger had been off the horn for half a minute. "Who—for the love of Pete! Asey!"

"Yup. It ain't measles—just a bluff, so don't get upset an' don't say nothin' about us bein' here. Bill Hardin' inside?"

"Went home fifteen minutes ago."

"You uptown yest'day aft'noon 'round three?"

"I was up at Masonic Hall."

"Don't know anybody that seen Lem Dyer clammin' 'round that time, do you?"

"Uh-huh," Mr. Hopkins said readily, to my delight. Apparently Asey hadn't exaggerated about Weesit's curiosity. "May, she said she seen him. She was uptown gettin' lard. Seen him off the shore in the inlet."

"Wonder if she'd be sure of the time?"

"Well," Mr. Hopkins said leisurely, "she told me she seen him just as the church clock struck three. 'Course, the church clock might be three-four seconds out of the way, but May wouldn't."

Asey laughed. "Okay. So Bill Hardin' was at the meetin' yest'day?"

"Why, that's why he come over now, Asey. Said he didn't get back till real late, 'round supper time. Had to go on a special. Nunno, he wan't there."

10

M R. HOPKINS put one foot on the running board.

"I told him," he said, "that was the trouble with working on a railroad. You was always late."

"His is," Asey replied succinctly. "Thank you kindly, Nate. Just forget we was here, will you?"

Nate said cheerfully it would be easy to do that, and we left.

"Asey!" I said. "Mrs. Harding told us her husband *was* at that meeting, and now this man says he wasn't. And she said he came home early, and Nate Hopkins says he was late—and on a special. Asey, what do you think about it?"

"It would seem," Asey returned, "to be what you might term a lie, on the face of it."

"Don't be irritating! Bill Harding *must* have been to the tavern, as the colonel suspected! Perhaps he hadn't known that Eve was responsible for the accident till just recently. Perhaps he just found out. Certainly that would give any man a motive. Perhaps—oh, this seems to me that we're on the track of something at last."

Asey nodded. "But on the other hand, the only way

he could of found out was by the checks of this so-called Martin Smith. An' if he traced 'em an' his phony uncle back to Eve, I wonder, after all, if he'd kill her? Eve was the goose that laid the golden eggs, don't f'get that. An' Bill Hardin' always been crazy about Sadie. Without them checks—no doctors, no wheel chair, no nurses, no nothin'!"

"But if you remember the end of that story," I said tartly, "the gentleman who had the goose that laid the golden eggs, killed it. Are you going to go after Bill now?"

"Not t'-night, Miss Kay. He'll be home by now. It's shorter to his place, walkin', than it is by the road. We'd have to let Sadie know we wanted him, an' there'd be a lot of compl'cations. I don't want to get into 'em. He'll be in Hyannis t'-morrer night, an' we'll get him then. An' b'fore I see him, I want to meander through Eve's papers in her safe. Don't really want to, but b'fore we go interviewin' Bill, it'd be best to check up an' see how much of our s'posin' about the beach wagon was so."

"There's one thing," I said. "If Bill Harding did shoot at Eve, certainly he wouldn't—couldn't—have been the tripper, Wednesday night. That *must* have been some one in the house, Asey."

"Seems's if. But if you stop to think it all out, Mark was the only feller upstairs we really know about—"

"Asey! You're not suggesting—why!" I was too thoroughly angry to continue.

"All I said was, he was upstairs. But he was with me Thursday. Nope, you'n Tony's out, an' Norris, an' Anne, an' Betsey an' Lem. Leaves only Stout, an' Lila an' Bill. It's p'culiar. I been in some cases like this where I didn't know any of the people in it, an' somehow things just seemed to happen left'n right. Here, I know what's gone on b'fore, an' I know the people an' the lay of the land. An' all I can do is 'lim'nate. Huh. Maybe Quigley was right that lobsters an' clams was my forty."

We left the colonel's coupé in the clump of willows and made our way back to the shed. Asey unlocked the door, and once again we went through the passage, guided by the dancing spot of his electric torch.

He snapped it out when we reached the step before the panel that led to the front hall.

"No need," he said in a low voice, "to flash lights around sudden for Quigley's fellers outside to see, in case the hall lights is out. Grab onto my coat, an' I'll guide you if they be."

I followed him cautiously up the step. He opened the panel slowly. The hall lights were out.

A hoarse whisper came out of the blackness. "Hold it! And stick 'em up!"

Promptly my hands left Asey's belt and lifted themselves toward the ceiling.

My first confused thought was that Quigley or one of his men, or both, had entered the tavern during our absence, found us gone, and accordingly drawn the truth of the matter from the rest.

"I have you covered," the voice went on, "and I shall—"

It occurred to me that the Quigley faction did not employ quite that type of English.

"Mark, you ass!" I said. "You utter ass! What's the matter with you?"

"Kay—Asey? Thank God!" But Mark still whispered.

"What," Asey asked in his driest tones, "what seems to be the trouble? An' how about havin' a little light on the subject?"

"No! No lights! Asey, we—"

"Where's brother Just?"

"We carried him up to my room and rolled him into bed. He'll be there some time. Boiled to the gills. Asey, we—"

"Then if Just's out of the way," Asey interrupted, "what's all this goin's on about? Who's here b'side you, Mark?"

"Just Betsey."

"Where's every one else? What *is* the matter?" I demanded. "Can't you get to the point?"

"We could," Mark retorted, "if you two didn't ask quite so many questions. Tony's with Norr, Alex is with Lila and Jennie in Eric's room, and Lem's at the back door outside. Betsey was at the dining—"

"What," Asey asked exasperatedly, "is all the clusterin' an' patrollin' about?"

"They's some one in the house," Betsey said. "We don't know who, but he must—"

"Be a burglar, I s'pose," Asey said. "That's what I call a lovely, r'fined thought. Who in time would want to get into this house where there's measles? Who in time could, with Quigley's men?"

"Listen, Asey," Mark said, "there *is* some one here. There has been."

"Well," Asey answered reasonably, "don't let's stand here in the hall an' give 'em the ben'fit of our doubts if there is. Let's go somewheres an' turn on some lights an' get down to business. Why p'trol the house this way? Why not just lock 'em in or out?"

"You seem to forget," Mark said coldly, "that you have the keys."

"Deary me, so I have. Well, you hold your hosses an' I'll light some lights an' lock the doors. N'en—"

"Don't light the lights suddenly down here!" Mark said hastily. "It'll look funny from outside."

"Great boy for appearances, this Adams lad," Asey commented. "I'm goin' to lock the doors, Mark, an' pull down the shades, an' n'en I'm goin' upstairs an' start from the hall down, puttin' on lights till I get here. That suit?"

"But won't people suspect something? I mean, the lights have been out—"

"Can't a man," Asey demanded in virtuous indignation, "make himself a cup of coffee at any time of night he wants? Or heat up a little broth for a poor sick child? Pish-tush. No one ever suspects anythin' 'less you s'pect they will. We're goin' to be all open an' above-board here."

He moved out of the hall toward the back of the house, and Betsey and Mark and I stood there in the dark and waited while he locked doors and pulled down shades.

That front hall had never seemed tiny, but it was growing, in the blackness, increasingly larger. I had a strange feeling that half a dozen people had joined our silent trio. I felt things move near my ankles. By the time Asey turned on the hall light and nonchalantly walked downstairs, I was the sheepish possessor of a first class case of the jitters.

Once the light was on, however, my fright blessedly departed. I told myself firmly that some day I *would* confess, openly and unashamedly, the intense fear of darkness I've had since I was a child. Of course I never shall, and people will always think me brave, as Betsey did, simply because I've learned to control my facial muscles.

"To look at you," she said admiringly, "cool as a cucumber, it makes me ashamed of myself. I'm just drippin' pers'p'ration all over."

I was too, but I didn't acknowledge the fact.

"Now," Asey led us out into the kitchen, turning on lights left and right, "now, while I make some coffee, tell all. There was some one wanderin' around the tavern. How'd you know it?"

"He didn't," Mark said, obviously annoyed at Asey's

dubious acceptance of what seemed vastly important to him, "leave a calling card, Asey, but he left a hat. A gray felt hat with a black band. No initials."

I remembered that the scar-faced stranger whom Betsey had seen wore a gray felt hat.

"Let's see it," Asey said promptly. "Where'd you find it?"

"In the front hall by the newel post. I don't know if it was left there, or dropped from above, or what. But I found it. Wait—I left it on the dining room table."

His face, when he returned, was a study.

"There's no hat there! It's gone!"

"Mystifyin'," Asey said. "Completely mystifyin'. Can you get out of handcuffs in twenty seconds, too, or do you saw a lady in half better? The disappearin' hat trick's good, but all you really need is a piece of elastic an'—"

"Look here, Asey, there *was* a hat! This isn't any joke."

"Well," Asey said, "I b'lieve you, Mark, but you got to admit it's askin' a lot. Sure you didn't help Just by a little encouragin' accompanyin'?"

"I haven't had a drop to drink, and it's not my imagination, and the Adams family is not subject to hallucinations. Thank God, it's not even a family tradition. There *was* a hat. That's the truth."

"Okay. Betsey, where'd you put that devil's food cake we had for supper?"

"In the cake box right square in front of your face.

If 'twas a bear it'd bite you. Asey Mayo, there *was* a hat. I seen it."

"P'raps," Asey viewed the box thoughtfully, "there was a devil's food cake, too. But there ain't, now. I bet we have to call the doc real serious for little Rollo t'-morrer. That was a big cake."

"Asey!" Betsey crossed over and looked into the closet. "Well, for heaven's sakes! It's gone. An' I put it there myself!"

"Eric," I said. "Just Eric."

"Eric nothin'! That child's been upstairs all evenin' long. Nobody—not a soul's been in here."

"Where's the lamb?" Asey asked, looking into the refrigerator.

"Is that—well—Asey, some one's taken that, too! Now, Asey Mayo, will you b'lieve some one was here?"

"Betsey," Asey said apologetically, "an' you too, Mark, I take it all back. Every last single sol'tary word of it. A hat that ain't don't really mean a lot to me. But a devil's food cake an' a leg of lamb that was, an' that ain't, that's what you might call reas'n'ble proof. Always providin' that no one else of the party ate 'em. Though," he added hastily, "I don't see how they could of wanted anythin' after your supper, Betsey."

Betsey sniffed.

"Wait'll I gulp down this coffee," Asey continued, "an' we'll hunt."

"The panel!" I said suddenly, and rather indistinctly, for my mouth was full of cheese and crackers. "The panel—if some one's here, they might perhaps—"

"I don't think there's any chance of any one usin' that," Asey assured me. "That panel takes a lot of knowin'."

We began our hunt with the kitchen. We searched that kitchen as thoroughly as any kitchen could be searched. I even remember peering into the double boilers. From the kitchen we proceeded to the rest of the downstairs rooms, which were combed extensively. Then Betsey and I sat on the seat at the head of the front stairs while Asey and Mark did the second floor; we watched the door to the third floor steps while they proceeded through every single inch there and in the attic.

They found absolutely nothing.

"Mark," Asey said wearily, "we'll have a look at the panel and the passage. But if any one did have the dumb luck to get into that, they couldn't get no farther than the door. It's locked. Come along!"

But they found no trace of a soul.

"I guess," Betsey said with a yawn, "he climbed into a crack in the floor, or else melted into thin air, like a feller I seen once at B. F. Keith's ole theater in Boston. Cake or no cake, lamb or no lamb, hat or not, I'm goin' to bed."

Mark agreed with her, but Asey shook his head.

"You fellers got me started on this," he said. "You fellers proved there *was* some one here, an' now I got my dander up. I'm just muley enough to keep on tryin' to see what's at the bottom of this. You can all go to

bed if you want to, but I'm goin' to keep on huntin',
even if it takes the form of just settin' an' rum'natin'."

Suddenly Tony Dean, barefoot, and with a gaudy
dressing gown girt hastily around him, emerged from
Norris's room.

"Look, Asey," he said sleepily, "can't something be
done about those rats?"

Asey looked at him suspiciously. "What rats?"

"Norr's nearly frantic. He's complained of 'em before,
but this is the first time I ever heard 'em, too. Sounds
like a pick and shovel brigade demolishing the Grand
Central Station."

"Where do they seem to be?" Asey appeared extraor-
dinarily interested.

"Around the fireplace, somewhere. Not in it, but
around it. In the paneling somewhere. I—"

"I got it." Asey grinned and dived into Norris's room.
In a minute he was back, chuckling. "Yessir, I got it. I
thought them—wait a shake."

He knocked briefly on Alex Stout's door. There was
a muttered conversation, then Alex, looking very cross
and sleepy, joined our group by the second floor landing.

"Really," he said, yawning widely, "it's all in a good
cause, Asey, but after amusing Just all day long,
couldn't you let a man sleep in peace?"

"You an' Tony," Asey ordered, "go upstairs to the
room over Norris's on the third floor, an' stand by the
chimney. Betsey'll go with you an' show you where
the lights are—"

"I won't," Betsey said firmly, "stir a step if there's rats—"

"You b'gun this," Asey returned, "an' you will."

"What's it all about?" I demanded.

"Mark, you an' Miss Kay an' me, we'll go down to the green room, an' fix this business up once an' for all. No way out on this floor or in the attic, so we'll be able to get 'em. Oh, you all pull the shades down b'fore you turn on the lights upstairs. I yanked 'em up. Now—"

"I'm willing," Stout said sleepily, "to play any kind of game you like, Asey, but it would be so much more fun if we had some idea of what it was!"

"There's some one loose in the house," Asey said briskly. "An' they's rats in Norris's chimney. Only there ain't an' there is, if you see what I mean. Rats is of the two-legged v'riety. It's the feller we're after. B'hind the panelin' of these chimneys is a space that stretches b'tween the bricks of the chimney itself, an' the side of the panelin', if you get me. Runs par'lel to the chimney, see, an' it used to be 'bout two-three feet wide. An' runnin' up it is a ladder, 'tached to the chimney. Had it for lookin' after the chimney in the old days when they used 'em a lot more, an' also for many other sundry an' various reasons. I thought Eve'd done away with that ladder when she had the place fixed over, but it seems she didn't. Some one slid up the panel—it's part of the wainscotin' in the green room, an' climbed. Get it now?"

We got it, hazily.

"Then come along, Miss Kay, an' Mark. I'll try to get him out downstairs. If he goes out the third floor—if he *can*—you get him, Tony. Left side of the chimney."

Blankly, we followed him downstairs. From one of his numerous pockets, Asey had extracted an old .45 Colt, which he fondled longingly.

The shades were down in the green room; he turned on the switch and flooded the room with lights from the great chandelier. Then he crossed to the fireplace and pointed to the large panel at the left. Calmly he lifted it and disclosed an opening about two and a half feet wide and three feet high.

"There," he said. "I thought of this right off yest'day aft'noon, but the doc an' I found that the one in Norris's room'd been nailed down for about two hundred years. So I didn't think of it again."

He stuck his head into the opening and yelled.

"Hey, feller! I got eyes like a cat. Be glad to come up an' get you, or I'll shoot, if you'd rather."

At the word "shoot," we heard a distinct rustle.

"Intel'gent rats," Asey said. "Not only hear, but they understand. Come on, feller! Crawl down."

There was a silence.

"Yup, you're sittin' quiet, but the plaster's fallin', just the samey. Okay. I'll come after you. I—"

"Aw, let me!" Mark begged. "Let me, Asey—"

He disappeared through the hole and we could hear him climbing up the ladder.

A minute later there was a thud and a scuffle. Then Mark, looking a little like a coal heaver, appeared with a short, terrier-like man whose clothes literally dripped dirt.

I noticed with delight that he had beady eyes, and that a mole protruded from his very grimy neck. And on his right cheek was an unmistakable scar.

"It's—he's the stranger!" I said. "The one Betsey and Eric saw. And Mark—isn't that—?"

"It is." Mark removed a crumpled gray felt hat from the man's pocket. "The gent's our burglar, too. Say, who are you and what's your idea in—"

"Wait up, Mark," Asey ordered. "Listen a sec—"

A little shower of plaster fell at the opening of the hole.

"Got some one with you, huh, feller? Tell him the jig's up."

"Nobody else," the man said suddenly. "Nobody else. And put that rod away. It might go off."

"Uh-huh. Only first take his away from him, Mark. Under his arm, in a shoulder holster. Now, what'd Quigley send you for?"

"What?"

"One of Quigley's men?"

"Who? No."

"Okay. What you doin'—" inside the chimney space something fell. Asey leaned over and picked up a man's black shoe.

"Nobody here," he said cheerfully, "but the cobbler.

7EEE. Short an' plump. Mark, go up an' get the gent. He'd be above Norris's room, I think."

Mark needed no second summons.

We listened expectantly to a thump and a rattle and a series of thuds.

"So you're not—well, I wasn't so sure. Whose boy are you, mister?"

The stranger didn't answer. Instead he looked at me as though he didn't like me one bit; his glance toward Asey contained elements of distinct hatred.

"Whose?" Asey repeated, as the thumps above grew louder. "Need help, Mark?"

"No." Mark's voice sounded hollow and breathless. "He's a fatty, too. Got him stuck—"

There was a crash as two bodies came tumbling to the ground.

Mark emerged first, yanking some one by the collar. "R'calcitrant, huh?" Asey asked.

"My goodness gracious, yes! Didn't want to leave his perch at all. He's too big for indoor work like that, though. Like to get stuck. Stand up, Fatty."

He pulled the man to his feet.

And then I began to laugh. I laughed till the tears ran down my cheeks and dripped off the end of my chin. I laughed till I had to sit down on the couch. I couldn't stand.

In spite of the dirt and the cobwebs and the soot—in spite of his crumpled clothes and entirely negroid complexion, there was no mistaking the man Mark had yanked down, the man he had jeeringly referred to as Fatty.

Scarface's plump companion was undeniably none other than my dignified Bostonian brother, Marcus Adams II.

~~~~~~

11

MARK leaned over and peered at the chubby figure, then he too dissolved into bursts of helpless laughter.

Asey surveyed us pensively. I think he thought we had gone mad.

"Oh, Kay," Mark babbled. "I—Kay—you tell Asey! I can't."

"I wish," Asey remarked plaintively, "that you would. I'd like to join in the gen'ral festiv'ties an' rejoicin', myself."

"It's brother Marcus!" I said weakly. "Oh, dear Heaven, to think that I should live to see the day when Marcus should emerge from—Marcus, what are—what *were* you doing in that chimney hole with this—oh, dear!" I wiped my eyes.

Marcus cleared his throat. That bass rumble has quelled more than one stubborn board meeting and reduced any number of strong directors to limp, dithering things. But at that moment it served only to start me laughing all over again.

He waited until Mark and I were finally silent, then he cleared his throat again.

"I see," he said coldly, "nothing humorous in this unfortunate situation. Nothing whatsoever—"

"You couldn't," Mark told him sincerely. "You're not sitting where we are."

"Neither," Marcus went on, "do I entirely understand your presence here, Mark. Nor yours, Elspeth." He frowned.

"You've got nothing," Mark retorted flippantly, "on us. Suppose, sir, you explain first. Asey—this is my father, by the way—Asey, don't you really feel that father and his boy friend rate the stand first?"

Asey nodded solemnly. "I feel they—oho! He kept the bone, even."

Peeking out of brother Marcus's pocket was the end of the lamb bone, which, intact, had been our dinner's pièce de résistance.

Mark snickered and I giggled, but brother Marcus ignored both of us.

Asey rubbed his chin reflectively. "Yup, Mr. Adams, in the face of all this, s'pose you tell us how it happens you're trespassin'—my goodness, what a lot you're guilty of! Breakin' an' enterin' an' rob'ry an' ignorin' a quarantine, an' assault an' bat'ry on your own son! Yes—yes. S'pose you break down first. How come you —uh—dropped in? An' why? An' when? An' who's your—er—pal?"

"This gentleman," Marcus said, "is Michael Krause. He is in my employ."

"Tch, tch." Mark clicked his tongue. "Gunmen at your age!"

Marcus paid no attention to him. "He has been in my employ for over a year, since my friend Burton Fielding's son was kidnaped. His duty has been to follow Mark at all times. It seemed a sensible and necessary step, in view of Mark's usual lack of responsibility and of reasonable care for his own personal safety. I saw no reason why my son should be harmed if I could help it."

Mark and I looked at each other. This was news to us. And it showed me that my brother cherished his son more than I'd suspected.

"Mark was to sail for Rio a week ago Wednesday," Marcus continued. "Krause telegraphed me, however, that while he went to New York, he failed to take his ship. I ordered Krause to follow him, and he reported Mark's arrival at the tavern. He was to keep Mark under surveillance till he should take the airplane—"

"You—knew about that?" Mark asked blankly.

"Certainly. Krause followed you to the booking office. I decided not to interfere, and to let you carry out what extraneous plans you had in mind, as long as you arrived in Rio on the appointed day. Krause was looking after you in the interim. I trust my explanation is satisfactory?"

"It sort of gives us a basis for Krause," Asey said, "but it still don't exactly extinguish the subject. I don't still quite catch why you're here, breakin' in, hidin' in chimney holes, stealin' cakes an' left-over lamb."

It took practically all of my brother's dignity to proceed before such charming sarcasm.

"As soon as Krause heard that Eve Prence—"

"Where's this feller stayin', by the way?" Asey interrupted.

"I'm sure I—Krause, where *are* you staying?"

Krause grudgingly parted with the information that he had a room in a tourist camp in Eastham.

"Go on," Asey said. "This is very interestin'. I'd ask you to set down, Mr. Adams, but you ain't in the best of c'ndition to set on clean chair covers. Go on."

"Krause telephoned"—Marcus is never guilty of 'phoned'—"that Eve Prence had been killed. I told him to interview Mark and find out what could be done for Anne Bradford."

Mark's jaw all but hit the carpet. "You—you knew about Anne, sir?"

"Certainly. I remembered instantly who she was when Krause reported on her during your first extended visit here last winter. Her father was Jonas Bradford of Bradford and Prence—excellent old firm. Had you come to me and told me the facts in the case, without resorting to childish subterfuge, most of this unpleasant situation would never have taken place. You have, as usual, taken your usual careless and irresponsible attitude—"

"You approve of Anne, sir?" Clearly it was being difficult for Mark to digest his father's speech. It had amazed me considerably, too.

"Of course I approve," Marcus said casually. "I knew her father well in a business way, and the reports on the young woman have been very good indeed." He spoke as though Anne were an unexpectedly fine crop of coffee. "But you hardly could expect me to proffer my opinion before I was informed of—"

"But, sir, I thought you wanted me to marry that Courtenay girl. The horsey one with the inherited beak!"

"Bradford and Prence," Marcus announced in his most positive tones, "were a far better firm in their day —far sounder, mind you—than Courtenay and Company. But—to continue this ridiculous recital. Krause could not, in view of the quarantine, get in touch with you, Mark. As the headlines became increasingly lurid, I felt it my duty to come here myself. I drove down earlier in the evening, met Krause in Orleans, and we drove here in his automobile. Krause had an idea, gleaned from some native, that possibly the quarantine was not entirely sincere."

That understatement, I thought, was almost worthy of Asey himself.

"After dark," Marcus went on coolly, "we entered the kitchen door and remained in a closet till we thought every one had retired. Then we went to the front of the house, intending to go to Mark's room, about which Krause knew. But apparently we had moved too soon, for some one was being carried upstairs, and a woman screamed and said there was a burglar—"

"Wait up," Asey said. "I forgot about them fellers on the third floor! Run up, Mark, an' tell 'em the news. Go on, Mr. Adams."

"Krause and I ran, which, I will admit, was very

silly of us, back into the kitchen. Then there was a silence, and we thought people had given up any thought of investigating. We were very hungry, neither of us, in the press of excitement, having remembered dinner. We—er—raided the larder. After an interval, I decided that it might be best for us to leave, but some one suddenly appeared outside by the kitchen door. I—"

"Lem, I guess," Asey said. "Must of swung down over the balc'ny."

"I had no real desire to leave," Marcus said, "for I wanted to see Mark. On the other hand, I did not care to stay for—er—obvious reasons. It is," he concluded with some force, "not pleasant to be called a burglar."

Asey nodded. Personally I wanted to laugh again. It was the first time during the fifty years I have known my brother that I had a chance to laugh last, longest and best. In fact, looking dispassionately over the past, it occurred to me that it really *was* Marcus's first embarrassing moment. Marcus never lost garters or spilled soup or sat on pins. It occurred to me, too, that it was the first time I'd ever really looked on him as a human being.

"N'en what?" Asey demanded. "How'd you find that chimney hole?"

"We made our way, cautiously, when we finally realized that a concentrated attempt was being made to corner us, from the kitchen into the dining room. Krause put out a hand and found his hat—he had previously dropped it in the hall when the woman screamed—on the dining room table. We went into the hall and then edged in here. I was," Marcus added parenthetically, "very nervous by then. I felt that if Mark were not present, explanations would be difficult indeed. Then we heard voices in the hall, and the lights went on."

I thought grimly to myself that I had been right when I felt people moving about my ankles; my jitters were far more justified than I had thought.

"Then," Marcus said, "Krause and I edged around to the far side of the fireplace. I remembered that our old house in Weymouth, and other similar houses, had sliding panels by the fireplace. I tried this, and it did. That's all, except that it was really very dirty and exceedingly cramped."

He seemed rather annoyed about it, as though some one else were to blame for his mussed clothes and general sardine-like confinement.

Asey looked first at Marcus's figure and then at the chimney panel.

"I can see," he said, "where that might be. Now," he yawned in spite of himself, "s'pose you tell us, Mr. Krause, all about Thursday aft'noon. Say from half past two on."

Mr. Krause closed his beady eyes. "On Thursday, September twenty-seventh," he began in a sort of singsong, "at two-thirty, I was perceding along a small path on the rear 'v this present prop'ty with the 'ntention 'v perceding further to town to 'plenish supply 'v gasoline, same having run out 'v car. Just previous to that time, met cook 'v this present 'stablishment, same being able to crob'rate 'foresaid statement."

"Same," Asey said, "is already crob'rated. Where was your car, an' what was your gen'ral intentions, an' if you got your gas, why was you wanderin' near Hoss Leach pond later on?"

Krause opened his eyes and sighed. "I was meeting a girl," he said, dropping the sing-song. "Car was up on the Hollow road. Going to meet her at three-fifteen. Thought I could get to town and back with the gas. Found I couldn't. Turned back. Met her by the big oak, and we walked—well, we walked around. Then I walked home with her. She had to get back, because she's one of Colonel Belcher's maids. And—"

"One of Belcher's maids?" Asey said. "Sure?"

"Yes. And I had to get back because," he looked at Marcus out of the corner of his eyes, "I thought it was about time that young Mr. Adams was getting back. I seen him go off with you, Mr. Mayo, and I knew he was safe for a while." ·

"One of Belcher's maids. Huh. See any one around the house after you changed your mind about gettin' gas, an' turned back?"

Krause shook his head. "I didn't see her. I come back by the road out front. The short cut the cook told me about run into a bog. I come back by the road."

"Now," Marcus said, "tell him what you told me about the woman, Krause. That woman was the real reason for my coming down here and wanting to see Mark."

"Any p'ticular woman?" Asey asked.

"As I come back by the road," Krause said, "I seen a woman start up the driveway to these premises; that was at five minutes to three."

"Sure of the time?" Asey demanded.

"It's my business to be sure," Krause replied loftily. "D'scribe her."

"Red hat, red coat, about five feet four, weight—um. Hundred and ten to a hundred and fifteen. Blonde."

"Lila Talcott!" I said. "Was it Lila Talcott, Mr. Krause, or don't you know her?"

Krause was cautious. "I seen Mrs. Talcott wear a red cap and a red coat, and she's about five-four and one-ten. But I've no reason to believe said woman," he lapsed into his official manner, "was Mrs. Talcott on basis 'v 'foresaid ev'dence. Description however crosponds to 'foresaid lady."

Asey smiled. "That," he said, "is what I been waitin' for, 'mong other things. Thank you kindly, Mr. Krause. At this point, s'pose we go to bed. I'll find a place for you two on the third floor, Mr. Adams, an' I hope you'll be good enough to—uh—stay put there. I'll try to get you out when I can, but I don't want Quigley's fellers to find out about you. An' stay away from windows, an' don't get up till I call you. We got an 'ficial guard in the house. He's what you might call out of the picture now, but you can't tell."

"But," Marcus said, "I have many things which I wish to discuss—"

Asey smothered another yawn. "I know. They's a lot

of things I want to talk over with you, too, an' with
Mr. Krause. But I been up since six, Mr. Adams, an'
I went to bed at four, an' day b'fore I didn't sleep at
all, an' it's now past four. I kind of feel whatever we
got to say'll sort of perc'late better after a few hours of
just r'laxin'."

Reluctantly, Marcus permitted himself to be led upstairs. Asey carried an alarm clock under his arm.

"Only sure way I know," he said as he left me at
my door, "of risin' in the world."

Bed was an entirely acceptable spot to me, but I found
that sleep was more or less out of the question. We had
found out too many things since the start of our noc-
turnal excursion for my mind to give way peacefully to
my subconscious in any nice, restful slumber.

Krause's report of the woman in red was of course
uppermost. Without doubt it had been Lila Talcott.
Alex Stout had said that she hadn't known that Eve
was his wife, but it was entirely possible that he might
have been mistaken. If she were pursuing Alex—everything pointed to an unmistakable marathon—and if she
knew about Eve, there was no difficulty about a motive.
Krause said she entered the tavern just before three.
And Asey had already caught her up when she suggested that one of the daggers from the pair of flintlock
pistols was the weapon used.

Then there was the problem of Bill Harding. There
was no doubt whatsoever in my mind that he had been
the one who shot at Eve the previous Saturday. He'd
lied about his whereabouts Thursday afternoon both to

his wife and to Nate Hopkins. He had motive enough. He could have entered the tavern, because Tony and I had been in the far end of the blue room, and the door to the hall had been closed. He might well have known about the guns, for, as Asey had said, the townspeople knew and had known for many years all about the tavern and its furnishings.

The scarfaced stranger was explained, and I knew that if he were in Marcus's employ, he was completely out of the picture. There was, of course, Alex and his duplicate key; I knew I could speculate about both of them for hours, probably without getting anywhere at all. I let my subconscious tackle the job.

At two o'clock Saturday afternoon I went downstairs for breakfast, to find Asey sitting at the dining room table, surrounded by a crumpled heap of newspapers.

"Mornin'," he said. "Miss Elspeth (Kay) Adams is figgerin' again t'day. Say, when'd you walk from New York to Boston? I missed that one b'fore."

"In 1918." I dived into the grapefruit Jennie Mayo brought me. "For a liberty loan drive. I collected an enormous sum of money for it, and spent several thousand dollars afterwards on myself for chiropodist's bills. My feet have never been quite the same since. What do the papers say?"

"Wa-el, a payroll rob'ry in Charlestown sort of pushed this off on page five. Ed'torials 'gree that Quigley's quick 'rest is a sample of what Mas'chusetts can do when she tries. Life in the ole gal yet, that's kind of the way they feel. No startlin' d'sclosures, 'cept Syl sent me a note sayin' Quigley's sent some more state cops to p'trol this place an' make sure we *are* quarantined. Doc told him there was more to Eric's measles than met the eye. Might be chicken pox. Quigley thought it was smallpox, I guess. He ain't sent for the knife, an' the doc's all but got rheum'tism from bein' out on the marshes. Just to be on the safe side, I had Syl, b'way of Hanson an' Lem, get hold of Steve Crump."

"Crump? Why, he's a wonderful lawyer, Asey, but he's awfully expensive!"

"Yup. But he's a friend of mine, an' I ain't in the poorhouse yet. That's all my affair. Just's d'cided to stay in bed t'day; Eve's gin did a better job'n I hoped for. He called Quigley an' said he was lookin' out for everythin'. I'm takin' a likin' to Just. N'en I found out about Uncle Martin Smith, the Hardin' lifesaver."

"Was it really Eve?"

"Seems's if. She's got an account in a Tacoma bank under the name of Martin Smith. How an' when she got it, I wouldn't be a one to know, but she usually wandered 'round the West for a spell every winter. Anyways, her checks to that bank is from her 'count in New York, an' her checks from it is all payable to Bill Hardin'. Sort of clinches the matter. Can't find the number plates to that car out in the shed, or anywheres else, but they're prob'ly a lot of rust in the Atlantic Ocean right now, if I know Eve. Thorough. Well, we'll tackle Bill t'night."

"Where's Marcus?"

"Havin' his clothes cleaned an' pressed while he waits in the pr'serve closet. Mark's doin' the job for him. He—uh—through? We'll go up an' harry Mrs. Talcott a little. I must say since this 'nforced c'nfinement, she's been doin' her duty by Eric like a shot. Amusin' him first rate, though I got a sneakin' feelin' he's more amused than she thinks."

We found Eric seated on the floor of his mother's room, which looked, as Asey said, like bedlam let loose.

"See," Eric said. "Aren't they swell?"

He pointed with pride to the lines and lines of paper birds of varying sizes which littered the floor and the furniture.

"Look." Eric picked up one of the largest and pulled its tail. "You hold it in the middle and yank this—and it flops. I learned to make 'em in Madrid a couple of Christmases ago from the padre that taught me how to make clay figures for the nativity scenes. See, we've made faces on 'em. Here's Mussolini. We got him off a box of Italian matches. And here's Lincoln. We just copied him off a penny."

"Very nifty," Asey said. "'F you'll give me a sheet of paper, I'll try to make you a necklace chain. Mind you, I ain't sure it'll m'terialize. It's a long time since I tried this. Bigger pieces'n that, Rollo."

With professional recklessness, he split and tore the paper.

"Where'd you learn to do it that way?" Eric asked delightedly.

"Feller I shipped with once used to be a paper artist

in a Barnum an' Bailey sideshow. He was on a tramp steamer that went 'round the Horn. Lots of cold winter nights when 'twas a pleasure to tear paper. I used up ten ton—there—"

He made a few deft pulls and pushes, and we all crowed like children over the result—as neat a lei as you would care to see. Eric was no whit less entranced than Lila and I.

"Wonderful," Lila said. "Simp-ly wonderful! I wish you'd show Eric—"

"Much as I'd like to set an' amuse the young for you," Asey told her, "I got too much to do. What's your theories about this business here, Mrs. Talcott?"

From his delightfully casual, purring manner, I knew he was setting his trap.

"I'm absolutely no good at this sort of thing," Lila said. "I'm really too helpless. But usually, it's a dull sort of person who hasn't any enemies, and Eve wasn't dull. She had—well, almost more than her share. But no one here could have killed her. Good heaven, we wouldn't be here if we didn't—hadn't—liked her. I think you're going to find out that it was some local citizen who·believed the stories about her. Some of them were pretty lurid, even for the most broad-minded."

"You mean," Asey said, "some pur'tanical New Englander, like they draw 'em in cartoons, just up an' stabbed Eve on what you might call gen'ral phil'n-thropic motives?"

"Exactly. That's just exactly what I think."

"Might have been." Asey got up and strolled over

to the window. "Might have been, if Eve wasn't a Cape Codder herself. If she'd just settled down here in town, an' done what she done, without bein' a Prence, I might maybe almost be half 'nclined to 'gree with you, p'raps. But she was a Prence of Weesit—" He stopped short and pointed to the window sill. "When," he demanded sharply, "when did those come here?"

On the sill were two brownish circular spots.

12

~~~~~~

LILA stared at them.

"What are they?"

"Never seen 'em b'fore?"

"Never."

"Who's been here this mornin'? An' this aft'noon?"

"Why, practically no one. That is, Alex came in, and Eric's been here off and on. And Tony. And Mark bummed some cigarettes. And that Mrs. Mayo came in and made the bed and cleaned up, earlier."

"You," Asey murmured, "an' Robinson C'rusoe. Yup. Prac'ti'cly alone. Rollo, you run down an' tell Betsey to bake you a cake. Or show your necklace to Mark's father. Yup, he's here. Now, Mrs. Talcott, you closed your window when you got up this mornin', didn't you?"

"Yes. But I'm sure I didn't notice those spots then. But they might have been here, I suppose. Really, Asey, I don't notice things the way you do. And what earthly difference do they make? I suppose I left a cigarette burning. That must be it. Burned down from an ash tray. Slipped, or something."

Asey sighed. "I s'pose."

"Well, what else could they be?"

"There," Asey said, "you got me. So you think an outsider done this, huh?"

"I do," Lila said positively. "At first, when the doctor told us, I thought it must have been Alex. But that was too absurd to think of a second time. Heaven knows, though, that poor Alex has had plenty of encouragement and stimulation—Eve simply would *not* divorce him—" She stopped, aware that she was saying altogether too much.

"You knew," Asey said slowly, "you knew Alex an' Eve was married?"

Lila seemed a little flustered. "Why n—I mean, yes. Yes, I did."

"Alex tell you?"

She hesitated and looked at Asey. "N—no."

"Did Eve?"

"No, she didn't."

"Well," Asey asked her patiently, "how did you find out? No one else in the house seems to know. At any rate, they ain't said nothin' about it."

"My husband—Jim—told me. A lot of people in Paris knew they were married, but they didn't get along, so they didn't live together. Alex came here a lot, though. I mean—well, Eve was a marvelous woman, but it would be difficult to spend any length of time with her. She was so temperamental."

"You never spoke of his marriage to Alex?"

"No. He never brought the matter up, so I didn't, either."

"Why did they keep it a secret, Mrs. Talcott?"

"They didn't, exactly. Some people knew. They really didn't care whether it was known or not. But they didn't yell about it. And Eve thought it wouldn't do her business any good."

"You knew, though, that Alex wanted to get a divorce, an' Eve wouldn't let him?"

Lila moistened her lips. "I—well, I'd heard so."

"Alex didn't tell you, an' Eve didn't tell you that?"

She shook her head.

"Then why did people," Asey accented the word ever so slightly, "why did people think Alex wanted a divorce, an' Eve wouldn't give it to him?"

His steady stream of questions was beginning to show some effect on Lila. She reached out and took a cigarette from a jade box, and lighted it nervously.

"Well, maybe—probably, well, I suppose it was mostly gossip."

"Yet you said," Asey quoted her own words back at her, "'Heaven knew Alex had plenty of 'ncouragement an' stimulation to kill Eve. Eve simply would not divorce him.' Now, Mrs. Talcott, if not a lot of people in this country knew they was married, an' if you never spoke to Alex or Eve about it, how come, just that you was so sure? Was Alex in love with some one else? D'you really know Eve r'fused to divorce him?"

"Oh, it was gossip," Lila said rapidly. "Just gossip. I didn't mean to insinuate that Eve was an obstacle in Alex's path. I just heard—I mean, it was all gossip."

"I see. Now, where was you just, Thursday aft'noon at three o'clock?"

"Why, out walking! I told you so. I was—it must have—I guess—I mean, I was walking by the ponds."

I recalled Asey's statement that he was going to wait before he got Lila's story, to wait until she knew her lines too well. His flood of questions she hadn't expected about the spots and about Eve and Alex, had confused her just enough so that her answers, probably pat enough once, were now garbled, muddled phrases.

"How'd you know there was a dagger in that gun, or daggers in the guns, in Norris's room?"

"I didn't know. I just guessed."

"Had that room last year, didn't you? Did you guess it then?"

"Oh—oh, I don't know. I suppose I guessed when I first saw the guns. I don't remember when."

"Guessed it an' didn't mention it, huh? Didn't ask Eve, to make sure. Let Eric play with 'em, without knowin' for sure whether he'd hurt himself or not. Stab himself. Stabbin', after all, ain't no simple thing. You should—"

"Don't!" Lila crushed out her cigarette. "Oh, Asey, don't! Please!"

There was a note of desperation in her voice, and the knuckles of her right hand, gripping her chair, were white.

It seemed to me that she had suddenly dropped all her pose of studied helplessness, laid aside her part of poetess and widowed young mother. She became herself—another slightly bewildered young woman who had never entirely solved the problem hand which life had dealt her. I wanted to tell her during that moment that it was a far more appealing character than the one she had chosen to assume.

"I knew you'd question me, Asey. I had the answers all ready. You knew it, and I knew you'd get at me sooner or later. But please, Asey, don't bring in Jim. And stabbing. Tell me what you know and what you want to know, and I'll tell you the truth. I promise it."

"Very well." Asey spoke more gently. "I don't want to touch your sore spots any more'n you want 'em touched. Now, tell me about the fight b'tween you'n Eve over Alex. I overheard parts of a couple, even though I didn't want to much, but I don't know why they took place."

"Asey, I really didn't know they were married until a friend told me last year. It nearly ki—I mean, it broke me up. I'd known Alex five years, and he'd never mentioned it. I'll admit I like Alex. I never had any thought of marrying him." She drew a long breath. Very plainly, I thought, she had. "Not," she continued, "not after I heard about Eve, anyway. He seemed to like playing around with me, and I went places with him and we had a swell time together, but that was all there was to it. But some one told Eve, or wrote her. She chose to make a scene, and told me I was trying to take Alex from her, and that she'd never divorce him. She said if he tried to divorce her—well, you know what Eve could say when she got started."

"In three languages," Asey assured her. "I know. Did you tell her she was wrong?"

Lila smiled faintly. "Did you ever try to tell Eve that she was wrong? I was going to be perfectly honest with her. Tell her that I liked Alex, and thought, once, that I might marry some one like him if I ever married again. But that after I found out about her, I put the whole matter out of my mind. And I did. You see, Asey, I have a certain feeling of loyalty toward Eve. After Jim died, she proved herself a perfect brick. We'd been broke. She sent us money and settled our debts and then came and got us out of Madrid. A lot of people said they were sorry, but Eve was the only one who did anything. Because of that, even if I'd still wanted Alex, I'd never have done anything about it. Simply because he was Eve's husband. Not even if they threw things at each other and fought and loathed each other—you know what I mean."

There was more than a ring of truth in what she said, and her story of Eve was entirely consistent with Eve's character.

"How'd she take that?" Asey asked.

"She didn't believe me, of course. She said I was a snake and a viper, that she'd started me on the road to success—which was true enough. She took some foolish poems I'd written for Eric and got her agent to sell them. That's how Eric and I've managed to get along ever since. Well, she said she'd done everything she could for me, and I'd repaid her by taking Alex away."

"That happened Friday, didn't it?"

"Yes. I told her I'd leave at once, and she promptly

changed her tune. You see, if I'd left suddenly, there'd have to be explanations. She knew I'd tell Alex. If he found out about her—her scenes—she knew he'd leave, too. I rather feel—I've always felt—that Eve really loved Alex. For all her philanderings. Anyway, Eve apologized and said she was sorry. Somehow it all smoothed itself out. Knowing Eve, I never mentioned the incident again. After that, though, I tried very hard not to be alone with Alex if I could help it. But Eve, in her contrary fashion, seemed to try to throw us together all she could."

Asey nodded. "Now, what happened Thursday afternoon?"

"I told you the truth, Asey. Alex and I squabbled over jumping a mud puddle. You know, don't you, how perfectly silly little things can develop into a row? He came home, and in one way I was glad. I'd been taking an awful beating from Eve for being with him—not a beating, exactly, but—"

"I know," Asey said. "Fem'nine digs. Eve was a master at it."

"She was. Well, I walked around the big pond— Uncle Thoph's. I lost my way, and asked a man, who told me just how to go. But I must have misunderstood, for I got more tangled up than before. Then it got dark. I suppose I must have walked in the wrong direction. I never can remember how to tell which is east and which west, and I shouldn't have known any better which path to take if I had. Then, after absolutely hours, Tony found me, and then the doctor found us."

"Fix the time?" Asey was purring.

She shook her head. "I remember hearing a train whistle. At least, I thought it was a train, either just before or just after I met that man who told me the way. I can't even remember the time. My watch is being fixed uptown at the clock man's. Eric took it apart to see how it worked."

"Would you know this feller that told you the way if you was to see him again?"

"I think so. It seemed to me that I'd seen him before, but I can't place him exactly. I'm awfully vague about remembering people. I think he was some man in town. I called to him as he was turning onto one of the old wood roads. I was tramping through underbrush at that point. I'd given up roads entirely."

"Okay." Asey looked at her. "That's very well done, Mrs. Talcott. I was inclined to b'lieve the first part of your yarn, but now I'm handin' you the blue ribbon for the best this d'ramatic s'ciety's done yet. You said you'd tell me the truth, an' I been waitin' for it in vain, like Clem Smalley said when he left the Holy Rollers after waitin' three days an' three nights in the top of his elm tree for the new flood. Now, I baited you the other night when I said I seen you come in the tavern at three on Thursday. But now we got a witness to prove it. In the face of that, got any 'ditions or c'rections you'd like to make?"

"Asey, if some one told you that they saw me, they're lying. I've told you the complete truth."

"Feller that seen you," Asey said, "was the feller that Mark's father had here, trailin' Mark. He seen you, an' d'scribed you—"

Eric came in, looking very disconsolate.

"I busted it," he said, holding out the paper chain. "I'm madder than hell. I was going to keep"—he looked at his mother—"I'd intended to treasure this forever. Lila, where's the glue? Did I use it all up on Fergy Cohen's shirts?"

"Who," I demanded, "was Fergy?"

"He was an awful columnist Eve asked from New York. He wore pink shirts and I glued them all up and he left. Alex," Eric said cheerfully, "gave me five dollars. Oh, I know. Lila, where's the liquid cement?"

"On the desk, somewhere."

"It is not! Lila, did you throw that away?"

"I put it on the desk Wednesday afternoon, after you stuck up the knocker and forged together most of Tony's dictionary. And you know he can't spell! It was the most awful stuff, and I'm glad if it's disappeared—"

"Lila, where is it now?"

Asey took a hand. "Eric, you go tell Betsey to bake you another cake. There's some paste in the blue room. Now," he turned to Lila after the boy had gone, "what about this cement?"

Since Asey had already assured me that the cement had nothing whatever to do with the string that had tripped Eve, I wondered at his bringing the matter up with such seriousness.

Before Lila could answer, Alex Stout opened the door and strolled in.

"Secret conclave, or may I join? Lila, here's your cement. See what a swell elegant job it did on my favorite belt."

"When'd you borrow it?" Asey demanded.

"Thursday morning," Alex said promptly.

"Hm. You know he'd taken it, Mrs. Talcott?"

"No, she didn't, Asey," Alex answered. "I just snuk in and took it. Does it matter?"

Lila lighted another cigarette. "I begin to see," she told Asey, "what you're driving at. Eve told me Wednesday night that she'd been tripped. I looked for holes, too. At the head of the stairs."

"You mean," Stout sounded incredulous, "you're thinking about that tripping business? How perfectly absurd! I suppose you're thinking that string was stuck up there? Nonsense. In the first place this stuff isn't strong enough, and in the second place, there would have been marks left."

Asey produced his pipe. "You took it Thursday, huh? I thought, Mr. Stout, you told me that Mrs. Talcott didn't know Eve was your wife. She seems to."

Alex looked ready to weep. "Oh, Lila! When—I wanted—Lila, I can explain everything! I tried to divorce Eve. I really wanted to marry you, but Eve—you know how—"

"Don't explain," Lila said coldly. "Don't try to. Asey, I've just remembered that I tried to find that cement Wednesday, directly after dinner, to fix the tassel on one of the laces of my walking shoes. Are you quite sure, Alex, that you didn't take it Wednesday?"

"I certainly did not!"

"You—"

"Wait up," Asey said. "You got a casting rod, ain't you? Got it in the house?"

"Yes, but whatever has that to do—"

"Reels and line, too?"

"Yes," Lila answered quickly. "Yards of line. He had—"

"See here!" Stout was launching into one of his apoplectic furies again. "What are you insinuating, Mayo? I—"

"I wasn't insinuatin' nothin'." Asey lighted his pipe. "Mrs. Talcott was."

I understood his plan now. He was using the cement as a wedge to force Lila and Alex into betraying whatever they had been hiding. He was going to play them off against each other and let them do all the work. He already had them well started.

"I'm not insinuating," Lila said. There was a blotch of color on either cheek. "D'you recall, Alex, that game of murder we played at the Burroughs', last spring? You told Pen Burrough that a string, carefully placed six inches above the floor at the top of a steep flight of stairs, was the ideal way of killing any one? The person fell down, broke his neck. One removed the string, and the verdict was accidental death. No weapons, nothing incriminating about it. And d'you recall telling

me, last week, that there were times when you wanted
to kill Eve, be—"

"All right," Stout yelled, waving his arms about like
a windmill. "All right! You asked for this! If you recall, you said you preferred stabbing, because no one
would think a woman did it! You said it was a theory
that women use poison, or guns. And you were afraid
of poison, and you didn't like the sound of guns! And
all you needed, you said, was to know just where to
strike! You said it was sure. You said poisons were slow
and sometimes didn't take effect, and there was too
much chance of only wounding some one with a gun.
And your husband was stabbed! You didn't think I
knew, but I did!"

There ensued what Asey probably would have called
"general c'nfusion."

I thought I had some slight knowledge of fights. The
Adams family had done a lot in a well-bred way toward
making an art of fighting. But this was something
entirely out of my experience.

Eliminating her adjectives, some of which were new
to me and all of which were out of keeping with a
children's poet, Lila told Alex that he'd never cared for
her, he'd only played with her, he never intended to tell
her about Eve, he'd even killed Eve because he wanted
to marry that red-headed radio crooner who was a
kleptomaniac, a dipsomaniac, a nymphomaniac, and by
way of having no family tree.

Eliminating his adjectives, which showed me easily
why his books had come under Boston's ban, Alex

stated that Lila had killed Eve because she expected he would fall on her neck and marry her, which he wouldn't have done for the Morgan millions, the Mellon millions and Midas's millions. He added that she never intended to tell him her husband was stabbed. She was in love with that liverish Spanish guitar artist who made the red-headed crooner look like St. Ursula and all her eleven thousand virgins rolled into one. The crooner was not really red-headed, but Titian—

At that point, Asey broke in calmly.

"Now," he said, "that's really enough. I was part an' parcel of a fo'castle for some time, an' either of you'd rate A.B. on any lime-juicer I ever seen. It's been real nice of you to let me in on the truth at last, an' you've saved me a lot of time an' trouble, which I sort of hoped you'd do. It's kind of dull, just yankin' inf'mation out like so many rear molars. But you c'nvicted yourselves plenty, right now. No need to 'laborate. 'Cept, which one of you *was* it that tied the string?"

They glared at him speechlessly.

"Okay, Mrs. Talcott." Asey rose and beckoned to me. "You b'gun the 'cusin', so I'll give you the honor. That's all for now, but my, ain't it goin' to take somethin' to get you two out of this!"

"Asey," I said when we got out into the hall, "that— why—really—"

"Yup. Good's a play, wan't it? Artistic temp'rament. I wish I had their c'mand of the King's English, even if theirs did sort of smack of the scul'ry, now an' then. Well, we're gettin' somewhere."

"Which one d'you think—"

"Tied that string? T'be frank an' honest, I wouldn't be a one to know. I favor Lila. She hopped at the idea too soon. We'll soon find out."

"How?"

"I'll give 'em about half an hour to make up. Pretty soon, I got a feelin' Stout'll come an' tell me he's the one that pulled the string trick. He's got a lot of Gal'had in him, an' he couldn't of got so mad at Lila if he didn't love her. An' other way 'round. An' if Stout'd tied that string, he'd never admit it himself. He would if she had, though. P'raps they shared the notion, but I don't think so. B'gin to see, Miss Kay, where Eve was a pretty good tormentor?"

I told him that I did. "And yet—she helped Lila out. And probably she's done things for Stout, too. It's peculiar."

"It is, an' she has. I pumped Tony. He says Stout's first stuff was third grade, highfalutin' writin', but he's one of the best pop'lar writers there is, now, with all his Boston troubles. Seems like Eve's swipin' his plot made him a success, anyways."

At the foot of the stairs Asey started to turn into the green room, then he motioned suddenly for me to be quiet.

Brother Marcus was talking to Krause.

"You understand, now?"

"Yes, sir."

"Even if you are convinced to the contrariwise, you're to say that it was she."

"Yes, sir."

"And most important of all, Krause, never, never, never! say one word about that dagger in the gun. Mayo's sharp. But I don't think he's found it out. And you know how it will point. Not a word."

13

IN my eagerness to hear everything, I leaned forward and stretched my hand against the door jamb—and my bracelets promptly clanked out the warning of our presence. Marcus began rather loudly to comment on the weather, and I made a mental note to omit jewelry during future murder investigations.

"Don't worry," Asey whispered reassuringly. "We heard enough. Come."

In the room, I took one look at Marcus and laughed unrestrainedly. From his waist down, his stout figure was covered by a cashmere shawl.

"Why, Mr. Adams!" Asey said. "Why, Mr. Adams!"

"Mark," his father announced with a shade of bitterness, "left the iron on my—uh—trousers while he replaced a blown out fuse for the cook. She seems to feel that she may be able to repair the damage."

Asey's instant sympathy was a little too suave. I remembered how abruptly he'd broken off when he told me that Mark was furbishing up his father's clothes, and rather wondered if the tragedy had not been accomplished by his order. I'd rather felt that he had no intention of letting Marcus and his man leave the tavern.

"I've been commenting," Marcus said rather hurriedly, "on those knives hanging over the table." He nodded toward two daggers with wavy blades. "Er— Malay krisses, aren't they?"

He was clearly all set to reassure us as to his meaning if we had happened to overhear any of his conversation. I thought, offhand, that with Asey's eyes boring into him, he would have been wiser to have stuck to the weather. And I began to wonder if Marcus and Krause were quite as completely out of the picture as I had previously thought.

"One of the Prence cap'n's trophies," Asey said. "Prob'ly brought 'em from the P'ninsular. Seems to of run to knives, this fam'ly."

"Are there—others in the house?" Marcus asked eagerly.

"Lots in the attic." I thought Marcus seemed relieved at Asey's casual statement. "Now, Mr. Krause, we'll b'gin where you left off last night. You seen a woman with a red hat an' a red coat comin' in the house Thursday aft'noon just b'fore three. D'you think it might of been Mrs. Talcott?"

"I'm sure it was." Krause was very positive.

"Wasn't so sure last night."

"I've thought it over," Krause explained. "It must have been her."

"Um. Watch her all the way to the house?"

"Yes, I did."

"Was the gate open?"

"It was closed. The woman put out her right hand and opened it and—"

"Sure it was her right hand? Stop an' think."

"I'm sure of it."

"Good," Asey said cheerfully. "Then the chances are pretty much like I been feelin' for the last couple minutes. 'Twasn't Mrs. Talcott at all. She's a south paw. I seen her open that gate outside, an' doors in the house any number of times. Always uses her left hand, she does."

Krause was disconcerted and so was brother Marcus.

"I'm sure," the former said stoutly, "that it was Mrs. Talcott."

"I know." Asey unwrapped a stick of chewing gum. "I'd be sure, too, if some one paid me to say so. Why you so anxious to throw the blame on Mrs. Talcott, Mr. Adams? What you got against her, huh?"

Marcus spluttered for several minutes. When he cooled down, Asey repeated his question.

"No need," he added, "of denyin' it. We happened to hear a lot of what you two was sayin'. No good ever come of exclusive, low-toned conv'sations, as the feller said when he shot the turtle dove. Why, Mr. Adams?"

"Because it seemed to me," Marcus said sulkily—he is not accustomed to being so firmly questioned—"that you were getting nowhere at all, and that Mrs. Talcott was clearly the guilty one. If Mark's mind is made up about Anne Bradford, I consider it the sanest procedure to remove her as soon as possible from this situation. I do not want my son to marry a young woman to whom the stigma of murder—"

"So that's why you're takin' such an int'rest, is it?

An' yet I thought, from what Mark said, that you had another girl all picked out an' okayed. Quick switchin', wasn't it?"

Marcus turned a little pink. "If you must know, I thought opposition on my part might make the whole thing more romantic for Mark. Mark is a very silly young man, but occasionally I like to humor him."

Asey plainly didn't believe him, but I did. And Marcus went up another notch in my estimation. I said so.

"But for heaven's sakes," I added, "do tell us how you knew about those daggers in the gun before Asey traps you!"

I think Asey could have wrung my neck, and Marcus was none too pleased with me.

"Those guns," Marcus said, "once hung for some time —several years—on the office walls of Bradford and Prence. I knew about them, though I'd not known till Mr. Dean took me in to see his son, that they were here. I wondered at once if it weren't possible that one of the daggers might have been the weapon used, since it seemed impossible to believe Anne's knife was the weapon, if she had not committed the murder. You overheard me telling Krause not to mention them, because I felt that if you had not discovered the presence of the daggers, they must be unknown to the entire household. I realized also that if the fact were not known, and I mentioned it, it would only involve Anne more, since it was her father who showed me the daggers in the first place. Do I make myself clear?"

Asey nodded. "So Anne's father knew. Huh."

"Tell me," Marcus said, "hasn't the doctor been able to discover, from tracing the course of the wound, anything about the murderer? His height, or whether he was right or left handed, or anything like that?"

"I asked him," Asey said. "But he says it would be hard to tell. Y'see, Eve was sittin' down. 'Parently the person took real careful aim, an' let drive. Now he might been standin' or crouchin' way to the left or way to the right, or straight b'hind. 'F he stood way to the right an' used his left hand, chances are t'would seem right handed, an' vice versa. Make a diff'rence how he held the handle. Now this was 'parently a straight blow, aimed from straight b'hind at a level of her shoulder. You could sort of make theories if you wanted to, but you'd prob'ly be wrong. Any one that done as final a job as this wouldn't leave no d'cided left or right hand touches to this, 'less he was bein' cagey. An' lots of folks is amb'dextrous, anyhows. Now, what about that woman, Mr. Krause? Be nice an' honest, please. I'm kind of tired of fairy stories."

"Honestly," Krause said, not looking at Marcus, "I don't think it was Mrs. Talcott, even though it looked just like her. There was something different in the way she walked and the way she held herself. Mrs. Talcott lopes, sort of. This woman planted her feet solid, and moved her shoulders more. I thought it was Mrs. Talcott at first, then I remember thinking it didn't seem like her."

"An' then you went on an' met one of Belcher's maids, huh? Okay. Now, I'm goin' to ask you two to r'tire to the third floor. It's 'bout time for Just to rise'n shine. An' it'd be awful hard, explainin' you two."

"We must leave to-night," Marcus said. "I've important business to-morrow."

"Sunday," Asey said, "an' you ought to med'tate an' keep the Sabbath. B'sides, you can't go out 'less you're clothed! I'm 'fraid I'll have to ask you to stay on."

"But I want to get a lawyer!"

"I already got Steve Crump. The third floor."

Marcus and Krause departed.

"Well," I said, still giggling over Marcus's appearance from the rear, "what now? What d'you make of all this?"

"Not so good for Anne, an' better for Lila. Oh—"

Alex walked into the room. His ears were dark red and he looked very sheepish.

"I'm sorry," he said honestly, "for that scene. Miss Adams—Asey, I apologize, if it helps any. But Lila and I'd been keeping things in for so long, that when they broke—well, they—"

"They busted," Asey said, helpfully.

"That's it. It's all been a miserable situation. I think Eve really loved me. In a way, I loved her. But I wanted to marry Lila. I tried to get a divorce, but Eve just blew up. I didn't want Lila to know about Eve till I could explain it all and until it was all over. In a quiet way, I'd started divorce proceedings, and that's why I'm here now. I wanted to be here when the news was broken to Eve. Oh—it's—I feel silly, explaining. I—I was fond of Eve. She always fascinated me. If it hadn't been for her, I'd have written third class tripe all my life, and lived in hall bedrooms. As it is, I write second class tripe and rate villas in Mentone and suites on the *Teuton*. But, Asey—the minute Eve told me about the string, Wednesday night, I began to think of what I'd said at the Burroughs'. And then the stabbing—I was sick for fear Eve'd tormented Lila too much. It drove me crazy. And Lila was going through the same thing about me. And look here—I put the string up."

Asey looked at me and smiled.

"Okay, Gal'had. I didn't think you did. So Lila 'fessed up, huh?"

Stout made no attempt to circumnavigate. "Asey, I knew last week that Eve'd got notice of the divorce. She never said a word. But she's been taking it out on Lila. She made Lila's life a perfect hell on earth. And Lila took it because Eve'd helped her out when Jim Talcott died. Lila did tie the string. If I'd been through what Eve had been putting her through, I'd have done it. You know how she felt—and how she feels about it now. But Eve goaded her beyond endurance."

He paused and lighted a cigarette.

"At dinner Wednesday," he continued, "Eve said she was going to her room till she heard Asey coming with Miss Adams. Lila was at a point where she couldn't stand it any longer. She tied the string, thinking if any one found it, they'd blame it on Eric, and it would give her a reason to go. You see, she didn't dare leave without reason. Eve was doing a little blackmailing, about things she'd tell me if Lila went. But—well, I can't condemn Lila the way you probably are. Once, after the first week Eve and I were married, I did almost the same thing. I pushed her in front of a cab. But she saved herself. And," he inhaled deeply, "that's another reason for—for everything. Eve knew. And threatened me. Anyway, that whole episode up in Lila's room wasn't very pretty, but I'm glad you got us going, Asey. The slate's clean."

Asey nodded. "Well, the string business's solved an' done. An' after all, it didn't work. But I dunno about the rest of Mrs. Talcott's story, even now. An' I don't know about yours, with your dupl'cate key."

"Lila didn't come to the tavern Thursday afternoon. She's telling you the truth and so am I."

"Okay. But we got to prove it, somehow. You go keep an eye on her, an' Just an' Eric. An' don't look so glum."

Asey smiled after he left. "Ever play that game, Miss Kay, where you choose somethin' in a room an' then try to find it by the hot'n cold method? Well, I got a feelin' that we're gettin' warm. Lila pulled the string business; dollars to doughnuts Bill Hardin' fired that shot at Eve. We got our stranger fixed, an' a lady in a red hat—I always liked red—an' there's three anyways that might of done the final job. Oh, golly, if we could only get out of this house right now! But Quigley's stopped that chance durin' the day. Well, we'll go as soon as we can. You go sleep some. We got Reddy an' Bill to c'nsider t'night, an' then I got 'nother crazy fool insane idea that I want to look in if we got time."

"What?"

Asey chuckled. "Ever play bridge much?"

"Upwards of twenty years," I said.

"Bill Porter, he forced me to learn almost on the point of a gun. Ever play a no-trumper where some one started runnin' out a suit, an' you had to discard an' discard till you nigh went crazy, an' in all the worry of what to throw away, you f'got whether that five spot is good, or if it's a four or six the feller's holdin' for the endin' trick?"

I admitted that I knew what he meant.

"N'en you got a couple of face cards that you want to keep real bad, even though you know way down in your bones that they won't never do no one any good? Well, that's where I am now. I got an ole king an' a jack, but I'm holdin' onto the ole five, just's so if I can get one trick, I got it."

"What are you talking about? And what is the trick?"

"You can't tell," Asey said, "if it's good or not till the windup. We ain't there yet, by a long shot. Go get some rest. The red-coated lady's goin' to take time."

At six o'clock we went through the passage and started out the door of the shed. We hadn't moved ten feet when a figure loomed before us.

Asey stopped short and I tried to turn into a marble statue. It wasn't hard. I felt like one.

The figure stopped, too. For several seconds there was silence.

"Nice evenin'," Asey said at last.

The stranger laughed. "Very nice. But it's dark. I couldn't see Asey Mayo if he was six inches away. I told 'em at headquarters Asey couldn't get out of the tavern and not have us see him if he tried. I told 'em I didn't think he had any intention of getting out. He hasn't, have you?"

Asey chuckled. "Nary a one, Hanson."

"Okay. I'll stick here. We won't see you. We can't."

"Hanson, that's white an' thank you kindly. So long."

We hurried along to where the colonel's coupé still stood in the willow grove.

"Nice feller," Asey said. "Syl told me the boys was all posted. Great man, Syl. Well, we'll go see Dorcas Winter."

"Who's she?"

"Jabe's sister. She's sort of a famous person. Kinder folks just call her the Town Crier. She ain't got no bell, but she don't need one. She's got her father's spyglass an' a pair of twelve-powered Zeiss binoc'lars, an' they live on a hill that gives 'em a bird's-eye-view of town anyways. She's the 'Item' r'porter. Gets paid by the item, too, an' to look at the Weesit news, you'd think this place was a thrivin' m'trop'lis. If there was a red-hatted, red-coated woman in town Thursday, don't think Dorcas ain't already got it wrote out for the social notes. Thank heaven, I can make her keep still about us comin' to see her, b'cause once 'bout twenty years ago, she seen in the Boston paper where a man named Asa Mayo died, an' she thought it was me, an' wrote my obituary. Real nice one, t'was, too. She wound up with 'Thanatopsis' c'mplete. It was her first an' only error, an' she don't like to be r'minded of it. Else, she'd put us down in social notes, too."

We found Miss Winter eating beans in her kitchen. She was a long, angular woman, and though I'd often heard of a nose for news, she actually had one. Its tip was as pointed as an old fashioned ice-pick.

"I'm alive," Asey told her pleasantly, as she showed some signs of screaming. "So's Miss Adams, she's Mark's aunt. An'—"

"I knew it!" Miss Winter said. "She looks just like her pictures. Asey—"

"After all," Asey said, "she posed for 'em. Dorcas, we're real, an' we won't give you measles. An' if you was to offer us a slab of that brownbread, I sort of think we'd be ones to take it."

Miss Winter sliced the brownbread recklessly and demanded to know all about the murder.

"I can't tell you all now," Asey said, "b'cause I ain't got time. But there's one piece of real important in-f'mation you can give us. An' if you give it to us, an'll promise to keep quiet about our bein' here, I'll give you first whack at the real story if we run down who really killed Eve."

Dorcas put down her notebook promptly, and promised that she wouldn't breathe a word.

"Fine. Now. Thursday aft'noon there was a woman in town. She come to the tavern 'round three. She wore a red hat an' a red coat. Five feet-five, weighed 'round a hundred an' ten. Walked sort of sturdy. Planted her feet."

"I know just who you mean, Asey Mayo! I know! Celia—Delia—Gloria—Flora—Nora—Dora, oh, dear, 'twas somethin' like Gloria. Floria. Columbia.—Oh, I've got her name right on the tip of my tongue! Columbia—Gloria—"

"Hal'lujah, maybe?" Asey suggested.

"No! Land sakes, Asey Mayo! Whoever heard— what's that song? Gloria in excel—Gloria in *something!* Gloria—I've got it. Celeste. That's it. Celeste Rutton. That was her name. She was sellin' compendiums."

"Compendiums?" I said, puzzled. "What are they?"

"If you're thinkin' they're a-cordeens," Asey said, "you're wrong. I know what you mean, Dorcas. One of them Compendium of useful knowledges, with items to date includin' radio programs an' the pop'lation of Sarawak. She come here?"

"Yes. But we had plenty of compendiums, an' as I told her, the 'Farmer's Almanac' was good enough. I used to do her washin' for her when she stayed at the tavern."

"What?" Asey and I yelled in unison.

"Why, yes. Must have been—let's see. It was the summer we had all that dry weather. Three years ago. I remember b'cause she had so many white dresses that was always gettin' dirty. She was a writer, an' then things went bad with her, an' she took to sellin' compendiums. She was here about two o'clock."

"Dorcas," Asey reached for his hat, "where was she goin' from here? Down the Cape?"

"Why, yes. She was coverin' Eastham yesterday, an' I 'magine she'd be in Wellfleet now, Asey. She asked me about places to stay, an' I told her Lyddy Howes's in Wellfleet, so if she's there, that's where she'd be."

"Did she have a car?"

"She said she did, but she didn't use it when she went from house to house. Said people didn't like it to get ready for what they thought was vis'tors an' find a book salesman. She said she walked where she could. Goin'?"

Asey took another piece of brownbread. "Yup. Dorcas, thank you kindly. An' you still make the best brownbread on Cape Cod. An' I'll tell you what happens when I can."

We got into the coupé and shot off down the Cape.

"A writer!" I said as we sped along. "And she's stayed at Eve's—look here, it seems to me I remember hearing something about this Celeste Rutton. I connect her—oh, I'm sure I've got some books of hers at home. High society things, where every one wears top hats and gardenias and the women drip perfume and brown orchids—"

"Laura Jean Libbey up to date?" Asey suggested.

"In a way. They're the sort of things Mark gives me because he knows there's nothing I like so much as a good eternal triangle where everything ends happily. And it's desperately hard to find that sort of thing these days. This Rutton woman—I know I haven't read anything she's written for a long while."

"Can't you even r'member headlines?" Asey asked slyly.

"Not one. But I'll bet it turns out that the reason she's selling books instead of writing sentimental pap for the middle-aged—I'll bet you it'll be due to Eve!"

Asey smiled. "I won't bet. Wish I had my car! An' we need gas. Got plenty at home for my boat, but I don't want to take a chance of goin' there. Well, 'leven minutes'll do it at this rate."

It did. He drove with the nonchalant speed of a Malcolm Campbell. Ten and a half minutes had elapsed when we pulled up in front of a Cape Cod house just off the main road in Wellfleet.

"Home ter'tory," he said. "Oho. There's some one goin' in. Maybe—Miss Rutton?"

The girl on the doorstep turned at his call and slowly walked toward the car.

"Miss Rutton, I wonder if you'd be willin' to spare me a few minutes? I'm Asey Mayo of this town, an' this is Miss Elspeth Adams."

I could just make out Miss Rutton's features from the light of a very dim street lamp. She was about Lila Talcott's height and build, and she was blonde. But her features were larger and stronger, and she had one of those determined jaws. Even in that light, I could see that she wore a red hat and a red coat.

"I've expected something like this." She had one of those husky modern voices which just escapes being raucous. "You want to know what I was doing at the tavern Thursday afternoon, don't you?"

"Just so."

"Very well. I went there to show Eve Prence what she'd done to me by her filthy tales. I wanted to let her gloat. And the knocker was stuck. After that first second, I lost my courage about going in. If the knocker had worked, I'd have gone in, but it saved me. In more ways, I guess, than one. So I turned and went out of the driveway. And the unpleasant part of that for you is that I can prove it. I walked to the next house down the road and was there at one minute after three."

"Sure of the time?"

"Thank God, yes. The clock-maker was there, tinkering with an old grandfather's clock. He was striking the hour when I came in, and then he pushed it ahead one minute. I corrected my own watch at the time. It was slow. And I stayed there an hour and sold four books. That blessed Mrs. Knowles is going to give 'em for Christmas presents, which is the smoothest method of revenge any one ever thought of. Consider her friends and relatives, having to sit down and write her—'Thank you for the lovely compendium. It was just what I wanted and hoped for.'"

I laughed with Asey, though I admit that I've seldom been more disappointed.

"But if you're the famous Asey Mayo," Celeste Rutton went on in her strident voice, "I'm amazed that you haven't tumbled to the dagger business yet. Anne Bradford's innocent, of course. I've known Anne for years—

went to school with her when we were both rich and pampered. The knife the papers talked about is all hooey. You want to get at those guns up in the front left bedroom, the pair of pistols that hang up over the fireplace, on the panel. They've got daggers in 'em. And the rest should be easy." She stopped, knowing full well that she had us standing on our ears. "Easy as any little pie you ever saw. Ask why."

"Why?" Asey asked obediently.

"Because all you've got to do then is to grab the lad that showed them to me three years ago when I had that room. Alex Stout."

14

∼∼∼∼∼∼∼∼∼∼∼∼∼∼∼∼∼∼∼∼

"UM," Asey said, "an' likewise huh. Say, Miss Rutton, will you squeeze in here with us an' drive 'round a bit? Lyddy Howes is b'ginnin' to peek through her lace curtains, an' I don't feel like advertisin' this exp'dition."

"Certainly." Miss Rutton got into the car. "I suppose it's unwise to accept rides from strangers, but if you have any notions of kidnaping me for ransom, the joke would be on you. I'm far more likely to swipe your pocketbooks."

"We'll take the chance," Asey told her. "I got to get gas, too, an' there's not one single station in this town that I feel like stoppin' at. I'm too well known. S'pose you two dump me here, an' get the gas? G'rage's down the road a mile or so."

"Amazing man," Miss Rutton commented, as I slid behind the wheel and we started off. "Powerful personality."

I agreed heartily. "Further acquaintance," I added, "increases my admiration for him. You know, that clock-maker incident was very fortunate for you."

She smiled. "I felt that the instant I gaped at yesterday's papers. There have been brief moments in my career when luck's perched on my shoulder, in spite of himself. Or herself. Which is it? And I think the tank's full."

I paid the garage man and we drove back to the wooded side road where we had left Asey.

"I'm burnin' with questions," he said. "Mostly about Alex. But first, d'you mind tellin' us about your set-to with Eve?"

"Mind? My dear man, I'd have told you anyway. I was getting along very nicely in the writing business. Then, after I stayed at the tavern three years ago, Eve wrote an article about me. There was absolutely nothing in that article for which I could have sued her, but it laid the foundation for some of the most loathsome gossip possible. There's very little publicity that's not acceptable or even profitable for writers, but what I got wasn't. And it was one of those things you couldn't up and deny. I got so worked up about it that the book I was doing just went to pot. Publishers wouldn't take it. Contract went. Other publishers weren't taking my type of stuff. It was a back-to-the-soil era, and orchids were out. I never could write short stories, though Alex Stout gave me his formula. I couldn't do action enough for the pulps, and the smooths had enough stories in their files to last during ten depressions. The upshot of it was that I was on my uppers, and all because I happened to have a boyish haircut when I stayed with Eve at the tavern."

Asey grunted. "I get the idea. Even r'member some of the stories."

So did I, now. Celeste Rutton, I thought, had due and sufficient reason to be bitter about Eve.

"That's all over now, though," she went on. "This selling books has been hell on toast, but it's had its amusing sides. I've found out a lot about human nature, if you want to call it that. My God, I made more money last month than any three of this foul company's four hundred salesmen! After next month, I'm going to have a desk job back in New York. Real white-collar labor. And I've got a novel half done. It's a damn good thing, if I do say so. Girl's got herself in hand."

She lighted a cigarette and passed her case to me. "But, now that I'm perfectly safe and out of this, I'll admit that I'm delighted at Eve's death. That doesn't sound well, but I think I've reason to feel that way. I'm sorry she was murdered, but I'm glad to think that the time will never come when I shall have to face Eve Prence again."

"Did you," Asey asked, "say—this is personal, but I'm sort of curious. Was you friends with Alex Stout?"

"I've known Alex for years. You're right, Mr. Mayo. Eve started all that business about me just because she thought he was paying me too much attention. Eve's always been crazy about him herself. I wondered how she was getting back at Lila."

"You wasn't by any chance the one that told Eve they was goin' around together, was you?"

"No," Celeste Rutton answered frankly. "I've too much feeling for any person to give Eve Prence a chance to retaliate. If Eve thought that affair serious, she'd have made Lila's life undiluted hell. I think I know who might have told, though. A guitar-playing Spaniard who was all the rage last winter. He fell for Lila, and she turned him down. He'd be the knife in the back kind. Curly Vance, a reporter I know, wrote me about Lila and the Spig a long time ago."

"You think Alex knew about them daggers?"

"Think? I know he did. I'd been in that room about a week when he mentioned 'em. Said he'd found out by accident and was playing a little game to see how many others noticed. He said no one had. Called it a lack of sense for details, and ranted on about people who can close their eyes and count steps and telephone poles, and all that visual memory stuff.—Though what good it does a writer to know that there are sixty-three steps in front of the Soldier's Monument is to me a moot question."

"You really think Alex done this?"

"I'll wager money on it." She laughed. "I can say no more."

"Not a comb'nation of Lila Talcott an' Alex, or Lila alone?"

"Not a combination. Two heads are less hot-headed than one. Not Lila. She's not the helpless idiot she tries to make you think. That's a lot of defense mechanism, even though it works. People always send her home in cabs, and see her through customs, and look after her baggage. But she's shrewd enough to know she's not intelligent enough to get away with murder. But Alex—he's an entirely different proposition. He's both shrewd and intelligent. Somehow you never take seriously a man as thin as he is, just as you never take a fat man seriously. But Alex isn't some one you get at one glance or one meeting. You have to know him quite a while before you realize how intensely clever the man is."

I agreed with her. Alex Stout hadn't impressed me at first sight, but I'd begun to see where there were many sides to his personality.

"Take one of his beautiful bursts of temper, when he's likely to do or say anything," Miss Rutton continued. "He flies into the most amazing rages for a thin man. Probably all glandular, but he does."

I privately wondered what writers did to sum people up before the more minor glands came into popular knowledge.

"Okay," Asey said. "We'll drop in on lady Knowles an' check up on you, just for sure. You helped a lot."

"I expected you would, but you'll find it's all true. To me it's the final sign that my luck's changed. If I'd gone in that house, I have a feeling I'd be in Anne's shoes right now."

Asey drew the car up before Mrs. Howes's. "You would," he said. "Oh—I d'pend on you to tell Lyddy we was a couple of travelin' salesmen. An' you might send me a dozen copies of the Compendium." He drew a bill fold from his pocket.

"You don't have to—"

"I want 'em," Asey said, "for Christmas presents. Lots of folks I know need knowledge."

"Very well. It's very decent of you. You know, it really *is* an amazing tome. I've read myself to sleep for two years over the chapter on self-control. I'll be here till Monday morning, and I'd gladly do anything I could for you."

"I like that girl," Asey said as we raced away up the Cape. "She's luckier'n she knows, even. Huh. I r'member Bill Porter showin' me that article about her. 'Twasn't pretty. Huh. More we stir this mess, less ed'ble it looks. I'm goin' to drop in on a cousin of mine—yup, another—an' make a few phone calls."

I waited outside in the car while he checked the girl's story, which was affirmed by Mrs. Knowles and the clock-maker. Then we set off again, up the Cape.

"What about Alex?" I asked. "Aren't—"

"We got him all bottled up to home. We're on our way now to Hyannis an' Bill Hardin'. I know where he used to stay."

But Bill Harding had moved, and it took us several hours to track him down. We found him at last in a boarding-house on a dim side street. It was a square frame building, badly in need of paint, and the hall smelled vaguely of disinfectant and cabbage. The front room into which the landlady ushered us charmed me at once. Its principal object of note, beside an oil painting of the battle of Gettysburg, was an upright piano, whose top was covered by an emerald green scarf on which a grimy plaster cast of the Winged Victory poised precariously. On the music rack were two sheets of music, *Dardanella* and *Trees*. The overstuffed furniture was electric blue, and the carpet was a bed of large faded peonies.

Bill Harding's face blanched when we entered the room and he began to tremble all over—whether because of us or the surroundings, I couldn't be sure.

Asey came to the point directly.

"Bill, we know the whole story. From the bullet on. All about Martin Smith an' the checks, an' the beach wagon, an' your not goin' to the Masonic meetin' like you told your wife, an' not bein' on the special like you told Nate Hopkins."

"Asey," Bill Harding was shivering from head to foot, "you—you don't think I killed Eve?"

"With the gaps like they are now, yes. Hate to say it, Bill; that's the way it looks. But if you'll tell me 'nough to fill in the gaps, an' tell me the truth, you needn't have no cause to worry. An' please, Bill, stop pretendin' to be an aspen. Almost nothin's as bad as you look."

"The bullet." Mr. Harding gulped. "Yup, Asey, I shot at her Saturday. They'd told me in Boston on Friday that they didn't think there was a chance of Sadie ever gettin' any better. Well—that's why I did. I—I ain't sorry, neither. The way I felt then, I'd of been glad if I'd hit her and killed her."

"How long you known she run Sadie over, Bill?"

"Eve? She come to me an' told me while Sadie was first in the hospital. Said she hadn't known she'd hit her. I b'lieved her. 'Tis pos'ble you wouldn't know, if your car was in a skid, an' hers was."

"That view," Asey said, "is what I call the cream

of the milk of human kindness. Yup, it's pos'ble. How come she had the beach wagon an' nobody knew it?"

"She'd bought it in New York an' was drivin' it home. She was awful worked up about it, Asey, when she found out."

Asey said nothing, and I had a mental picture of Eve Prence, hastily driving her car into the carriage shed, boarding up the windows, putting on locks—doing everything she could think of to keep the accident from being traced back to her.

"She really was," Bill continued, "an' I felt bad, too. She said she was willin' to pay anythin' to keep Sadie under the best of care, f'rever. Said she was willin' to acknowledge the accident as bein' her fault, even though it'd mean pretty hard times for her, b'cause people wouldn't think she was tellin' the truth about her not knowin'. I said if she'd pay the bills, that'd be all right. She said she'd tell Sadie, but I didn't want her to, somehow. She give me money then, and checks always come every month afterwards, from Martin Smith. She did that so's Sadie wouldn't know, an' folks at the bank wouldn't talk. Then one day soon after she talked with me, I was chattin' with Lem Dyer, an' he said he didn't see how Eve'd got home from New York that trip when she did. He said she just appeared there the day after the accident, and hadn't come by train. Next day I seen him, an' he said Eve'd told Betsey some friends brought her in a car from New York, and then went on to Provincetown. Y'see, Lem an' Betsey wasn't there the day she come back."

"That's about all Eve could say," Asey commented.

"Yup. But it seems, Asey, she'd told Betsey that—the very next day after the accident! An' she hadn't come to me for over a week, see?"

We saw, only too clearly.

"That meant," Bill Harding went on, "that she'd hid everythin' b'fore she'd a chance to see the papers to know she'd anythin' to hide. She must of known then, right off, that she'd hit Sadie. So—well, I didn't know what to do. Eve was a queer sort. I was afraid if I accused her of runnin' away delib'rate, she'd deny everythin' an' never give me any more money. I hadn't no proof 'cept her word, an' she had money enough to hire lawyers to laugh me out of court if I said she told me she'd run over Sadie. So I went to her an' told her I wanted her to come see Sadie every week when she was in town. I thought—well—"

"Nem'sis," Asey said. "Vengeance plus."

"Uh-huh. I thought it'd sort of hurt Eve, maybe, an' it was nice for Sadie to see some one that was what you might call out an' around in the world. Sadie likes to talk about books an' people an' things, an' though folks are awful nice to her, they ain't Sadie's sort, really. Well, everythin' was all right till that doctor told me about Sadie last week. Asey, I was content till then. Eve gave me all the money I could ask for for Sadie, an' we was doin' all we could. But that sort of busted everythin'. I just sort of went crazy. I'd got to wonderin' about that car, too, an' what she did with it. I wondered if it was in that boarded up shed.—Lem said Eve told him the kids'd been runnin' wild in it, but I thought different. It kind of kept poppin' up in my mind. I found myself wanderin' around the tavern an' the grounds. Day after I shot an' missed her, I seen her showin' that Adams boy the tree where the bullet was. I went an' dug it out. I was ashamed of myself by then. Seem's if when I fired that shot, I lost all my crazy feelin's to kill her. I seen it would just be worse for me, 'cause there wouldn't be no more money for Sadie."

"Okay. Now, what did you do Thursday aft'noon, Bill?"

"I was goin' to that meetin', Asey, but it was a lovely day, an' Masonic meetin's are sort of all alike. It was a holiday for me, too, so I went up an' walked to the back shore, an' around the ponds. On the way home, I met old Step-an'-Go-Fetch-It Carver, an' he told me about Eve's bein' killed. I was near insane. I didn't know what to do! It meant the money for Sadie'd stop, an' there was always a slim hope if we kept up the treatments, she might walk again in spite of what the doctor said. I—I was just crazy."

I believed the man's story, although his tale of walking around ponds and shores was, after all, as much without proof as was Lila Talcott's recital. I felt myself mentally championing the chubby conductor, whom I'd considered at first just another garrulous busy-body.

"Bill," Asey said, and from his voice I knew he was for the Hardings, too, "Bill, is there any way on earth you can prove you walked, an' when an' where?"

He thought a moment. "Yup, Asey, there is. I met that woman Lila Talcott—the one that's got that hellion son. I met her around Uncle Thoph's pond at three. She was lost, an' I yelled to her which was the right path. I think she missed it, though."

"How d'you know it was at three?"

"Well," Bill Harding said, "I looked at my watch, for one thing. An' for another," he added with a touch of pride in his voice, "that watch's been right by the South Station clock for ten years, ever since I had it."

"But," Asey said, "we can't prove it, Bill."

"Yup." Bill's color was beginning to return. "Sure can. The train whistled."

"Get out, Bill, there ain't no train at three!"

"There was a special, Asey. Ole eight-forty was doin' duty on a special for this vice-pres'dent that wanted to go to Provincetown. I was supposed to go on it, but Barney Fisk got sent instead. An' you know how they toot for Sadie? *Wah*-wah-wah-*wah-wah*."

Asey nodded. "Yup. '*Come* all ye *faith*ful.'"

"That's it! Well, Pete Brady tooted it, even though he knew I was home. It's a joke of his, sometimes, to do it when I'm home. When I heard that, I looked at my watch, an' it was three, exactly. I met Mrs. Talcott a couple minutes later."

Asey looked at me and smiled.

"It checks," I said. "Don't you remember Lila said there was a whistle, just before or just after she called to that man?"

"It checks," Asey said, "if Pete Brady does. Is he

here, Bill? Good. Get him. Yes," he continued, as Harding bounded out of the room, "if Brady says he tooted at three, Bill an' Lila is out. On just Bill's say-so, we couldn't be sure. But since both of 'em noticed the whistle, then there must have been one. An'—ah."

Bill Harding returned with a large florid man, half of whose face was covered with shaving lather.

"I brought him this way," Bill said, "b'cause I was afraid you'd think I might be primin' him if I waited. This is Pete Brady."

Mr. Brady seemed a little ill at ease; justifiably, I thought. The only sillier sight than a man half covered with shaving lather is a woman half covered with cold cream.

"Bill talked to you about this whistlin' business on the special Thursday?"

"No," Brady said. "You mean, my toot for Sadie?"

"Just so. When'd you toot?"

"At three, exactly. I looked at my watch. But I'll tell you how you can check that. We went through the Weesit station at three-two, and it would be on the report."

Asey rose. "Thank you. An' don't worry, Bill. Ole eight-forty was a miracle special from heaven as far as you was concerned. If I was you, I'd kiss that engine, rust'n all, Bill, an' hang wreaths about its nozzle. Got any ideas about this, b'fore I go?"

"Well, I read about it in the papers, Asey, an' I decided it must be that big feller, Tony Dean. Take a powerful man to stab like that. 'Course it ain't Anne. It couldn't be."

"It ain't. But with a dagger like that one that was used, you wouldn't have to be very strong, Bill," Asey said. "An' sad as it is, 'cause that was my first thought, he an' Miss Adams here was together during' the crucial time."

Mr. Harding looked at me reproachfully. "You're Elspeth Adams, an' you let me go on about you an' your nephew!"

"It wasn't nice of me," I admitted, "but you told me a lot more about Weesit than you would have otherwise. Who's your second guess, Mr. Harding?"

"That kid of Mrs. Talcott's. After what he did to that coach when he come down on eight-forty, I wouldn't put anythin' beyond him at all. Why, he smashed two windows and busted the water cooler and six seats, and spilled glue all over a dozen more. And he tore the handle off—uh—'Men.' I collected damages from her at the end of that trip for near onto eighty dollars, which was what we figgered it'd be for r'pairs."

Asey laughed. "He's d'structive, but Rollo ain't entirely d'praved. Okay, Bill. We won't mention this to Sadie."

Mr. Harding shook his head. "I s'pose not. Don't know how I'm goin' to explain about that uncle dyin', though. It's goin' to be hard."

"May not have to tell her." Asey opened the door. "An' forget we was here, too. Yup, Bill, I had to look through some of Eve's papers, an' I'm sure Uncle Martin'll continue to crash through. We'll give Eve that much credit. Night."

Before Bill Harding could pour forth the gratitude which was clearly seething inside of him at Asey's announcement, I was bustled out to the coupé, and again we raced away into the night.

"I'm glad," I said after a while. "Glad about the Rutton girl and Bill Harding both. And for Eric's sake, I'm glad Bill cleared Lila. But Asey, in spite of the fact we know Alex knew about the daggers in the guns, how *are* we going to *prove* anything? We've got plenty against him, and we've done a lot to-night, but we haven't *got* anywhere!"

"Don't f'get," Asey said, "first step in goin' 'round the world is fallin' down your own doorsteps."

"This is no time," I said, "to paraphrase Chinese proverbs. What are we going to do? To-morrow's Sunday—"

"It's been Sunday some time. Don't worry. We got a day left, an' a king, an' a five spot."

It did not occur to me until I was ready to slip into bed, a good hour later, that brother Marcus and his detective were undeniably the five spot.

15

I WAS up and about on Sunday morning at the earliest hour since my arrival at the tavern. I didn't want to get up. I don't think I was ever more tired and sleepy in all my life, but wild horses couldn't have kept me in bed any longer.

Since the meaning of Asey's mysterious five spot had filtered through my brain the night before, I'd brooded constantly about Boyce Adams. Boyce Adams was a great-great-great—and possibly even another "great"—uncle, who had nonchalantly stabbed his wife for supposed goings on some time during the days of Andrew Jackson. According to those in the Adams family who dabble in matters genealogical, brother Marcus is supposed to be the spitting image of Boyce, both in looks and in temperament.

I admitted to myself in the cold clear light of dawn and reason that the parallel might not necessarily extend to stabbing, but after the events of the past few days, practically nothing seemed too fantastic or too futile to consider. I felt that if some one looked me firmly in the eye and announced that my astral body had sneaked off and murdered Eve Prence, I should have been inclined to give the matter my most serious attention.

After all, as Asey had said the night before, the theory of detecting a murderer was nothing but a combination of sheer exuberant fancy and stark common sense.

"First off," he said, "you take all the pos'bil'ties, n'en you take the most prob'ble pos'bil'ty, an' then you add what common ord'nary hoss sense God give you, an' then you stir well. Only flaw is that usually the spoon gets taken away from you 'fore you get a chance to stir, an' then you got to go start all over again."

Just as I finished breakfast, Asey and Doctor Cummings came into the room. The doctor, who generally oozed spick and spanness, looked exceedingly disheveled.

He apologized at once.

"I'm not at my best," he said, "but believe me, Miss Adams, there's due reason. Mrs. Cooper had twins around three o'clock this morning, and then after I was sure that mother and girls were doing well, I drove up to see friend Quigley. He demanded that knife yesterday in such a firm fashion that I took it from the bank and carried it to him."

"But—"

"But I think we've forestalled any nasty plans he may have. Jimmy Bell, the local photographer, took pictures of it and the blade first, with a scale, and he's going to enlarge 'em. If they play any games, we're going to have the goods on them. And I saw Syl and Anne. Both all right. Anne sent her love to every one and a note to Mark." He yawned. "In my next incarnation I hope I'll be a librarian. I'd enjoy a nice sedentary existence with fixed hours. Well, I'll be getting along, Asey. Let me know if any of the patients need help."

"Patients? Is any one sick here?" I demanded.

"Any one? Norris has an earache, your brother has a cold, and Just is in awful shape. Too much of Eve's bad gin again last night. The wages of gin, in his case, is not only breath, but death, he thinks. He was saying very harsh things to a rosary about it. I told him he *would* probably die if he got up, so he's nicely out of your way. I'll drop in later."

Just as he was leaving, Krause came into the room, sucking his thumb vigorously.

"Hey, doc," he said, "I got a splinter. You take it out?"

The doctor opened his bag, delivering the while a polysyllabic lecture on the folly of allowing open wounds and the juices of the mouth to come in contact with each other.

"By the way," he said, in that forcedly jovial tone all doctors use the instant they begin any operation, no matter how minor, "by—don't jump. It's in deep, but it'll only be worse if you wiggle. By the way, where were you Thursday afternoon when all this was going on here at the tavern?"

"I—ow! I was out with one of Colonel Belcher's maids. She—"

"What! Out with—" The doctor shot a look at Asey.

"That's right," Asey said firmly. "That's where he

was. Out with one of Belcher's girls. Colonel seems to have an eye for good-lookin' help."

The doctor nodded. "Yes, indeed. There, run along, Mr. Krause, and don't chew that finger again. Or any other finger, for that matter. Miss Adams, unless you think you require my professional services, I'll depart."

I assured him that I was in comparatively excellent health, and he said I looked it.

"Incidentally," he added, "if you want to do a good turn to humanity in general and Tony Dean in particular, give him a bit of relief from Norris. That boy is indulging in an orgy of self-pity the like of which I've never seen before. Dean is ragged. He told me he was trying to finish a play, and I told him he'd finish himself if he wasn't careful."

I promised that I would.

He and Asey strolled out of the room, and for nearly ten minutes they conversed in low tones by the front door while I nearly burst with curiosity. There is nothing which drives me more nearly crazy than just being able to hear the sound of buzzing voices when I particularly want to hear words.

I felt sure they were talking about Krause. Their exchange of glances had not escaped me. I felt sure there was something wrong about Krause's story of Thursday afternoon. It all strengthened my belief that Marcus and his man might be more deeply involved than Asey had let me know.

Asey chuckled when he returned. "You look," he

said, "like you'd been eatin' sour pickles an' butter-milk. What's the matter?"

"You're holding out on me," I told him, "about this five spot."

"What d'you mean, Miss Kay?" He seemed a little taken aback.

"You know perfectly well what I mean. About Marcus and Krause. I suppose you—look, what's all this lifting of eyebrows about Belcher's maid? Wasn't Krause with her after all? You've been funny about that for some time."

"Krause is your brother's hired man," Asey said. "He's hired to tell the truth."

"I suppose you're insinuating he's hired to tell lies," I said hotly, "just because Marcus wanted to get Anne off, and was willing to force Krause into lying about Lila to do it! Asey, you don't think for one instant that Marcus and Krause had anything to do with this, do you? Marcus is a pompous thing, I'll admit. He's positive, and used to having his own way, and sometimes he's dull. But he does care dearly for Mark, and that's the only reason he came here. I never realized myself until the last day or so how much he did care for the boy."

"That bein' the case," Asey said, "wouldn't he be willin' to get Eve off the scene, if he'd found out from Krause that Eve was against Mark an' Anne's gettin' married?"

"Nonsense. Utter nonsense!"

"Yup. But he wanted Lila to take the blame—"

"Look here," I said, "you've got me so worked up about this that I've even been thinking of ancestors who stabbed, and wondering about heredity." I told him the story of Boyce. "But," I added, "it's no less absurd than— Asey, do you think Marcus and—are they your old five spot?"

Asey hedged. "Now, Miss Kay, you heard all I heard an' you seen all I seen. An' don't forget we ain't through with Alex, not by a long shot. We—"

Marcus came into the dining room. His face was very pink and his nose was red. Apparently he was in the throes of a head cold of no mean magnitude.

"I've been talking with Norris Dean," he blew his nose. "He's a particularly talented young man, Elspeth. I don't care for his poetry, but I must say that his knowledge of music is remarkable. Have you heard him play?"

"No, I haven't." Marcus's interest in music has always been more than casual. For years and years he has made up symphony and opera deficits, and he is a better than average violinist himself. I think it has always hurt him that Mark can't carry a tune one-sixteenth of an inch.

"Really remarkable," Marcus said. "Mr. Mayo, have you any clews in the offing? It seems to me that time is getting very short indeed."

"We got a real nice clew," Asey informed him, "only thing is, we don't understand it one bit."

"M'yes," Marcus said half to himself. "Yes. The spots."

"What spots?" Asey asked silkily.

"Oh, those brownish circular spots on the window sill in Norris's room," he answered, apparently unaware of my frantic high signs. "His father and I discussed them yesterday. And I understand from Mrs. Talcott that you found others in her room. Are you quite sure about Mrs. Talcott? And have you found out about the woman Krause saw?"

"Feller in town," Asey said, "who was five miles away from here at three o'clock Thursday aft'noon, was also a couple hundred yards away from Mrs. Talcott. An' it can be proved. An' the one Krause seen is all checked. You notice them spots yourself?"

"Mr. Dean showed them to me."

"Did, huh? Mr. Adams, where was you Thursday afternoon?"

"I," Marcus blew his nose again, "I was out driving."

"Alone, I s'pose?"

"As it happened, yes."

"When'd you leave your office?"

"As a matter of fact, I didn't go to my office at all on Thursday."

Asey pulled a piece of paper from his pocket and gazed at it solemnly. "No," he said, "so you didn't. Hm. An' you was two minutes late Friday—"

"I was *not* late," Marcus interrupted indignantly. "I have never been late to the office for thirty-three years. I pride myself that I arrive before most of my—"

"I'm told," Asey said, "you was late."

"You—you have the arrant audacity to—have you spied upon my comings and goings, Mr. Mayo?"

"Why not?" Asey asked. "You always spied on Mark's, didn't you?"

"But I—I—" Marcus reached out his hand as though to snatch the paper from Asey, but Asey calmly passed it to me.

Unconsciously I read what was written on it.

It said: "Stew meat. Dog biscuit. Roq. Cheese. Pay paper bl. Get rope. Gas."

Asey, apparently, was bluffing brother Marcus.

"You just tell us the story of Thursday aft'noon," Asey said calmly.

Marcus did, with heat and detail. There were at least twenty people who could, according to him, vouch for the way he spent each single and separate moment from the time he rose till the time he went to bed. He was busy writing down names, addresses and telephone numbers when Asey at last stopped him.

"All right," he said. "That's plenty. But what about Krause?"

Marcus was just as earnest and long-winded about Krause. If Asey hadn't stopped his list of gilt-edged, gold plated references in behalf of his detective, I think my brother would have continued for the rest of the day.

"That all sounds nice," Asey said, "but you sort of can't get away from the r'mainin' fact that Krause's story is first class cheese. Full of large-sized holes. Y'see, he says he was out with one of Belcher's maids—"

"If he says so," Marcus interrupted, "he was. Krause is entirely reliable."

"Shouldn't wonder. But y'see, Belcher's maids left here Wednesday aft'noon on the train for Wash'nton. He's only got an ole top-sergeant of his lookin' after him now."

"Impossible," Marcus said positively. "Entirely impossible. Call him in, Mr. Mayo. I assure you there has been a mistake. I understand why you have been feeling that he and—call him in."

Asey strolled out and returned in a few minutes with Krause, who seemed very embarrassed indeed when Asey demanded the name of his lady friend. He even blushed.

"I don't know," he said finally. "I—I just called her Molly."

"Was it her name," Asey inquired, "or do you call all your girl friends Molly?"

"Oh, it was her name all right. Only I—well, I didn't know her well enough to of found out what her last name was."

Brother Marcus seethed at that commentary on modern manners and social customs.

"Deary me," Asey murmured, "what'd Em'ly Post say to that? Are you sure, Krause, that she worked for the colonel?"

"Why, she said so. And I always left her at the fork of the road by his house."

"What she look like?"

Krause, who had Celeste Rutton's description on the

tip of his tongue, seemed curiously tongue tied. She was good-looking, he said, and she wasn't exactly short or exactly tall, and she wasn't thin; but on the other hand, we weren't to get the idea that she was any heavy weight.

"I take it," Asey remarked after several minutes of that sort of maundering, "that you're one of them as don't let business interfere with pleasure. Snap into this, feller. Get p'fessional."

"Uh. Five foot—uh—three. Weight about one—oh —four. Medium light. Around twenty. Wore bright clothes—"

"Not uniforms?"

"No. She always wore earrings, too."

"That don't tally with any of the colonel's girls," Asey said. "Can't you do any better inventin' than that? Now if I was tellin' this yarn, I'd make up a good-lookin' girl while I was at it."

Krause looked stunned. "Say," he said, "this is true! Look, she told me she was—"

"I s'pose you didn't come into the tavern yourself, Thursday aft'noon?" Asey interrupted. "On the orders you got from Mr. Adams here?"

Marcus and Krause boiled over simultaneously.

"That's okay," Asey said. "But here you been tryin' to get Mrs. Talcott in wrong, an' a red-hatted an' red-coated lady. Now, I'll take Mr. Adams' word he was where he says he was, but you got to do a lot of provin' about your yarn, Krause."

Krause suddenly became full of details. "She had a

widow's peak, and high cheekbones, and small ankles. She talked French, too."

"French, huh? I—"

Asey stopped as Doctor Cummings burst into the room. If he'd seemed disheveled on his earlier visit, he was now apparently completely disorganized.

He flung himself down on a chair, got up, strode up and down the strip of hooked rug before the fireplace and literally tore his hair.

"What you goin' to give us?" Asey asked interestedly. "Spartacus to the Gladiators, or are you goin' to launch the Curse of Rome?"

"Asey, I've just been back to my house. Listen. I told you Jimmy'd taken scale pictures of the knife, to keep Quigley from pulling anything?"

"Yup. Nothin'—"

"Listen. I got home and found my wife and Reynolds, the Wellfleet man, working over Jimmy. Martha'd called Reynolds because she didn't know where I was. He—"

"What happened?"

"This is the story, as I got it. I—my God, I'm speechless! Two hours ago, some one called Jimmy on the phone. Sounded like me, he says, and the person said it was me. Told Jimmy to bring the photographs and negatives at once to me, out on the end of the stone crusher road. Not to tell any one he was going. And Jimmy, knowing something'd been up, since I'd told him not to talk about the pictures, thought it was all right, and went and did!"

Asey nodded. "I b'gin to get it. Is he all right?"

"Yes. He got there, got out of his car, and some one grabbed him from behind. You know the tangle of underbrush at the end of that road! They beat him up, swiped his prints and negatives, and beat it. Somehow he got into his car after he came to, and drove to the house, pretty much all in. Martha got Reynolds and they fixed him up. He'll be all right—"

"Didn't Jimmy have any other prints or pictures at home?"

"He did. And his mother told us when we phoned her that she'd given 'em to a man that came and asked for 'em! She'd never seen the man before, didn't notice him or his car particularly, or anything like that. But she gave him the prints, without question. Just as she said," the doctor's scorn reached heights, "he asked for 'em! Asked, mind you. He *asked* for 'em!"

"Jimmy know the men?"

"Didn't even see 'em. They got him from behind, and had a blindfold around his eyes before he knew what was happening. Plain ordinary bandanna handkerchief you could buy in any five and ten. Of course it was Quigley's bunch. He asked me again to-day about the knife and if I still thought it wasn't the right one. Probably they've been watching me and my house. Never entered my head that they might! Jimmy came there openly, and every one knows he's a photographer. He had his camera with him. They just spotted him and acted accordingly. And believe you me, when that knife appears, it's going to be just as thin as it should be!"

"But—why, the very fact that Jimmy was robbed and beaten," I said, "will prove—"

The doctor shook his head. "They'll say some reporter wanted a picture awfully badly. Don't think there won't be an explanation. Asey, that's the absolutely bitter end! We could produce the other knife from the gun—and we'd still be no better off. If you haven't got the real murderer now, the chances are pretty much against your getting him by to-morrow afternoon. It means that Quigley knows there's more going on here than has met the eye. I'll bet there are a dozen more men hanging out around this place than when I came here earlier. And Anne will—"

Asey stood up. "I've said," he announced quietly, "that I'd get her off, an' I intend to. Doc, you be careful about yourself after this. You get any strange calls, an' you just stay home. Wouldn't be a bad plan to keep some one with you in the car, an' with your wife too—"

"Asey, there's no hope in this world that you—"

"Go home, doc, an' get some sleep. Forget about this knife business. We got this afternoon an' t'night an' t'morrer mornin'. Ain't licked yet."

The doctor left reluctantly.

"I feel," Marcus said, "that the doctor is right. I—"

"Mr. Adams," Asey looked at him wearily, "you just please take your hired man an' find out how you can prove his story of the lady named Molly. I don't want to see you again till you got it proved, either."

"I—"

"Krause," Asey said, "has dug himself an' you a nice hole. You don't—"

Rather stiffly, Marcus left the room. Krause followed.

"What about Krause's story, Asey?" I asked. "D'you believe it?"

He sat down and pulled out his pipe. " 'Fraid I do," he said. "When he said she spoke French, I got it right off. The girl's Molly Doucet. I thought it might be when he mentioned the earrin's. She lives in a shack near the edge of Belcher's 'state with her good-for-nothin' father. I was holdin' that out on Krause more to upset your brother than anythin' else, in the hopes of gettin' a few pearls of wisdom out of him. I didn't. We'll go an' see Molly t'night an' check Krause. Huh. Let's go into the blue room. I seem to think better in there, an' God A'mighty knows I need to think."

"How black it's getting outside," I said as we walked down the hall.

"Yup. Cloudin' up plenty. Sunny an' nice 'nough early, but the wind's shifted. I got a feelin' we're in for a no'theaster. That's about all we needed, a good storm. Guess Heaven ain't with us."

In the blue room we found Eric, curled up in a chair. He was peacefully reading a volume of Pepys' Diary.

"Hi," he said. "Say, Asey, d'you see my glasses over there? I think I left 'em on the stool next to you."

Asey looked down on the footstool, and then beyond to the window sill.

I don't know exactly how to describe the sound that issued from my throat as Asey picked up the battered shell rimmed glasses,—both bows were held together by dingy lumps of adhesive tape.

The circular brownish spots were explained at last. They'd been made when the bright sun, earlier in the day, had hit Eric's glasses, left slantwise on the sill.

∿∿∿∿∿∿∿∿∿∿∿∿∿∿∿∿∿∿∿∿∿∿

16

"ERIC." Asey pulled a piece of paper from his pocket and scribbled on it. "Will you take this to Betsey?"

"Sure." He bounced off.

"What," I began, "what—"

"That's just a note to tell her to keep him busy. Huh." From another pocket he pulled a small folding rule. "Woman sent me this," he said, "last year, with a magnifyin' glass. Never knew, quite, if she was bein' helpful or funny, but t'would seem now she was a help."

"What," I began again, "what—Eric—"

He looked at the ruler, lying between the two circles on the sill, then looked at me and smiled.

"'Twas glasses all right, Miss Kay, but they wasn't Eric's. We're pickin' up a lot— God A'mighty, an' to think I laughed at Tony for C'lumbus an' the eggin' about them daggers! I ought to of known what these was!"

"But if they weren't Eric's glasses that made the spots," I said, "whose were they? And why are you so sure they weren't his?"

"I don't know whose made the spots in Norris's

room. But these is the same as the ones in Lila's room, an' a little underhanded measurin' on them showed me later that they wasn't the same as the ones we found first. Smaller. Lot less space b'tween 'em. Eric's got a narrow head. Frames of his glasses is small, an' his eyes is closer t'gether than most people's. Likewise, I'm just plumb sure it wasn't Eric."

"But who made the others?" I persisted.

Asey smiled. "That's a little problem I'll leave to you. Every one in this place but Anne wears glasses—golly, I can't get over how dumb I am! There it was up in Norr's room, plain as day. West room, sun pourin' in there the aft'noon Eve was killed. Then in Lila's room. East. Sun in there all mornin', an' so was Eric. If you got a dunce cap handy, I'll put it on."

"How are you going to find out whose glasses were responsible?" I asked. "Can't you collect them all and line them up on a sill—"

Asey pointed outside. It was pouring rain.

"Seems's if we couldn't. B'sides, if you stop'n think this out, reasonin's goin' to get us farther'n 'xperimentin'. Lots'd d'pend on the slant of the glasses, too."

"What do you mean, reasoning? Why, if you can prove that one person's glasses were on that sill in Eve's room, you've got the one that did it, haven't you?"

"Just so. We'll go harry Alex."

"Look," I said as we went upstairs, "I've forgotten Norris. I told the doctor I'd relieve Tony. You carry on with Alex yourself, and report to me later."

"Tired of d'tectin'?" he asked with a grin. "So'm I.

I'll go in to Norris with you. Alex'll keep. We can harry him this aft'noon just as easy."

Norris greeted us sullenly.

"Come to relieve dad, have you? All right. I'll be amused by you two for a while. Don't pretend you don't want to hurry, dad. You know you've been itching to get out of this room and onto that script for two hours."

Looking very unhappy, Tony left.

I recalled his comment Thursday afternoon about Norris's intensity, and accurately decided that the boy was concentrating all his efforts toward making the rest of the household as acutely and bitterly miserable as he felt himself to be.

"How's your earache?" I asked.

"Worse," he said. "God, I wish we could get out of this rotten spot! I wish we could go this minute and leave it all behind us forever—"

"You can, soon," Asey said soothingly.

"Soon? Like hell we can! We've got to stay here for another month, no matter what happens in the meantime."

"Another month? How come?" Asey asked.

"Because Dad's paid up, that's why. And we haven't another cent till December. Dad made a mint last year, and I didn't do so badly, but Dad put everything into his bank, and it went screwy. He *would* have to pick the only bank in the country that's still closed after the bank holiday!"

"Oh, come," Asey said, "it ain't your father's fault!

They's a lot of banks that ain't opened, an' I take it yours is payin' off in driblets. That's better'n a lot—"

"My God, Pollyanna!" Norris snorted. "There's no reason to blame Dad, except that he wanted to come to this foul place, and he insisted on staying. And look what it's brought us!"

"If I recall rightly," Asey said, "your father told me over a month ago that he was all set to go to Maine, an' you wouldn't have none of it. He said you insisted on comin' here. An' insisted on stayin'. Said he didn't want to very much, but if you wanted to do anythin' enough to fuss about it as hard as you was, he was willin' to change his plans for you. Seems to me you're kind of bein' unfair. Av'rage father would have packed you up an' left. Yessir, I call it unfair."

"Unfair?" Norris launched into a long and slightly tiresome tirade against the tavern and its occupants and his father and every one and everything else he could think of.

I had a vague feeling that he had perhaps read, when he was very young, a description of literary temperament, and was doing his best to live up to it. It was all very picturesque, and he looked a little like Byron in his youth as he sat there on a steamer chair before the fire. But I wanted to spank him.

Asey sighed. "Yup," he said ironically, "you live an awful hard life. But don't it ever 'cur to you that the rest of us don't want to stay here in this tavern, either? Dif'rence is, we ain't actin' like a lot of blubbin' babes over it. Think of Anne, feller, up there—"

"Anne deserves everything that's happened to her and a lot more! I'd like to strangle her with my own hands!"

That aroused me. "See here," I said, "you're going a little too far, Norris. And it just so happens that we have a witness who can prove that Anne was doing just what she said—"

"Witness, bah! I wouldn't give tuppence for any of the witnesses you and this Mayo could rake up! With your money, he could get you a thousand witnesses, if you wanted them. But let me tell you, your witnesses aren't going to get by me! I told Quigley I'd see Anne got the chair, and I intend to! He's coming for me to-day."

"What?"

"He told me Thursday he would get me when things started, and Mr. Adams said that was to-day. After all, I was here. I know what happened. And Eve—dear Eve—she—"

Asey looked at him curiously. "Very fond of Eve, wasn't you?"

"Fond?" Norris said. "Fond? Oh, you damned fool! I was going to marry her!"

I gasped and looked at Asey, and he gasped and looked at me. I remembered Eve's solicitude about Norris Wednesday night, when Eric went in to listen to the radio. Perhaps she had realized that she couldn't keep Alex; perhaps that was why she had kept quiet about the divorce. Perhaps she was turning to Norris— it was all rather horrible.

"Why do you 'oh' and 'ah' like that?" Norris was on the defensive. "Is there any reason why I shouldn't have married Eve?"

We knew of one perfectly good reason, but if Norris didn't know about Alex, I knew that I, personally, would never be the one to break the news.

"Any reason you gulping dolts can think of?" Norris demanded.

"Tell me," Asey said, "how long have you known Eve?"

"Why don't you say what you mean, Mayo, instead of New Englanding all over the lot? I never saw Eve. I didn't have to. Any one with her glorious voice couldn't have been—oh, there's no use talking about it with you! Or any one! I've just got to sit here in this miserable rotten spot and think—for the love of God, tell Mr. Adams to come talk with me. He's some one I can talk with. At least he knows music, which is more than you fools do!"

Asey shrugged his shoulders and departed to find Marcus. We left the two of them, a few minutes later, knee deep in a technical discussion of counterpoint which left me slightly dazed.

"That," I said, "will be the last philanthropic visit I make to that—that boy! Asey, d'you suppose he was serious about marrying Eve? It—why, it doesn't seem possible!"

"Nope, it don't. But Norris was pretty def'nite about it, an' I hardly think he's the sort that'd ever make any statement like that just for fun. It's what you might call a compl'catin' factor, ain't it? Y'know," he grinned, "if I was a writer, writin' up this story, y'know what I'd call it? I'd call this story 'Ex-It.' Seems's—"

Tony Dean came up the stairs to where Asey and I sat on the cushioned seat at the landing.

"Is Norr's ear worse?" He tucked a handful of manuscript under his arm. "I hope he—"

"Mr. Adams is amusin' him," Asey said, "an' doin' a better job'n we ever could. Seems like Miss Kay an' me is just a couple of gaspin' ole fools. We don't know nothin' an' it was a ter'ble chore, the whole business."

Tony shook his head. "He's been rude again? I'm sorry, and I apologize for him. Sometimes he gets streaks when I actually don't know what to do about him. But they usually pass. This business of Eve, though, seems to have made him lose all sense of balance."

"Did you know," Asey asked, "that he was intendin' to marry Eve?"

Tony turned white and sat down limply beside me. "Marry—Eve? My God—no! You're joking! Did—did he say that?"

"He just told us. That's why we was gaspin' fools."

"Marry—Eve! Good God,—well, that explains what's been the matter, anyway! I suppose it was her voice—heaven knows that was a gorgeous thing. But—marry her! Asey, I can't get it through my head. And Alex—I—oh, I just can't understand!"

"What d'you mean, Alex?" Asey asked.

"It's nothing. He told me last night that you knew the whole story, so I assumed you did."

"What whole story? Or," Asey smiled, "which part of what whole story?"

"If you don't know about it, Asey, I've really no right to mention it. I'd rather not. It's none of my business."

"Uh-huh. But—I think you better."

"It's nothing, really. I don't know what made me— It's just that Eve was once married to Alex, when he was much younger."

"Once—you mean they was divorced?"

"Why, yes," Tony said. "That is, I assumed so. That's what I was thinking about. They must be, if Norris said that about Eve. I mean, she'd have told him if she were still married, certainly. Norris wouldn't have made a thing like that up, or spoken of it, if it weren't so. And it wouldn't have been so if she hadn't divorced Alex. I wondered if she'd told Norr about that, or her first husband."

If Tony had continued and announced that Eve had married as many times as Peggy Hopkins Joyce and the Mdivanis combined, it wouldn't have surprised me. I was approaching that condition which comes over one occasionally in a dentist's chair. You've ouched so many times over minor twinges that when the dentist finally and firmly begins to drill on a live nerve, you think practically nothing of it.

"First husband?" Asey said. "Who was he? Did you know him?"

"Why, in a way. I—"

Alex strode out into the corridor, waving a sheaf of yellow manila paper.

"Listen," he said energetically, "I've got a grand story. You sit right there, all of you, and listen and tell me what you think of it!"

"We," Asey told him patiently, "are only a couple of pantin' porpoises of laymen, Miss Kay an' me. You come round some other time with your papers when Tony's not busy with us. You get him—"

"Nonsense. You've got to listen. It came to me the other night, and you'll see why. It's—"

"See here," Asey said, "if you got to come bargin' into tetey-tetes, s'pose you listen to me. Whyn't you tell us you knew there was daggers in them guns in Norr's room? An' had known, for three years anyway?"

"Would you have told, Asey?" Alex returned, apparently not in the least disturbed. "Would you have told, under the circumstances? I don't think you would have. Isn't—wasn't there enough against me already? You just assumed that I didn't know because none of the rest did. You never asked me about 'em. If you had, perhaps I might have admitted knowing. It's been a game of mine, seeing how many people have stayed in that room who never noticed that handle might be a dagger handle. Lila came near it, but she didn't take the trouble really to find out."

"An' you never told her? But you told Miss Rutton."

"Celeste? What's—"

"We won't go into her," Asey said. "Tell me, did you know Eve'd been married before you met her?"

"Yes. She told me. Listen, Asey, I want to tell you about this story. It's superb. Simply—"

"Did you know that Norris was contemplatin' marryin' Eve?"

Alex dropped his manuscript. "What! No. How—hadn't that woman—hadn't—didn't—didn't Norris know we were still married? Tony, didn't you know she was still married to me? Why—how could you have let her play with the youngster like that! He'll never understand—never could have—and Eve—oh!"

"I didn't know about it," Tony said, "till Asey just told me that Norr'd told him. I didn't know anything about it. And I thought you were divorced, anyway."

"I was trying to. Perhaps that's why Eve— Tony, you don't suppose that Norris expected to marry her, and then found out somehow that she was still married to me—" With Tony's eyes fixed on him, Alex found it difficult to finish his sentence.

"If you're insinuating," Tony said, "that Norr killed Eve—well, don't, Alex. My temper's worn thin. I'd probably pick you up and shake you till I'd broken every bone in your thin body. Besides, Norr can't even move with crutches. This—this gets worse and worse. Asey, can't you pin it on the scarfaced man? Where was he during the time all this happened?"

"Gallivantin'," Asey said briefly. "Now, who was Eve's first husband, Alex?"

He shrugged.

"You don't know?"

"Not his name. I know he wanted a home and family, and so Eve divorced him. Always wished I'd known him. We'd have had a lot in common."

"Didn't Eve mention his name ever?"

"Never. That first marriage was always more or less of a mystery. I never knew any one who did know about it. It happened when Eve was little more than a schoolgirl. I know it was during the time she was in Rome, supposedly studying singing. I've always thought the man was an Italian."

Asey turned to Tony. "Can you shed any light on the subject? You said you knew him."

"Only in a way," Tony said. "I never knew his name, either. This—the whole story sounds absurd. I was on a street car in Paris, just after the war. It so happened there was an item in the Paris *Herald* about Eve's being decorated by the French government. She'd done a lot,—ambulance work and nursing and what not. Anyway, a fattish man sat next to me and read over my shoulder, which always annoys me intensely. I asked him coldly if anything was wrong, and he pointed to the item and said that he was sorry, but he'd seen his wife's name. I didn't believe it, at first, but he said more than enough to convince me. When I asked him his name, he hopped up and jumped off. But he was no Italian."

Asey sighed.

"Well," Alex said, "Italian or not, he certainly hasn't any place in all this. Now, listen. I want you to hear my story. It's important, because I just looked at my check book and something's got to be done in a hurry."

"The wages of the pen," Asey murmured, "bein' penury, I s'pose."

"May I use that?" Tony and Alex spoke together, and Asey laughed.

"Fight over it." He smiled at me. "An' I'll give the loser some gen'wine local color."

"It's mine," Alex said, "because I provoked it. Now, listen. The woman thinks her husband is unfaithful, and the husband—"

"Name 'em," Asey said. "If we *got* to have it."

"Very well. The woman is—Moira. Greek for fate—always effective. Moira suspects Michael of being unfaithful. Michael suggests—um—"

"'Field and Stream,'" Tony said, "crossed with 'What the Well Dressed Man Will Wear.'"

"Krause's first name," Asey suggested, "is likewise Michael."

Alex ignored them both. "The other end of the triangle is Olga. Well, Moira finds a strange key lurking in her husband's pockets— Asey, don't ask me if she went through 'em regularly! She asks Michael what it is. He says it's Olga's, at which Moira throws a fit. But Michael says he's never used it. Took it only to keep Olga quiet. Moira doesn't believe him."

"The nasty old skeptic," Tony said. "Shows you what the modern woman—"

"Moira doesn't believe him," Alex went on, "but she

loves her husband, and so she goes to Olga's apartment, with the key, intending to—"

"I know," Tony said. "And by her passionate entreaty on behalf of the generation to come,—what is home without a father?—she compels Olga to go from wherever she is. Usually, *I* make it London to Paris, though you can vary it and make it Paris to London. And Olga's that overcome that she won't even take Moira's check. Fadeout, with a deep lavender spot. Only trouble with your bright idea, Alex, is that it seems to me I've written that story of yours sometime before. So have you."

"If you'd let me tell this," Alex said, "we'd get along a lot better. Moira goes to Olga's apartment with the key—but—here's the big moment. This is the effective bit. The key—doesn't fit!"

"When the pigeons throw peanuts to the man," Asey said, "that's—that's news! I s'pose, Alex, this was all brought on by that key business?"

Alex nodded eagerly. The flippant comments about his story didn't seem to have bothered him in the least.

"I began to think," he said, "of all the keys that have got people into trouble and smashed their lives, and how probably, if people hadn't gone off half-cocked, they'd have found out that at least half the keys didn't fit. Now, I've half a dozen duplicate keys for my luggage. But I challenge any one to open my hat box and my trunk with their respective duplicate keys. Just can't be done. I—"

"Is this prop'ganda," Asey drew from his pocket the

duplicate key to Stout's room, "'bout ole—let's see. Ole EP2T19?"

"It really isn't a hint," Alex said honestly. "I know that key's all right. That is," he added hastily, "Eve turned it back and forth in the lock when she gave it to me. The door was open, but it worked all right then."

"We could try it, anyway," Asey said, getting up from the seat.

Alex put out his hand. "Don't. Truly, Asey, I didn't mean for you to do anything like that. You've got me pretty cold, and I know it. The key works. I'm Eve's husband, and I wanted to divorce her, and she didn't like the idea. You can't get away from all that. I knew about those daggers in the pistols. I've—well, you *are* going to make me sub for Anne, aren't you?"

"I'd like to," Asey admitted, "as a last r'sort. Only stone in this gooseb'ry jam is that everythin' about it is all a lot of circumstantial ev'dence, an' I'm frank to admit it. If I had one single sol'tary bit of real proof, I'd snap you up like a whip. So happens I got a clew. But I can't use it on you. So there you are. I'm 'fraid, too, if I was to pr'sent you, all tied up with pink ribbons, to Quigley, with just what there is against you now, he'd simply clap you into a cell an' keep you in case Anne didn't pan out the way he expected. After all this public'ty, he couldn't switch."

"Well," Alex drew a long breath, "I—well, Lila and I've been talking it over. After the—the string episode, and all the—the rest, I'll gladly go to bat if you say the word, Asey."

Asey nodded. "I told Miss Kay you had the Gal'had spirit. Now, just for fun, we'll try this key."

It worked beautifully when the door was open.

But when the door was shut, the key—for reasons known only to heaven and its maker,—stubbornly refused to budge.

17

"**D**EARY me," Asey said, grinning at Alex, "an' I meant to prove the op'site. Huh. Hoist with m'own p'tard an' whitewashed with m'own bucket, that's what. Yessir, I guess we'll have to let you out 'longside of Mrs. Talcott. She—"

"Lila," Stout interrupted, "you mean, you've proved her story is all true? You've cleared her?"

Asey nodded. "Uh-huh."

"And you never told her! My God, man, you'd torture an innocent, helpless woman—"

"You may r'lieve the damage, Gal'had," Asey said. "An'—hey, wait!"

Alex champed back impatiently.

"Well, what is it?"

"R'member," Asey said sternly, "Rollo goes to mil'-tary school. The one he wants near Boston. See?"

Alex smiled. "He does," he said briefly, and dashed up the hall to Lila's room.

Tony sighed. "This," he said, "is all beyond me. I'm going down to the green room and work on my script, if Mr. Adams is looking after Norr. I've got to get that done. Shakespeare may have lived and flourished in turbulent times, but I'll bet even he couldn't achieve much in all this frenzy."

Asey and I followed him downstairs and went into the blue room.

"See here," I said, "you've thrown your king with Alex, your five spot's no earthly good if you feel that Krause is telling the truth—and, Asey, you've got less than twenty-four hours—"

"Wa-el," Asey drawled, "you just stop an' ponder on how much can happen in less'n twenty-four hours. See what you fell into from the time you left your boat Wednesday aft'noon till Thursday aft'noon. Proves it don't take much time to—"

"But what d'you think about all this now?" I demanded. "What d'you *think?*"

"Think?" Asey chuckled. "If you was settin' on a stick of driftwood in the middle of the Atlantic Ocean durin' a Feb'ry no'theaster, what'd you think?"

"I shouldn't think," I told him promptly, "I should pray."

"That's just what I'm doin'," he informed me cheerfully. "I'm prayin', only I'm tryin' to work in a little logic at the same time, like Timmy O'Connor used to say when he told about duckin' John L.'s left. There must be somethin' we slipped up on, but it's kind of hard seein' just where, the way things is now."

"I'm sure I can't see any slips," I said bitterly. "We've gone through everything. Betsey was with Sadie Harding at three. Lem was clamming. Bill Harding and Lila were both five miles away. Tony and I were in the blue room. Celeste Rutton was at Mrs. Knowles. Anne was out by the chicken yard. Mark was with you. Norris couldn't have moved or seen, even if he was in the room. Eric's out. You say his glasses couldn't have made those spots on Norris's sill. And—"

"An' Krause's out, I feel sure. He told me he thought he seen Rollo around the pond when he was comin' back from leavin' his girl. From what he said," Asey laughed, "I gathered the boy's yarn 'bout walkin' the turtle home was true. Krause couldn't of made that up. B'sides, Molly's the kind of girl'd think it lifted her up a couple pegs in the social scale to call herself one of Belcher's maids."

"And Marcus?"

"Look at that list of names he give me," Asey said. "He couldn't c'rupt the whole dum length of Beacon Street, could he? Nope. He's out."

"And the key's finished Alex," I said. "The last white hope. Asey, isn't it possible, just the same, that he might have had still another key, that *did* work? That he might have put the duplicate that didn't work there for us to find? That story of his was so—so infernally pat!"

Asey nodded. "'Twas. An' like the Rutton girl said, Alex is no slouch when it comes to brains. But if he did have a third key that worked, we'd never find it now. An' somehow, his story is just silly enough to be true."

"I still can't understand why that key works when the door's open and not when it's closed," I said.

Asey went into the matter in some detail.

"May not be a proper expl'nation," he concluded,

"but I think it's due to that little ridge, like I said. Not bein' an expert locksmith, I can't give any more reason'n that. Sort of r'minds me of Bijah Cutts an' the rooster's egg. Bijah was a little daffy, you see, an' some of the fellers give him a pullet's egg once, years ago, an' told him 'twas a rooster's egg. He was real pleased, an' went 'round showin' it to every one, an' course, he got sort of laughed at. Folks told him it wan't in the nature of the beast to lay eggs. Explained real careful all about it. Bijah listens grave an' intent an' says, fin'ly, 'So none of you folks ever seen a rooster hereabouts lay an egg. Huh. Any of you ever seen a forren rooster from forren parts?' An' they had to admit that forren roosters was out of their ken. Bijah just smiles happy an' says, 'Well, that's the answer, then. 'Twas prob'ly a forren rooster.' Well, Miss Kay, this was just a forren key."

I laughed. "Just the same," I said, "this is disheartening. Thirteen people, more or less, and all of them with alibis."

"That's the princ'pal trouble, far's I can see," Asey said. "All these fellers was elsewhere, 'cept Norris an' Krause. We're sure of Norris, an' I bet you we'll be sure of Krause. It just plain ain't natural. An' knowin' Weesit, I don't think any outsider could of come to town by train or car, in broad daylight, without some one knowin' or seein'. Don't think it's any bolt from the blue stranger."

"But no one knew that Marcus and Krause came."

"They come at night, an' followin' folks an' not bein' seen is Krause's business. Just the samey, when I called Mrs. Knowles about the Rutton girl, she told me she'd seen a scarfaced man hangin' around this way lately, so you can see even an expert ain't got much chance. B'sides, whoever done it sort of knew the routine of this place, knew folks wandered off durin' the aft'noons, knew Eve's fav'rite chairs an' all that."

"Asey, it's just got to turn out that Alex has another key. Don't you remember how he wanted to go out Thursday night? I'll wager he was going to get rid of it then."

"Uh-huh, but I still feel he's tellin' the truth. Y'know, there's somethin' I been thinkin' of. S'pose, Miss Kay, you take a compass an' draw a circle. N'en you take everythin' inside of that circle an' give it the once over, like we been doin'. An' you draw a blank, like we have. Now, they's two ways of surveyin' the r'sults. Either some one's lied plenty—"

"Alex," I began firmly. "He—"

"Maybe. But when you lie a lot, you get yourself into a lot of dif'culties. Things you make up won't tally with things other folks say. Alex's story is silly enough to fit in. Anyway, either some one's yarn is fishy, or else it's what I think. We just chose the wrong center for the circle in the first place, see?"

"No," I said. "I don't. Any more than I grasped what you meant by your old five spot. What other center can you have that would work? What other but the one you've used?"

Asey smiled as he got up from his chair. "I ain't give up that five spot yet," he said. "I—"

"What! Who—"

"Nope. Time'll tell. Even if we don't ask. You realize we spent since Thursday night worryin' about time? What time was this, an' what time was that, an' where was you at such an' such a time? Somehow whenever you think of time, there's more to it than you figgered at first. Time shows up what your brain couldn't get when things was happenin'. Time busts up all the thoughts you had that wasn't sound, an' c'ments the things you thought of, but wasn't sure of. Now, we got what you might call three d'mensions here, but the fourth, time—"

"Asey," I said plaintively, "is this any place to launch into a philosophical discussion on time? I'll grant you that all the clichés about time are true. Time's proved 'em. Time flies. Time and tide wait for no man. But, proverbs and philosophy aside, what *are* we going to do?"

"Eat," Asey said with a smile, as the dinner gong rang. "Dig into our roast beef, an' let time c'nceal what is now shinin' in splendor, like McGuffey's Third Reader used to say."

It rained all through dinner, a steady pelting rain that beat against the windows as though some one were playing a hose on them. Then the wind began to roar. The shutters rattled and the walls and floors creaked with that patient regularity you can find only in really old houses.

Betsey was driven from her kitchen by the smoke from her stove.

"You take a no'theast wind," she said, wiping her reddened lids, "an' that stove won't go worth a cent. Never has an' never will, spite of spendin' money on that chimney as long's I can r'member. Lem says they got the hurricane signals flyin' from the hill. Land's sakes, I should think they would have!"

Asey saw me surveying the elements and laughed.

"Don't look so good, does it? I'll prob'ly get rheum'-tism or somethin'—"

"I'll give you both a horse chestnut to carry," Betsey interrupted, "an' then you'll both be safe from that!"

"Good idea for me," Asey said, "but don't bother with any for Miss Kay. Little Cape drizzle shouldn't faze her after copin' with real water like the Hels'-pont."

"If this," I retorted, "is a drizzle, heaven preserve me from a real Cape storm. When do we start to check Krause's Molly?"

"Not for a couple hours. I'm 'fraid we got to walk, too."

"Walk?" I looked outside and shivered. "Why?"

"Well, I was up attic, huntin' out an ole saddle I seen there for Penrod to gallop on over a chair, an' I took a peek out the attic window. Couple of Quigley's extra plain clothesmen was sendin' two troopers I didn't know over that path we use goin' to the car. I ain't goin' to take no chances now. We'll walk. It ain't far."

"But if we get out, how'll we get in?"

"*If* we get out," Asey replied, "we *will* get in."

"And," I brought up the problem which had been bothering me for some time, "suppose that something does turn up. How are we going to get out of here tomorrow?"

"Cinch. Doc'll just ruin his pr'fessional rep'tation, an' c'nfess he took a ptomaine rash for measles. Or else we'll lay it on Eric. Say the kid dotted himself with mercurochrome for fun. His rep'tation'll take it lyin' down. Any other mental conflicts?"

"What about Norr's story that Quigley's going to use him as a witness?"

"If we're still licked t'morrow, the quarantine'll be on, an' the doc'll see to it Norr don't leave. If we got somethin', it won't matter one way or another. Now, we'll leave a couple minutes b'fore eight. Lem says these fellers change guard at eight. We'll go while they're changin'."

At one minute after eight we slipped out of the side door of the shed into the pelting rain.

It was pitch dark and the wind seemed to blow through me as though I were a screen door. Somewhere in front of the tavern I could see the flashes of electric torches. I shivered and prayed that no one should suddenly decide to turn the beams our way.

Slowly, with me dangling along behind, Asey moved into the woods. The man must have had eyes like a cat. While I could barely distinguish his figure from the encirling gloom, he led on as unconcernedly as though it were broad daylight. Every now and then I could hear a dull booming—it was the surf sounding from the outside beach.

After fifteen minutes, Asey stopped. "There," he said, "guess we can stop an' get our breath. They'd have been after us with lights if they'd suspected."

I wanted to know where we were.

"Dead end, Miss Kay. We're just b'tween the Meth'-dist an' the Con'gational cem'teries." At my snort he continued cheerfully, "We ain't far from Molly's. All set?"

I grabbed onto his belt, and we squashed our way through a strip of marshy meadow land and yards of slippery, clayey surface to a tiny tar-papered shack. I thought at first it was a chicken house, but it turned out to be the Doucet home.

The young girl who answered our knock also answered Krause's description to a T, even to the earrings. Showing no emotion other than a faint glimmer of vague surprise, she checked Krause's story and agreed not to mention our visit. Asey thanked her perfunctorily and once more we went out into the rain.

"Well," I said, "what now?"

"Goin' to the colonel's. Only a few yards, an' we'll use the back door."

The colonel himself let us in. When he saw who we were, a streak of lurid blue-tipped words flowed from his mouth.

"My God," he wound up weakly, "d'you know who's just been here? Quigley. Some of his men found the coupé in the woods. He wanted to know what it was doing there. He's just left. What happened? Did they get on to you?"

"They didn't get the chance." Asey told of our walk. "Say, did he go near the g'rage? If he seen my car—"

"I squelched him too thoroughly, but I sent Lorne out to stand guard. Lorne'd put the roadster in the old stable and covered it with a tarpaulin, and the place is locked and bolted. There are some old buggies there, covered over, too. I told Quigley the coupé was undeniably just stolen, that I'd used it this afternoon, that it was the business of the police to protect car-owners, and so on and so forth. I forget whom I said I'd call in on the matter, but I know I mentioned the marines and something about pasting ugly mugs if I were annoyed again. Quigley apologized before he left, and Lorne was out of the door as soon as they were. You're safe from him. How are things going?"

"They ain't," Asey said. "I want to use your phone."

"Go to it. I—"

"May take me some time."

"That's perfectly all right. You can phone all night and charge fifty calls to Siberia if it would help get Quigley. I don't think he'll be back here to-night, Asey, if ever, but if you don't want to sit out at the hall phone, there's the extension in my study. Throw everything on the floor and make yourself at home. I always wanted a chance to ask Miss Adams about her putting."

Asey grinned. "She can swim, too," he said, and departed.

For fully an hour the colonel held forth on his ideas about putting, and then demanded mine. Somehow putters and balls appeared, and an indoor imitation green was brought out from under a couch. By twelve o'clock we had laid out an entire course in the living room. There were half a dozen pillow bunkers and a water hazard in the shape of a pail of water. Both of us forgot entirely about Asey, and Eve Prence, and the murder. Golf affects many people that way.

We didn't even notice Asey's entrance, sometime after one o'clock.

"You crazy loons!" he said, laughing till the tears ran down his cheeks. "You loons! Lucky you were both golf fiends. 'Twould of been awful if one of you went in for polo. Well, you can c'ntinue this later. Right now, colonel, I want you to help us get back to the tavern."

His plan was beautifully simple. The colonel was to take a car and drop us near the woods. Then, giving us ten minutes to get as near the shed as we could, he was to drive up to the tavern and raise what Asey called a rumpus.

"Don't care what about," Asey added, "but just fuss enough about something so's the guards'll get int'rested in the front of the house. Anythin'."

The colonel put on his coat and smiled briefly.

"Let's go," he said.

The rumpus he raised was audible even to us, standing there in the dripping rain by the edge of the pines. Half a dozen flashlights started to move forward, and Asey gripped my elbow.

Five minutes later we were in the tavern.

"Now," I said, after Asey had assured himself that everything was all right, "what did you find out? What were you checking? Marcus? Did you prove your five spot?"

"I didn't prove anythin', exactly, but I got a lot of hope. Now you're tired—a little golf goes a long ways—"

"Asey, don't you dare tell me to go to bed, and that time heals all and that we've still got a few hours! To-morrow afternoon Anne Bradford—and Asey, the whole thing's my fault for not looking after Eve, and—"

He propelled me gently upstairs toward my room.

"Miss Kay, I got hope, an' time does heal all. An' nothin' I found out'll be sure till t'morrer, if then."

"Asey—"

He opened the door of my room, pushed me in, and softly closed the door.

Bed for me Sunday night was simply the grave of lost illusions.

I was up at eight Monday morning; Tony joined me as I went downstairs.

"No less," he said, "than fifty million men with shotguns are patrolling this place. Quigley's going to make sure none of us gets out to help Anne. You know, the more I think of that man, the less I like him. Well, I hope Asey's lawyer is on the job."

"He is." Asey greeted us both at the foot of the stairs. "Syl sent a note to me. Crump's on the job, an' so's the doc an' the colonel. Syl says Quigley's orders is that no one leaves here on two feet, an' he thinks Quigley's comin' down to get a statement from Norris. But in case anythin' turns up, the doc's got everythin' ready to call the quarantine off."

"In case? Asey," I said, "you still don't think you have any chance?"

"Six hours," Asey said. "Lot can happen in that time."

"Speaking of time," Tony said as we went into the dining room, "have you got Eve's clock keys? I looked for 'em in that blue jar in her room, but they weren't there. Norr's just reminded me that the clocks have to be wound at nine. If they're not, they stop and get out of order. Eve never could be bothered winding them one by one at various times, so she did the whole bunch together on Monday mornings."

"I know," Asey said. "I r'membered an' got the keys."

"Want me to wind 'em for you? I often have."

Asey shook his head. "Don't bother. I will."

But at nine o'clock he demanded a fourth cup of coffee from Betsey.

"Don't forget the clocks," Eric said anxiously. "It's time. Look—this one's stopping."

"I'm through," Tony said. "Eric and I will—"

"Don't bother. I'm goin'."

But it was quarter after nine before he left the dining table and beckoned for me to follow.

The dining-room clock had stopped at 9:02, and the blue and green room clocks had both stopped at 9:03.

"Asey," I said, "what *is* all this? What are you looking so grim about?"

"I told you time'd tell," he said, "I'm hopin' it will."

"Why—you—you weren't serious about—did you really mean *time?* I thought you were just philosophizing—"

"I know." He led the way up to Norris's room and opened the door.

Norris, still in bed, demanded that we should get out and leave him alone.

"Son," Asey said, "you just keep very still. See, Miss Kay?"

He pointed to the clock on the mantel, whose clipper-ship pendulum was still busily ticking back and forth over the painted waves on the glass door.

"Now—quiet, Norris. We'll just make sure if time's goin' to tell."

"What—" I began, but Asey shook his head.

"Got to be sure. Wait."

At 9:43, the clock stopped. Asey drew a long breath and looked at Norris.

"D'you remember a train whistle Thursday aft'-noon?" he asked.

"What in the name of God has—"

"Do you?"

"Yes, I do! The damned thing tooted for hours just as I picked up my violin to play! What—"

Asey turned to me.

"We got it," he said quietly.

18

"**W**HAT—"

Asey steered me out into the hall and closed the door.

"Asey! Norris—what!"

"Time," Asey sat down on the cushioned seat at the head of the stairs, "time's crashed through. Just like I thought an' hoped an' prayed it would. 9:43. We'll give it three minutes leeway. That leaves forty. Twenty-five after an' fifteen b'fore. Yup, I been thinkin' about that clock ever since Norris first opened his mouth an' talked about askin' Eve questions that she didn't answer to. He said there was only a flat, dead silence. An' if the clock'd been tickin', he'd of noticed an' said so. An' the whistle tooted when he picked up his fiddle. Yup, time's done it."

"Time? But what is this about clocks and time—and the train whistle? It tooted at three, Asey. Pete Brady said so. And at three, the program was just beginning! Norris said he picked up his violin to play, but he simply couldn't have. He—"

"Miss Kay, I told you I thought we'd drawn our circle around the wrong center. We had an' we did. At three, every one was out an' 'counted for. The things they said all jibed, like Lila an' Bill, an' Krause an' Molly, an' all the rest 'cept Alex. An' like I said, I b'lieved him. All the d'tails was true. An' that bein' the case, then it seemed to me maybe the time was wrong. It was."

"But we *know* Eve was alive at three, Asey," I protested. "The program began then, and she talked to Norris. Eve was alive at three!"

"We was told that, but we didn't know it. Last night at the colonel's I phoned Berlin. That program went on at 9:45, not 10:00. That is, at 2:45, not 3:00. Y'see, Hitler, he d'cided he had a message to d'liver. I knew that last night, an' I was pretty sure my five spot was goin' to be good. But I didn't see how it was done. I s'spected, that is, but I didn't know's I could prove it. Not by a long shot."

"But what—how could any one know the program was changed? Who is this five spot?"

"He knew, 'cause it was announced, just once. It'd of been around 1:15, here."

"But who—Asey, I just don't get this!"

"Okay. Y'see, Tony—"

"Tony?" The hall seemed to be whirling around me. "Tony?"

"Yup. Y'see, Norris was on the balc'ny out back till after lunch. He ate out there. Tony set the radio for that three o'clock program b'fore he brought Norris in. Got the news of the change, prob'ly just by ac'dent. Just happened to pick up the 'nouncement. He left the dial set, brought Norris in, an' then went out for his walk. He planned to come back b'fore 2:45. He had his alibi, y'see, in that play."

"Asey, you're stark staring raving mad!"

"Nope, but I wish I was. All he had to do was to find some one he could read the play to from the time he come downstairs, b'fore three, till 3:25. He'd set the clock at 3:25. See?"

"Set the clock? Asey, I feel stupid, but I can't believe this! I can't understand it."

"I knew the time was wrong last night, like I said. That was somethin', but it wasn't all. Now, Tony went upstairs at 2:30. He's awful quiet for a big heavy man, but when you stop an' think it out, most heavy men do move quiet. Like your brother Marcus—he's light on his feet. An' Tony's used to bein' around Norr when the boy's asleep. Anyways, he didn't make no noise that woke Norr up at that time, even if he had at times b'fore. He got the gun down, an' took out the dagger. At 2:45, he shoved the clock hand ahead to three. Clock struck. Then he shoved the hand to 3:25, an' stopped the pend'lum. N'en he crouched down b'hind the chair he knew Eve always set in. Norr heard the clock strike. It waked him up. He turned on the radio. Eve come in."

"But the glasses, Asey! What—"

He smiled. "I thought you'd got that when I told you reasonin'd go farther'n experimentin'. If the glasses was on that sill durin' the time of the murder—well, the murd'rer wasn't near sighted, but far sighted. Eric's near sighted. So was every one here, but Tony an' Alex.

But when Alex read from that story yest'day, he put his glasses on. An' the key finished him."

I remembered suddenly how on Thursday afternoon, Tony's glasses had been perched like aviator's goggles on his forehead while he worked on his script in the blue room. He'd probably worn them while he was out walking, but when he worked over the play, he'd slipped them up.

"Asey," I said, "I'm a fool. And he didn't have glasses on when he came back downstairs."

"But they was on the mantel when I come into Norr's room at 3:30. You see, he knew the timin' of that play. Knew how long each act'd take. He had a sound thirty minute alibi. At 3:24—or even b'fore— Miss Kay, he'd already started upstairs b'fore Norr's cow bell rang, hadn't he?"

I nodded. "He said he wanted to have Norris read the second act from his Braille copy. He opened the door, and then the bell rang."

"Uh-huh. An' he was ahead of you. Not more'n thirty seconds, like you said, but he had time enough to push the pend'lum an' start the clock goin', an' to put his glasses from the sill onto the mantel. With all that happened after, Norris wouldn't be thinkin' about the clock's b'ginnin' to tick. If he did, well—there'd be the clock goin', an' all c'rect. You'd just say it was his nerves that made him think it was so quiet."

"Still, Asey, I can't believe this! I can't. Why, he sat down there and read that play to me! He couldn't have killed Eve just minutes before!"

"R'member he writes plays. He's used to parts. R'member he was the only one that s'gested finger prints? An' he's like to wear a golf glove with fingers on his right hand, when he goes out walkin', b'cause he always carries an' swings a big blackthorn stick. He'd just been walkin'. An' that glove was down on the floor with his wet shoes, when we carried Norris into his room. There wasn't no fingerprints, an' he knew it. Others didn't even think of suggestin' it. The only flaw was the time. But with Norris tellin' of the clock strikin' three, an' the clock goin' all right, the chances was a million to one it'd get by. Papers didn't even mention anythin' but that at three o'clock, when a radio program begun, Eve Prence was alive. No one even asked what station it was. 'Course, if Norris hadn't waked up an' turned on the radio, it'd of been all off. But he did. An' if he'd been awake when Tony first went up, it'd of been off. But he knew the boy was sleepy from bein' out in the sun. It was a chance in a lifetime, an' he was dram'tist enough to see it. I wanted to get this over with last night. I knew the time was wrong, an' I knew Tony's glasses was the spots. But how he worked it wasn't clear."

"But if you knew about the glasses, or guessed, wasn't that enough?"

"He's got half a dozen pairs of glasses, an' he could of said he'd left a stray pair there all the time he was out. I thought I'd have to bully an' wangle it out of him. But this clock's done it. Y'see, I figgered the only way he could of done it was to push the clock ahead, an' stop it. If he hadn't, the clock'd of struck an' Norr'd of known. An' the time'd of been all wrong. I hoped he wouldn't dare to fiddle with the clock, figgerin' it'd be wound at nine, or seein' to it that it was. I just had to wait for time, like I said. When he spoke about the clock keys an' windin' the clocks, I knew for sure. Clock had forty minutes more to run than it should. An' Eve boasted of these clocks like her father did b'fore her. They're ac'rate. Every one here knows it."

"Why, didn't he change the clock?"

"When you come right down to it, I can't think of any way he could of. You can wind a clock if it's goin' to stop 'fore it should, but you can't unwind less you're an expert. Fiddlin' with it might have stopped it, called 'tention to it. Folks might say, if it was out of order, maybe it was wrong Thursday. Easier to let it be. If the clocks'd been wound, as usual, an' kept on bein' wound as usual, he'd of been safe. At first, y'see, I d'cided the program was fourteen minutes or so, Norris played five or six minutes, an' the rest of the time he spent waitin' for Eve to answer b'fore he rung the bell. Really it was nearer twenty minutes he played, an' the rest waitin', prob'ly. Norr wouldn't be able to tell how long he played."

"But if Norris hadn't played, or waited—"

"He always played after that program. Tony knew it an' banked on it."

"And Tony—oh, Asey, why should he have?"

"For Norris. He'd do things for that boy that he'd never do for himself. An'—'member my theory about motives 'n all? You heard Norris say they couldn't get away. An' Tony prob'ly knew about Norris an' Eve an' didn't like it. An' somethin' else. You notice yest'day how he brought up the subject of Eve's first husband, an' then shied off when he found we didn't know about the feller? An' then, when he found that even Alex didn't, how sort of vol'ble he got? All about that fat man on a street car? I think—"

He broke off as Tony appeared at the top of the stairs.

"He," Tony said quietly, *"was* Eve's first husband. You're right. He couldn't get away from her or here, or even get Norris away, because he was broke. He did it for Norris because he can't look after Norris much longer, so the doctors say, and he wasn't going to let Eve do it. Not the boy whose mother Eve had all but hounded to death. Was it the spots that set you going, Asey?"

"In a way. Mostly it was odds an' ends. The timin' of your play. Your noticin' the time when you come in the room. The way there wasn't no plan stickin' out. Almost like it'd been done b'fore—written out. Like a play or a book, where you don't notice plans. Y'see, you gen'raly do, in real life."

"It was inspiration," Tony said, "well worked out. I thought it was air tight, with Norris there to hear the clock strike. Even if people found out about the program being switched, I was safe, and I thought, with every one else out of the house, it would just go down in history as an unsolved case. I remembered the glasses

I'd left on the sill just as I began to read to Kay. I knew I could say they'd been there all afternoon, but the spots were more than I'd counted on. I'd just time to start the clock and put the glasses on the mantel when Kay came in the room. I didn't expect you back so soon, Asey, either. I was trying to stall and get her to phone for you so that I could have a whack at taking them off—but you came. After that, I didn't dare touch 'em. And I thought the clock would solve itself, just by seeing to it that it was wound. Anyway," he drew a deep breath, "Norr's out of Eve's clutches. The money in that bank'll be enough to look after him. I made a lot last year."

"How," Asey asked, "an' why did you come here?"

Tony shrugged. "Broke. Norr thinks we're paid for. We're not. We're charity patients. Money's always floated from me, Asey, as fast as I've made it. I made a lot, but I always managed to spend just a little more. Last year's is left just because the bank is closed. Eve knew I couldn't keep money. I—well, I'm ashamed to say she's financed me more than once in the past. Many times. She knew my weak spot, and she played on it. After we were divorced, I—that was why Mary—well, we won't go into that. We were broke, and Eve saw me in New York in the spring, found out about the bank, and offered to have us stay here. Then she began on Norr, who could only judge her from her voice. She was decent to him, but she taunted me. I knew what would happen after Alex and she were divorced. I couldn't bear it for Norr, to find out the other sides of

Eve. And I knew I wouldn't be around a lot more to look after him. A year at most. On Thursday I saw my chance to save him, and I took it. Then when Anne appeared, I saw what I'd done. It would have worked in a play, but it wouldn't work offstage. And Asey, I'm not really sorry."

Outside a siren sounded. We went to the front window. An open touring car was rolling up the oyster-shell drive, followed by a dilapidated sedan.

"Quigley," Asey said, "with the doc behind him. They're comin' to get a statement from Norris, Tony, but I'm 'fraid we got to give 'em you."

Tony looked down at the car. "It didn't work," he said. "But I'm—I'm not sorry. Asey, will you give me just ten minutes?"

"Tony, I can't let you off that way. I'd like to. But I said I'd get the girl out of this, an' I got to. An' I can't do it if I let you—"

"See here, Asey, the whole damn thing's written out and signed for you. It's in an envelope down in the green room. I just wrote it. I knew I'd have to when you kept the clock keys. And it's the finest third act finale—"

"But," Asey said, "we can't have no ep'logue. We just plumb can't."

"I swear, Asey—I give you my word of honor. I won't kill myself. Just ten minutes!"

"If I got your word, okay."

Tony went into Norr's room and shut the door. Asey and I silently looked down at Quigley's car. The window was open a few inches and we could hear the exasperated voice of the doctor as he expostulated with Quigley.

I cried, and I didn't try to stop myself. We'd won. We'd accomplished what we set out to do. Anne would be freed. Asey had picked the truth from the great mass of tangled detail. But it was a bitter victory, if it was a victory.

Asey brushed his shirt sleeve across his eyes. I think he felt about the same way I did.

Tony returned. He wore an overcoat, and he held a felt hat in his hand. Somehow I got the impression that for him the play was only beginning.

"Let me go down alone," he said to Asey. "Will you?"

"I—look—gee, Tony, I can't—"

"I've got three minutes, and I gave you my word."

He shook Asey's hand, then mine, smiled and went downstairs. We heard the front door open, and almost immediately the doctor came racing up.

"Asey!" he said, "what—"

Asey was lifting the window. We heard Tony speak.

"Mr. Quigley." He stepped on the running board of the car. "Mr. Quigley, I've got a story to tell you. It may not seem—well, may I tell it?"

"There ain't much," Quigley said complacently, "that you can tell me. Shoot."

"Thank you. Did you ever hear of Mock Duck, Mr. Quigley?"

"Huh? Say, what—"

I could feel Asey grow tense beside me. Apparently he knew what Tony was talking about.

"Mock Duck," Tony went on, "was a Hip Sing hatchet man whom they still tell tales about down on Pell Street. I write plays, and I've always meant to put him in a play some time. He used to wait, Mr. Quigley, for the On Leongs to gather, and then he'd rush into the middle of the crowd, squat down, shut his eyes tight, and empty his revolvers. One in either hand. It was very effective."

"Say," Quigley said, "what's this got to do with Eve Prence?"

"Practically nothing," Tony said coolly. "But I've just learned that my plays aren't perfect, and I've thought of an improvement that could be made in a play about Mock Duck. He could keep his eyes open, and use one gun—"

Tony's hand came out of his overcoat pocket, and Asey pulled me back from the window as Quigley slumped forward and a perfect fusillade of shots rang out.

When they stopped, I pushed away from him and the doctor and looked out.

Quigley was still slumped forward on the floor of the tonneau. Sprawled above him were the men who had been sitting on either side of him.

Tony was striding down the oyster-shell drive, apparently unhurt, though the two men in the front of the car held smoking revolvers. State police ran up, and Tony pointed his gun at them.

"It's empty," Asey muttered. "He's askin' for it—but by Heaven, he's keepin' his word!"

The driver of the car steadied his gun hand and took careful aim.

That epilogue was more dramatic than any Tony Dean had ever put on the boards.

The following Monday I set out on the "Gigantic" for my winter in Capri.

Anne and Mark were already on their way to South America—without Krause. And I had sent no detective stories to the boat. I felt they were entirely superfluous. Marcus had taken Norr back to Boston with him. He hadn't said so, but I felt it would become a permanent arrangement. Eric was at General Naseby's, bursting with pride and brass buttons. Alex and Lila were in New York.

The end of Quigley had been the end of the Quigley régime. Asey and Colonel Belcher, and what the colonel called the outraged peasantry, had seen to that. And the peasantry *was* outraged, for Tony's statement had been published, and the doctor had added his story of the knife with numerous other personal observations.

And credit had gone, of course, where it belonged—to Asey.

Eight bells sounded and some one knocked on the door of my cabin. I let in a small page who was almost staggering under the weight of an enormous brown paper package. I opened it hastily—all my friends had sent their good-by offerings ten days before to the "Merantic," and I was missing them this time.

Under three layers of brown paper I found six copies of Celeste Rutton's bulky compendium, but Asey's fly-leaf note on the top volume was characteristically brief.

"Flowers fade. The Hellespont is okay, but you still ought to try Gull Pond."

If it means seeing that remarkable man again, I am strongly tempted to do so.